Death and the Blind Tiger

A Max Hurlock Roaring 20s Mystery

By John Reisinger

Glyphworks Publishing
2013

Death and the Blind Tiger
A Max Hurlock Roaring 20s Mystery

Glyphworks Publishing, 2013

Cast of Characters

Maryland and the Eastern Shore
Max and Allison Hurlock
Isis Dalrymple- librarian
Duffy Merkle- moonshiner
Chief Vickers- Easton Police
Chip Carswell- Easton newspaper reporter
Tom Hawkins- owner of horse farm

New York City
Ellsworth Connelly- wealthy bridge expert
Constance Tibbet- Connelly's housekeeper
Gunther Von Grunewald
Helen Arness- Connelly's ex-wife
Mandy Jewell- Connelly's current lady
Harold Darwin- NYPD detective
Bill Fulton- Connelly's chauffeur
Gwen Perkins- jilted Connelly lady
Horace and Martha Porter
Martin and Dianne Forsythe

Historical people
Dorothy Parker
Robert Benchley
Duke Ellington
Texas Guinan
Izzy and Moe
Harold Ross
Edna Ferber

Chapter 1
Fall, 1923- Dropping in

The sudden silence when the engine stopped would have been restful and pleasant if the biplane had not been 2,000 feet in the air at the time.

Max and Allison Hurlock had just turned their Curtiss Jenny (affectionately named Gypsy) for home after a flight across the Chesapeake Bay to Maryland's Western Shore when they first heard the engine sputter. Allison picked up the speaking tube.

"Max, what's that?"

"Trouble," he sighed. "I think Gypsy is about to be cantankerous again."

"Drat. She could have waited until we were back on our side of the bay at least. See any place to put her down?"

Max continued to adjust the controls, and that was when the engine died. Finally, he scanned the ground below.

"We're over the Worthington Valley, northwest of Baltimore. There's a big area down there. Lots of grassy fields. We can easily glide there."

"Wonderful," Allison replied. "Next time I'll wear my light fall suit."

Gypsy descended with only the sound of the wind whistling through the bracing wires between the wings.

Allison looked below them then turned to Max in the rear cockpit. With the engine silent there was no need for the speaking tube now. "Look out, Max. There's a bunch of horses down there."

1

"I see them. We've got plenty of room."

The ground got closer and closer until a few seconds later the biplane was bouncing to a stop in the middle of a rolling green field. The air smelled of hay and freshly mowed grass, with only the faintest hint of manure. In the middle distance, white painted barns with identical red roofs stood against a backdrop of gently rolling green hills and white pasture fences. Several horses stood impassively a few dozen yards away and regarded them curiously.

Allison turned to Max and pulled off her leather flying helmet. Her Auburn hair waved in the breeze.

"You know, Max, that day I pulled into the service garage in my father's car a few years ago and saw that handsome grease monkey offering to wash the windshield, I never dreamed it would lead to this. I guess the fact that it was raining at the time should have been a hint."

"Yes; well I had to do something to pay my way through college," said Max, lifting the engine cover. "Chatting up passing Goucher College girls was just a fringe benefit."

Allison smiled. "It was for both of us."

A minute later, Max was examining the engine, burning his fingers in the process.

"Looks like the magneto again," Max pronounced.

"Lovely," said Allison, taking off her flight jacket to reveal a green and black dress underneath. "So now what do we do?"

"We wait until it cools down. An hour should do it. Then all we have to do.."

He was interrupted by the sound of a Model T approaching. "Looks like we have company."

The Model T bounced alongside Gypsy and a beefy, red-faced man got out.

"You folks had some trouble?"

"Afraid so," Max replied. "I'm sorry to barge in on you like this, but we didn't have much choice. It'll be fine in an hour or so, though. Then we'll be out of here."

The man looked over the airplane, then nodded when he saw Allison. "Well, why don't you folks come back to the barn with me and freshen up while you're waiting."

"I'm Tom Hawkins," the man said after Max and Allison had introduced themselves. "This is Hawkins Pride Farm. We board and train thoroughbreds here."

"Race horses?" said Allison. "How exciting."

Hawkins pulled up to a large, red-roofed barn, one of several on the property.

"We're doing some time trials right now. You folks might find it interesting. I'll have someone get you some lemonade."

A horse and jockey rounded the final turn and tore down the straightaway past the three figures standing by the rail. The thundering blur of the hooves pounded the ground and kicked up little clumps of the dirt track in their wake.

"A great run," said Hawkins, looking at his stopwatch. "Tigress beat her best time by almost a half second. I have to make a note of it. Mr. Connelly will be very happy."

Max and Allison were still looking at the horse receding in the distance as a dust cloud lazily drifted across the track.

"I take it Mr. Connelly is the horse's owner?" asked Max.

"That's right. He lives in New York and keeps Tigress here for training. He comes down every few months to look in on her. He's due here today as a matter of fact. You can meet him. He's quite a character."

"That must be an expensive hobby," Allison remarked.

Hawkins chuckled. "Believe me, Mr. Connelly can afford it. In addition to his house and a large yacht in Florida. He's a self-made millionaire several times over. He used to be married but now lives the life of a rich bachelor. Quite a man with the ladies I understand."

"Mr. Hawkins," said Allison. "I write articles for various magazines. I've always wanted to do one on horse racing. Could I interview you on the subject?"

Hawkins blushed slightly. "Of course. I've never been in a magazine article before."

"While you're answering some questions for Allison's magazine article, I'll take a quick look at that barn we passed," said Max. "It has an interesting roof line."

As Max disappeared around one side of a nearby barn, a shorter and heavier man appeared around the other. He spied Hawkins and walked rapidly over.

"How's Tigress doing, Tom?"

"Great, Mr. Connelly. She just beat her best time by a half-second. She's ready to race any time you say."

The newcomer nodded enthusiastically. "Wonderful! But I ..."

He suddenly became aware of Allison and abruptly turned all his attention on her. "Hello. Why, Tom, who is this exquisite creature?"

"This is Allison Hurlock. She dropped in on that airplane out in the south pasture. She's researching a magazine article on thoroughbred racing. Mrs. Hurlock, this is Ellsworth Connelly, owner of the horse you just saw fly by here."

Connelly grasped Allison's hand and kissed it in the continental fashion. "Charming; an absolutely charming creature."

Allison smiled politely. "Why Mr. Connelly; I thought the only creature you came here to see was Tigress."

Connelly smiled broadly. "Allison, you are as witty as you are beautiful. I like that in a woman. Have you had lunch? I know a delightful place nearby."

"If Tigress moves as fast as its owner tries to," said Allison, shaking her head, "my advice would be to enter her in the 1924 Preakness without delay."

Connelly turned to Hawkins again. "Beauty, brains and a sharp wit. Tom, I just love this woman."

"That makes two of us," said Max, reappearing from his trip to the other barn.

"Ah, Mr. Connelly. This is my husband Max. Max, this is Mr. Connelly. He owns Tigress."

Connelly's smile didn't waver. "Please call me Ellsworth. I was just talking to Allison, here. She's an extraordinary woman."

"I like to think so," said Max dryly.

"You're a lucky man, Mr. Hurlock. Do you have a card?"

Max handed Connelly his card.

"Investigations?" Connelly asked, looking at the card. "How exciting. Are you a private eye of some sort?"

"I'm more of a general investigator. I try to find the facts and put them together whenever there's a problem or a question to be resolved."

"Very interesting. Have you discovered any facts about me, Mr. Hurlock?"

"You mean besides the fact that you have good taste in women?"

Connelly laughed. "Guilty as charged. Anything else?"

"Other than the fact that you're left handed, your valet is ill, and you seldom attend the movies, not a thing."

Connelly was silent a moment, then applauded. "Why this is amazing. How the devil did you know all that?"

Max smiled slightly. "Just a little observation. You have a wristwatch on your right wrist, something left-handers often do."

Connelly nodded. "That makes sense, but what about the valet?"

"A man who owns race horses is likely to have a valet as well, but you apparently shaved yourself this morning; you missed several spots and have a small cut. Since your valet didn't shave you, I surmised he might be ill."

"Actually, my valet just quit and I haven't found another yet, but you were right about me shaving myself."

Max shrugged. "Well, it was a stretch."

"What about the fact that I seldom attend the movies? You were right about that, but how did you know?"

"That was easy. You never said Allison looks like the actress Mary Miles Minter. Everyone else seems to."

He put the card in his coat pocket "Very impressive. Well, Mr. Hurlock, as it happens, I am in need of someone with your talents at the moment. It regards a very sticky and possibly dangerous situation in which I find myself."

"What sort of situation?" Max asked.

"All in good time. Before I entrust you with my secrets, I have a little test for you. I will send you a clue to my situation and see what you infer from the clue. Then I can see if you are as good as you seem."

Max frowned. "I'm not a performing bear, Mr. Connelly. If you have doubts, you might be better off with someone else. I have plenty of other clients."

Connelly smiled even more broadly.

"Oh, come now, Max. Surely you'll indulge me this little whim? I like a demonstration of something before I agree to invest in it. Besides, where's your spirit of adventure? Where's your thrill of the hunt? The game is afoot, eh what?"

Max thought a moment, then nodded. "All right. Send your clue and I'll decide what to do next."

"Excellent! Meanwhile, I'll be delighted to assist your charming wife with her article...whomever she resembles."

"That was Tigress's last run for the day, Mr. Connelly," said Hawkins. "She'll have to be walked down, and then Scottie has to wash and brush her before she gets settled back in her stall."

"Then that's where we can have the interview," said Connelly, brightening up. "I'll show you the fine points while Tigress is being washed down and groomed. Come along, Allison. It's just a short distance."

Max looked doubtful, but Allison took him aside. "Don't worry, Max; I think I have him sized up. He thinks he's catnip to women, and maybe he is to some, but I find him highly resistible. He does know a lot about racing from an owner's point of view though, and that's what I need. Besides, the groom will be there, too."

"All right, but I'll be looking in on you once in a while; in case you need rescuing."

"My hero. But if he tries to get too fresh, he'll be the one who needs rescuing."

Max grinned. "I almost feel sorry for him."

"So how did you get started as a racehorse owner?" Allison asked Connelly as they walked to the barn.

Connelly frowned for the first time. "I have to credit my ex-wife for that, I'm afraid. God knows there's little enough else she did that turned out well, but she introduced me to one of her society friends who knew someone who had a stable. That was in 1919, and Man O' War was starting to tear up the tracks. Everyone was talking about it and I got interested. Yes, my ex-wife set me on the track, so to speak. Her name is Helen, Helen Arness; Hell-in-a-Dress I used to call her. I had just made my first million and I found myself the object of a great deal of female attention. That all came to a halt when I met Helen. We had a whirlwind courtship and got married on Long Island at some estate or other. Helen's family was solid middle class and lived comfortably, but that wasn't good enough for her. She had to have all the luxury and servants and mansions I could afford, and a great deal I couldn't. We had a large and comfortable house on West 70th Street in New York, but she wanted a mansion in the Hamptons. Well, this went on for a year or so, with the two of us arguing over cars, houses, bank accounts, parties, and all the rest of it, until I couldn't stand it anymore. We divorced and she got half of everything."

Allison looked at Tigress walking majestically past, her muscled flanks shiny with sweat. "You seem to have enough left to keep body and soul together."

Connelly smiled and Allison could have sworn she saw his eyes twinkle.

"Helen got half of everything I owned then, about $600,000 or so. Since that time, I've made another million. Helen has spent most of her money on attorneys trying to get her hands on the rest of it, but she's too late. The terms of the divorce were quite clear."

Allison looked at him critically. "So now you're living the unfettered bachelor life Miss Arness interrupted." It was less a question than a statement.

Ellsworth Connelly looked surprised, then thoughtful. "Why, Allison, you're quite right. That's very perceptive. I was right about you; you are an extraordinary woman. Your husband is a very lucky man."

"So I suppose you'll have to look elsewhere."

Connelly laughed. "You'll have to excuse me, Allison. You're correct that I lead the bachelor life to the fullest, and that I love the ladies. When I see a beautiful woman, I express an interest in her and see if it is reciprocated."

"Even if she's already married?"

"That doesn't matter to me if it doesn't matter to the lady."

"And if it does matter to the lady?"

"Then I retire from the field gracefully, though in your case, with genuine regret."

To Allison's surprise, Connelly bowed slightly.

John Reisinger

Chapter 2
Some trouble up in New York

Two weeks later, Max was working on Gypsy's engine in the coolness of his barn. After an hour, he emerged into the daylight and walked around to the front porch or their house. Allison had been a little under the weather for the past few days so Max was glad when he heard the sound of a typewriter. He turned the corner to see Allison sitting cross-legged on a porch chair in front of a low table that held a glass of lemonade, a dictionary, some pages of notes, and her old Remington. A sheet of cardboard in the window next to her bore the number 25 written in crayon to tell the ice man how many pounds of his product was needed for the icebox on his next delivery. She did not look up.

"Hey, Allison.."

"Wait....there. I wanted to finish this sentence before I forgot."

"The horse article?"

"Right. I think it's coming along, but I need an angle, something for readers to hold on to. After all, most people have never even been to the track, let alone owned a horse."

Max sat down on the other chair. The September day was warm, but the stifling heat of summer had faded and the lush green leaves were not yet dappled with yellow, red, and brown. Cicadas hummed while ducks periodically squawked from the marsh.

"You know, I've read about Man O' War and I even went to the Preakness at Pimlico once," Allison

11

continued, "but I never realized how much was involved in horse racing. Apart from the time and expense, they handicap the fastest horses by making them carry more weight."

"It's a good thing they don't do that with people."

"So are you taking Gypsy up today?" she asked.

Max shook his head. "I think there's a storm coming. The wind is out of the northeast."

Allison looked around. The leaves on the trees were barely moving.

"How can you tell?"

"The smell. It's heavier and damper than usual. Then there's that other smell."

"You know, I noticed that too. It's sort of a sweet yeasty smell."

"It's the Merkle brothers' still," said Max. "They're cooking up a fresh batch of corn liquor I imagine. They'd better be careful or the Prohibition agents will smell it too."

"Aren't they the ones who have that pig farm?"

"Right. If the Prohibition agents really wanted to find the places with the biggest stills, they should look for the places with the fattest pigs. It's a dead giveaway, since they feed them the corn mash. It gets rid of the mash and covers up the smell."

"Why Max you're just a font of local lore. I wouldn't be surprised if National Geographic didn't send someone to interview you for your anthropological insights. So what do they do with the, er, product?"

"Oh, most of it's for local consumption, but they ship some out to thirsty speakeasies all over the area. It gets loaded onto rumrunner boats in Crisfield or maybe Cambridge. The Coast Guard grabs some of them, but most escape."

Allison shook her head. "Ah, the sleepy rural backwaters of Maryland. Beneath the bucolic surface is a seething world of law breaking and intrigue. I feel a whole new article coming on."

A v shaped formation of ducks flew overhead squawking as they began the long trip south for the winter. As the sound receded, Max and Allison heard the faint sound of tires crunching on the oyster shell road surface.

Max stood on his toes looking though gaps in the surrounding woods to try to see the source of the sound. "Are we expecting anyone?"

Allison shook her head. "Must be one of your friends. Maybe the Merkles are stopping by to drop off a complimentary bottle or two."

Max looked again and saw a car approaching. "It's the Police. Looks like Chief Vickers. What's he doing out here?"

"I knew it was one of your friends."

Vickers stopped in the drive and waved as he approached the front porch.

"Good afternoon, folks." The chief was a small man with a soup strainer moustache, but he had a no-nonsense air of authority that commanded respect.

"How are you, chief," said Max. "Have a seat. Can we get you some lemonade?"

The chief sat down on a porch chair, pulling it closer as he did so, and setting a brown parcel at his feet.

"Thanks. I'm here on business, I'm afraid."

"Business?" said Allison. The sweet smell of the sour mash in the air was stronger than ever, and she wondered if the chief had followed his nose to the wrong place. But the chief didn't seem to notice, or if he did, chose to ignore it.

"I got a call this morning from the New York Police Department. It seems, there's been a bit of trouble up in New York. They wanted me to ask you a few questions about a Mr..." he consulted a notebook. "..Ellsworth Connelly. Do you know him?"

"We met him on a horse farm over on the western shore about two weeks ago," said Max.

"Is he in some kind of trouble?" said Allison.

The chief made a note then looked up.

"Oh, no. Mr. Connelly is not in trouble. I'm afraid he's well beyond all that. Mr. Connelly has been murdered."

Max and Allison looked at each other.

"Murdered?" they asked in unison.

"How? When?" asked Max.

The chief shrugged. "That's about all I know. They never give us any details about these things; they just wanted me to ask you some questions since you're witnesses."

"Witnesses? We didn't witness anything. We just ran into him at the horse farm after Gypsy stalled out," Max said.

"According to the New York City Police, Mr. Connelly had your business card in his pocket when he was found, so I guess they figured you had some sort of professional relationship."

"Well, you can tell them for me that they figured wrong," said Max. "I gave him a card when we met, that's all."

The chief made another note and scratched his head. "I see. Now, they wanted me to ask if Mrs. Hurlock met him as well."

"Of course," said Max. "She was with me, and.. Oh, no. Allison, do you see.."

"I see perfectly well," Allison replied. "They know all about Connelly's habits and his taste for married women. They want to know if he did his bachelor on-the-make act with me and if you got jealous about it. Max, they're looking for people with motives to kill him, and they're looking at us!"

The chief looked uncomfortable. "Now, folks, I'm sure it's just routine. Besides, I expect there are a lot of others in the same boat as you."

"We are not in the same boat," Max snapped. "We're abandoning ship."

"Now, now," said the chief. "I understand your concern, but they have to ask anyone who had anything to do with the victim. You understand."

"I suppose," said Max dubiously.

"Now Miss Allison, when he was with you, did Mr. Connelly say or do anything you found objectionable?"

Allison shrugged. "We talked about race horses I'll show you my notes if you'd like."

"That won't be necessary. I think I have enough to satisfy the New York police."

"I still can't believe you came all the way down here to ask these routine questions," said Max.

"Well," said the chief, "to tell you the truth, there was one other reason I came down. Clem Grason over at the post office told me you had a package and I thought I'd drop it off."

"Chief, this is too much," Max protested. "Are you delivering the mail now?"

"This mail is sort of special, Max," said the chief handing him the package. "Here it is; you can see for yourself."

The package was about the size of a shoebox, tightly wrapped in plain brown butcher's paper, and tied with heavy brown twine, as if to prevent whatever was inside from escaping.

The return address was written in firm block letters.

ELLSWORTH CONNELLY
122 WEST 70TH STREET
NEW YORK CITY, N.Y.

"Now I understand why you wanted to deliver this personally," said Max. "Connelly must have sent it just before he was killed."

"Well, this is a first," said Allison. "We just got a package from a dead man!"

"That explains why the police chief is delivering mail all of a sudden. Let's see what's inside."

Max unwrapped the last bit of paper and opened the cardboard box.

"It looks like a porcelain statue of some kind," he said.

The object was a stalking tiger, about twelve inches long and highly detailed. The mouth was drawn back in a menacing snarl, complete with protruding fangs. The tiger was perfectly colored in orange, black and white stripes. The glaze reflected points of the sunlight filtering through the surrounding trees.

Max examined the figure. "A Bengal Tiger, and a very handsome one. What's this? Someone has painted what looks like a blindfold over the eyes."

"A blindfolded tiger? Curiouser and curiouser," said Allison, examining the object closely. "There's a label of some sort on the underside of one of his rear paws. It says 'Fine Ceramics, Ltd'. I suppose that's where Connelly bought it."

"And there's a tag or something around the neck," Max added. He removed the tag and read it out loud.

"'Puncheon'."

The chief frowned. "Puncheon? Is that supposed to be the tiger's name?"

"I don't think so," said Max. "Allison, how about handing me that old dictionary you keep by your typewriter."

"I'll look it up for you." She picked up the dictionary and thumbed through the pages. "It says here puncheon means a tool for making holes in leather or engraving coins. It also refers to a type of rum."

"A tiger with a blindfold and the name of a type of rum around his neck. So what does it mean, Max?" The chief was clearly puzzled.

Max frowned. "I don't know yet. I think Mr. Connelly may have been sending me a clue to test my deductive abilities."

"Maybe it's supposed to be a blind tiger," said Allison. "Blind Tiger is another term for a speakeasy. I came across it while researching my race horse article."

"So maybe he wanted to point me to a speakeasy that features puncheon rum for some reason," said Max. "Who knows? Anyway, it's all pointless now, of course."

"I'm not so sure it's pointless at all," said the chief. "Why that blind tiger thing might have a clue to who the murderer might be."

Max shook his head. "Look; if he really feared for his life from some specific person, I doubt he'd be dropping clues and subtle hints. He'd be reporting it directly to the New York Police."

"You're probably right," said the chief, snapping his notebook shut and rising from his seat. "It looks like a dead end. They'll have to solve the case without any more help from us. Well, so long, folks."

Vickers got in the car and started back to Easton..

As Max stood watching the Model T disappear down the drive, Allison sat in a wicker chair on the porch with the ceramic tiger in her lap, pretending to pet it. "Poor little guy. He wants to tell us something, but what?"

"At this point, I don't really care," said Max, pacing back and forth, "but I think I'd better learn some more about what happened in case anyone starts pointing fingers at us."

"Maybe the Star Democrat has some information on it," Allison suggested. "As for Mr. Tiger here, I think he'd look good on the hall table."

"I'll go into town and talk to Chip Carswell tomorrow. If the paper has any information on the case he'll know where to find it."

As they went up the stairs to bed that night, Max glanced back at the blindfolded tiger. The ominous statue stood silently on the hall table, illuminated only by a shaft of moonlight from a front window and looking more than ever as if it were about to pounce.

The cluttered office of the Easton Star-Democrat newspaper was in a modest wooden building on Harrison Street in Easton, not far from the courthouse. Max walked in the next morning and looked up Assistant Editor Chip Carswell, an old friend and fellow flying enthusiast.

"No, we don't get the New York papers down here," said Carswell, shaking his head, "but we do get news from United Press. That's the news agency that carries reports to all the papers. Now let's see. When do you think this was?"

"Probably between three and five days ago," said Max. "I think it would have taken that long to find out about me and chase me down."

Carswell flipped through a pile of papers, mumbling to himself as he went. "Connelly, Connelly....ah here's something. It's from five days ago. I think this is what you're looking for." He squinted at the paper in his hand as Max read over his shoulder.

E. CONNELLY, CARD GAME EXPERT AND RACE HORSE OWNER SLAIN
Found by Housekeeper After Being Mysteriously Shot While Sitting in Chair
Valuables Not Touched - Tragedy Follows Party at Waldorf

As Max began to read the dispatch, Carswell found another one.

"Here's an update, Max. Connelly was shot once through the forehead. He was last seen by his chauffeur who brought him back from some shindig at the Waldorf the night before and dropped him off around 2 A.M. The chauffeur lived elsewhere. Oh, get this; the chauffeur says Connelly wasn't alone; he was with his latest love, a young lady with the unlikely name of Mandy Jewell. The police are questioning her."

"I'll bet they are," Max observed. "Hey, is that another dispatch?"

"Oh, yeah; dated yesterday. Let's see."

He pulled out the dispatch and held it up to the light.

NEW SUSPECT IN CONNELLY SLAYING
Quarreled with Connelly the Night of the Crime
Letter, Phone Calls Revealed

Police continue to investigate the mysterious death of wealthy card expert and horse owner Ellsworth Connelly at his home on West 70th Street Tuesday. Police have revealed that Mr. Connelly had apparently been reading a letter when he was shot, and that he had made several phone calls earlier, including one to the farm in Maryland where he keeps his race horses. In addition, police are looking for Count Gunther Von Grunewald, an ex German Navy officer now a local architect who had attended the same Waldorf function as Mr. Connelly that night. Witnesses say Von Grunewald and Connelly had argued earlier, but Von Grunewald has not been seen since. The subject of the quarrel was not revealed, but police are investigating.

"Well," said Max, "it's still pretty early, but things seem to be pointing to this Von Grunewald guy. He certainly seems to be acting suspiciously, and he had a pretty good run in with the victim the same night as the murder."

Carswell looked at him sharply. "Say, you're not getting involved in another high society murder, are you Max? This sounds like one to stay away from if you ask me."

"Too late for that, I'm afraid. The only question is whether this thing will blow over if I just keep my head down. It sounds messy."

A clerk appeared at Carswell's desk. "There's a phone call for Mr. Hurlock. It's from Mrs. Hurlock."

"Max," came the voice on the phone. "Do you remember someone named Krauss when you were in the navy?"

"Henry Krauss? Sure. He was a Machinist's Mate in the engine room. Why?"

"His uncle is here to see you."

"His uncle? Well, I was just about to leave anyway. Tell him I'll be home in an hour or so."

After a drive down the St Michaels Road, Max jumped out of the Model T and saw Allison sitting on the porch with an angular looking blond haired man who rose as he approached.

"Good afternoon Mr. Hurlock." The uncle had the air of a military man, and one accustomed to command. "I am so glad you could see me. My nephew told me all about you and where you could be found."

"Mr. Krauss, any relative of an ex shipmate is welcome here any time," Max replied.

"Oh, forgive me," said the uncle. "Where are my manners? My name isn't Krauss. I am his uncle on his mother's side. My name is Von Grunewald; Gunther Von Grunewald."

John Reisinger

Chapter 3
Von Grunewald

"Von Grunewald?" Max repeated. "You're the fellow the police are looking for up in New York."

"Regrettably, yes, but I have come to you to ask for your help."

"Allison, please get in the house and call the police," said Max, placing himself between Von Grunewald and his wife. "This man is wanted in a murder case."

"Please," Von Grunewald pleaded. "Just hear me out. And I assure you and your charming wife that I haven't killed anyone."

"All right," said Max, sternly. "I'm listening."

Von Grunewald bowed slightly and Max could have sworn he clicked his heels. "My sincere apologies, Mr. Hurlock. I would have telephoned first, but I didn't want to risk being arrested before I had a chance to speak with you."

"Well, it's a pretty safe bet you're going to be arrested afterwards, so keep talking. What do you want?"

"Now, Max," said Allison, "give him a chance. He's here to ask for your help."

"Making us accessories to a fugitive is a strange way to go about it," Max grumbled.

"That was unfortunate but unavoidable, I'm afraid." Von Grunewald spoke with a slight German accent. "It is true as you say that the police are looking for me, and I intend to turn myself in as soon as we are finished here. I did not intend to run away. In fact I was in Atlantic

City the day after the murder, and heard about it from the newspapers."

"Then why didn't you contact the police?"

"From what I read in the newspapers it looked like the police were going to blame the crime on me. I decided I needed someone to investigate independently and I had heard of you through my nephew, so I decided I would appeal to you to help me before I turned myself in to the authorities. I am a wealthy man, and can pay you as necessary."

"Listen Von Grunewald; I'm flattered, but I know almost nothing about the details of the case, just a few newspaper stories. You need a local private eye, someone who knows New York and maybe knows the people involved. Besides, the police have been asking us questions because we saw Connelly a few days before he was murdered."

"Yes, your charming wife told me about that, but that is an advantage. It will make it easier to talk to the police and maybe gain access to the crime scene since you're not just a curious bystander."

"Right now," said Max, "being just a bystander sounds pretty attractive."

"What I am proposing," Von Grunewald continued, "is that you come to New York and investigate this case. I will pay all your expenses and put you up at a hotel as long as you need. Of course I will pay generously for your services as well."

"Why me?" Max asked. "The New York police department is a lot better equipped to deal with this than I am."

"I'm afraid that under the pressure of public opinion to arrest the killer, the police might not be entirely trustworthy. I am an American citizen now, but to them I am just a former enemy who argued with Connelly the night before he died. What better person to hang for this murder?"

"I fought the Germans in the Great War, too. Why trust me?"

Von Grunewald leaned forward slightly. "Because of what my nephew told me. You knew him as Henry Krauss, but his real name was Heinrich Krauss. He came to America years before the war, joined the American Navy when the war came, and was on your ship, the USS Carson, a destroyer; the kind you call a 'four stacker'. You were a junior Lieutenant. Heinrich told me about the stabbing on the ship, and how everyone wanted to find the German 'spy' they assumed responsible. My cousin expected to be arrested because of his background, but he wasn't because one man on that ship wasn't fooled. One man refused to accept the spy theory without evidence. That man was you, Mr. Hurlock. You found the real killer and probably saved my cousin. You have a talent for observation and logical thinking, but most of all, you have a sense of honor. My cousin is grateful to you for saving him, so now I ask you to do the same thing for me. You must help me prove my innocence."

"I never set out to prove or disprove anything, merely to find the truth, whatever it might be."

"Of course. That is all I ask."

"Moreover, I'm at a disadvantage since I'm not with the police and have limited access to the crime scene and the evidence. I may not be able to find the truth."

"I only ask that you try."

"And you have to turn yourself in, and I mean today."

Von Grunewald nodded. "I will turn myself in as soon as I have told you some more background."

Max drummed his fingers on the porch rail for a few seconds, and then sighed. "I have to admit it's an interesting case from what I know of it so far." He turned to Allison, who had been unusually quiet through the exchange.

"So that'll be three for dinner?" was all she said.

Allison's southern fried chicken was not the stuff of legend. She used to say that while other cooks' fried chicken made your mouth water, hers was more likely to make your eyes water. In fact, if the Eastern Shore cooks who made delicious southern style chicken were to stand in line, Allison would probably be near the end of it. Even so, the meal was passable and the atmosphere in the cozy dining room with the curtains at the open windows lazily moving in the soft breeze was pleasant. Von Grunewald ate with both enthusiasm and good manners, as if dining at the Ritz, something he had no doubt done many times.

"I've called Chief Vickers to come pick you up," said Max. He'll be here in about an hour, so you'll have time to fill us in. I understand you were a German naval officer?"

"I was *a Kapitan-Leutnant, Kommandant* of the U-73. We were trying to sink Allied shipping."

Max put down a drumstick he had just picked up. "A U-boat? I was trying to sink you."

"That is the nature of war, Mr. Hurlock. Fortunately, neither of us succeeded."

"I suppose you're right," said Max finally. "Now tell me about the argument you had with Connelly the night he died."

Von Grunewald sighed. "It was stupid, as most arguments are. We were at a reception at the Waldorf; a

26

charity benefit affair. He was there with Mandy Jewell, his latest conquest. I was with Helen Arness."

"Hell in a .. I mean Helen Arness? Connelly's ex-wife?" Allison remembered what Connelly had told her.

"That is correct. I have known her for years and we decided to attend the affair together."

"Well," said Allison, "that must have been somewhat awkward."

Von Grunewald smiled. "Not in the way you might think. Connelly was not jealous of my attentions to his ex-wife. He had no desire to reunite and he was far too busy with other pursuits. As far as he was concerned, Helen could go her separate way with his blessing."

"So what was the quarrel about?" Max asked.

"I consider myself a gentleman," said Von Grunewald, looking down and smoothing his napkin self-consciously, "so I would prefer not to say."

"Well, I would prefer not to take on a case for someone who would prefer not to tell me what he knows," said Max sternly.

"Of course. I will tell you, but I hope Mrs. Hurlock will not think me less than chivalrous."

Allison laughed. "No need to worry about that. The way you piled into my chicken tells me you are willing to sacrifice yourself to spare a lady's feelings."

"Nonsense. It was *wunderbar*, Mrs. Hurlock."

Allison turned to Max. "See what I mean? Old world charm right down to his shoes."

"What about the argument?" said Max impatiently.

As if to fortify himself, Von Grunewald took a long drink of lemonade, then continued. "As I said, I have known Miss Arness for several years. We were never romantically involved, you understand, just good friends."

Allison looked skeptical, but said nothing. Max showed no expression.

"We were in the corridor outside the main ballroom of the Waldorf. Ellsworth and Mandy Jewell were there when we emerged. We had seen each other on the dance floor earlier and greeted each other politely. One tries to be civil."

"One does," Allison agreed.

"As I said, I've known Helen for several years and she is a nice person for the most part, but.."

"But what?"

"She has a sore spot where Ellsworth is concerned. Why they ever got married in the first place is a mystery to me. They were, as I believe the English say, 'like chalk and cheese'. They were incompatible, in other words. Do you have that expression here?"

"On the Eastern Shore we say they're like two hornets in a bottle."

"Yes, I see; a very colorful expression. Well, she was especially bitter about the divorce and even more so about Ellsworth's romantic conquests. She had already seen Miss Jewell on the dance floor and made disparaging remarks about her to me, but she didn't let it end there, unfortunately. In the corridor, Ellsworth introduced everyone, calling Miss Jewell the 'jewel of my life'."

Von Gunewald noticed Allison wince.

"I had the same reaction, Mrs. Hurlock, but Ellsworth thought it was clever, and I'm sure he wished to flatter Miss Jewell. Helen just smiled, much the way Lady Macbeth must have, and said 'You'll have to forgive Ellsworth. He never did have any taste in jewelry.'"

"Ouch," said Allison.

"Exactly," said Von Grunewald. "I thought it was in extremely bad taste and was about to say so, when Mandy Jewell spoke up. She had been quiet up until then and I thought she was shy, but she just smiled and said '"His tastes have improved greatly in the last few years, especially his taste in women.'"

"Yikes," said Allison. "Somebody mop up the blood."

"As you can imagine, this brought Helen up short," Von Grunewald continued. "After a second or two, she replied in a low, cold voice. 'I do hope you haven't unpacked your bags yet, my dear. Your week is almost up.' That's when Ellsworth jumped in. He berated Helen for her bad manners and she said bad manners were better than bad taste, and for a moment it almost looked like they were going to come to blows, so I stepped between them and appealed for calm. Ellsworth told me to mind my own business and said he knew I wanted Helen for myself and that I had been chasing her for years. It was nonsense of course, but contact with Helen always seemed to bring out the worst in him. Well, to be truthful, it seemed to bring out the worst in her as well. Anyway, I told him he was imagining things and he should try to act like a gentleman. He said I seemed to be quite an expert on proper American social behavior for someone who was trying to torpedo American ships just a few years ago."

Max nodded encouragement, but said nothing.

"Well, before I had a chance to reply, Helen was pulling me away. It was probably a good thing she did. He turned as well and started in the opposite direction, but not before Helen got in a parting shot. She looked at him with anger in her eyes and said "You bastard. Someday you'll be sorry. Someday you'll pay."

"Uh, oh," said Allison softly.

"Did anyone hear her?" Max asked.

29

"Everyone heard her. The corridor was filled with people. It was all most unpleasant, Mr. Hurlock."

"I'll bet it was. Could either of them have been drunk?" Max asked.

"I don't know. There were a lot of hip flasks in that room, but I can't be sure that he had one. I'm sure Helen didn't."

"What happened after that?

"It was getting late at that point, so I took Helen home to her place in the Village near Washington Square. She was still seething when I dropped her off. All she would say was that Ellsworth had spoiled her evening."

"What time was that?"

"Around 12:30 or so. So you see why the police are so anxious to talk to me?"

As if in answer to his question, a car pulled up outside and they could hear the sound of someone on the front porch, then a knock on the door.

"That'll be Chief Vickers, I'm afraid. He got here in record time," said Max. "I'll take your case, Mr. Von Grunewald, but you have to be honest with me. You have to tell me all you know from now on, chivalry or not. I'll be up in New York in a few days. That should give you time to talk to the police and get released. I doubt that they're ready to press any charges at this point, but even if they are, you can get out on bail."

"*Danke*," I will see you then.

Allison was at the front door by this time, and opened it to find Chief Vickers standing there.

"All right," he said in his most official voice, "where's the Kraut?"

That night, Max and Allison sat on the front porch enjoying the coolness in the air and listening to the crickets.

"You know, Max," Allison said finally, "I never understand these people who say how wonderful it would be if women ran the world. You know; how if women were in charge we'd never have any wars?"

"So what don't you understand?" Max had the feeling he was being used as a straight man again, but didn't mind.

"Have any of these people ever actually met a woman? A woman like Helen Arness or Mandy Jewell that is. Thank God neither of them had an army or navy at their disposal. No war indeed; no survivors is more like it. A man might punch you in the nose, but some women will cut your heart out with their tongues. And they won't worry about the blood unless it clashes with their shoes.

"Whew. You sound like one of those anti-suffragists that tried to stop women from getting the vote."

"Oh, I'm all for equal rights for women," Allison replied, "and we should have gotten the vote long before we did, but that doesn't mean we should pretend that men and women are interchangeable in everything."

"That's my little rabble-rouser," Max chuckled. "So what do you think of Herr Kapitan-Leutnant Von Grunewald?"

"A very charming and sophisticated man, but he's lying to you."

"I know," said Max. "His reluctance to say bad things about Helen Arness was an act. He was dying to tell me, but wanted to look good."

"Yes, and he and Miss Arness were not just casual friends," Allison added. "A man isn't casual friends with

31

a woman for several years and through her marriage and divorce."

"Right," said Max, "and he doesn't take a casual friend to an expensive charity event at the Waldorf. Then there's the suntan."

"The what?" Allison was surprised.

"That's when I first knew he was lying, or at least being deceptive. His hands are suntanned except for a pale section around the ring finger of his left hand, indicating he usually wears..."

"A wedding ring." Allison finished his sentence. "So he's married and he didn't want you to know. I wonder why?"

"Probably to avoid awkward questions about why he was taking Helen Arness to the Waldorf and leaving his wife at home I would imagine."

"Some gentleman," said Allison. "So I guess you've gotten yourself into another murder."

Max nodded. "So it seems. I just hope it will be as easy to get out of it."

Chapter 4
New York, New York

Like a line of misty mountains looming in the distance behind some nearby foothills the hazy gray New York skyline appeared above the rooftops of New Jersey. In the Baltimore and Ohio Pullman car approaching the tunnel that would take it under the Hudson and into the city, Allison gasped and squeezed Max's arm.

"Oh, Max, it's as beautiful as I remembered it. There's no place like New York. It has so many great writers, the big financial houses, the finest restaurants and hotels, the great publishing houses, the best entertainment, and just about anything you could want."

Max took in the scene. "Anything except solitude."

Allison appeared not to have heard. "There's just something about the place, something vibrant and exciting. There's just no place like it."

"Well, not on the Eastern Shore, at any rate," Max admitted.

The train had turned now, and entered a downgrade that led to the blackness of the tunnel mouth. The passing buildings disappeared as the rumbling of the train's wheels echoed off the tunnel walls in the sudden darkness.

Above them, the Hudson swarmed with traffic. White-painted excursion steamboats took sightseers up and down the Hudson while barges, schooners, workboats, and even pleasure craft bobbed and scurried

33

over the gray waters, churning up boiling white wakes and leaving trails of black smoke from their stacks. As a backdrop to all this activity, the massive New York skyline rose silent and gray, its sharp angles softened by the haze.

As the train squealed and lurched through the dark tunnel, Max looked at his watch. "We'll be in Pennsylvania Station in a few minutes. Are you all ready for New York?"

"Max, I've been ready since we left Baltimore. I remember the last time I was here during the war. There were fancy horse carriages everywhere, all going to these huge plush restaurants like Delmonico's. They call them lobster palaces and all the well-off people eat there. It's sort of a ritual, I suppose. Of course, we'll stick to the smaller places."

"In keeping with our smaller resources. I doubt we'll be rubbing elbows with the Astors of Vanderbilts."

Allison shrugged. "Don't be so sure. Ellsworth Connelly traveled in some pretty snooty circles to hear Von Grunewald tell it. He hobnobbed with some extremely wealthy people. That reminds me; did you bring your straw hat?"

Max groaned. "It's in my bag. You mean I have to wear it too?"

"No, just be ready to take it out and show people when they look appalled at your old fedora. That way they'll know you at least own a decent hat."

"Well, I guess I can do that..."

"Of course you have to wear it."

Max grinned. "You're beautiful when you're sarcastic."

A few minutes later, the train squealed to a stop in a large underground concourse and Max and Allison emerged into the cavernous interior of Penn Station.

As they climbed the stairs towards the relative brightness of the street, the sound level rose the higher they got. They emerged onto a street swarming with traffic and waves of pedestrians crowding the sidewalk. Above the traffic noise, the air seemed to be filled with a steady dull rumble mixed with the tooting of horns, and overlaid by a staccato sound like distant machine guns.

"Is someone shooting?" asked Allison, a little anxiously.

Max looked above the line of buildings and billboards on the street and saw the gray skeletons of several nearby tall buildings under construction.

"No, I think what we're hearing is the sound of riveting on all the steel frames going up; the sound of progress, I suppose. Hey, there's a taxi."

Max threw the suitcases into the trunk of the taxi and they headed off to the hotel, dodging other taxis and threading their way through the traffic. The air was warm and muggy, and smelled of hot metal, strange cooking, and exhaust fumes. Max looked dubious, but Allison loved it.

The Wolcott Hotel's lobby looked as if it had been decorated with leftovers from Versailles, with ornate gold scrollwork, carved cherubs, marble columns, and heavy chandeliers everywhere. In contrast to this dazzling display of opulence, however, Max and Allison's room could most charitably be described as "cozy".

Allison stood by the bed and looked around. "What was that old vaudeville gag, Max? My hotel room is so small I have to go out in the hall just to change my mind?"

Max looked out the single window onto a fire escape. "Now, it's not that small, and it's clean."

Allison smiled. "You're right. I'm just spoiled by the wide open spaces of the Eastern Shore. So what do we do now?"

"You got me there. Von Grunewald just said to check in and wait for him to contact us."

"Max, he's been arrested. How is he going to contact us; by carrier pigeon?"

"He was a little vague on that point, I'm afraid. He had arranged for the room, although I noticed there was no message waiting for us when we arrived."

"So do we just sit here and wait?"

"No, I think we can make better use of our time than that. I've seen most of the newspaper stories about this case, so now I'm ready to look up the people involved, but first I'll visit the scene of the crime up on West 70th Street. Want to come?"

Allison wrinkled her nose. "As tempting as it is to see the place where a man I talked to a few weeks ago was shot through the head, I think I'll visit a few blind tigers."

Max raised his eyebrows. "You mean speakeasies?"

"Why not? New York is full of them and I've decided to do an article about them."

"But why are they called blind tigers?" Max shook his head. "You never said."

Allison pulled out a dresser drawer to stow some clothing and almost fell back across the room's only chair in the close quarters. "One article said it was from some place that charged a fee to 'see the blind tiger', then served drinks to the customers. The idea was to take advantage of a loophole in the Prohibition law that made an exception for free drinks."

"And they kept a blind tiger in a cage?"

Allison made an expansive gesture, striking the wall as she did so. "There was no tiger, blind or otherwise.

36

That's the whole point. It was just to try to get around the law. If a patron said he didn't see any blind tiger, the proprietor would say 'Don't worry; he didn't see you either.'"

Max sat on the edge of the bed, taking care not to hit his knees on the wall. "I'll never cease to wonder at the useful things you learned at Goucher."

"Nothing of the sort. I read it in Police Gazette while researching the horse racing article."

Max nodded approval. "A sound publication, though maybe not everyone's idea of higher education."

In the confines of the room, the sudden knock on the door sounded startlingly loud. When the door was opened, a bellhop was waiting with a note that Mr. Hurlock was wanted on the telephone in the lobby. Max left Allison to struggle with the rest of the unpacking and returned a few minutes later.

"That was Von Grunewald. The police grilled him, but finally decided he would not be charged with the murder, at least for now. He's taking us on a quick tour in about an hour, then he's taking us to dinner tonight."

"So in an hour we leg it for the open road again."

"I'm afraid so. He edged closer and put his arm around her. "You know, we still have time to.."

"No, we don't," said Allison. "Besides, as small as this place is, I'm not sure we even have room for that sort of thing."

Max sighed. "Then I'd better finish this case in record time."

Von Grunewald's green Buick was idling at the curb when Max and Allison got to the front door of the Wolcott 25 minutes later. Once again the noise of the city hit them as soon as they stepped onto the street. Von Grunewald, dressed in an immaculate gray suit, jumped out of the car and bowed slightly, while tipping his hat. He looked more like a German aristocrat than ever.

"*Guten abend.* Please get in and make yourself comfortable." Once again he kissed Allison's hand gallantly.

Von Grunewald had no chauffeur, so Max got in the front seat and Allison the back. The German skillfully maneuvered the car through the traffic and towards Broadway and Times Square.

"I trust you have found your accommodations comfortable; yes?"

"They're adequate for a day or two," said Max, "but I'm afraid we'll need something a bit more spacious after that."

"Of course. I spoke with the manager and he assured me they have a suite available in a day or two."

"That would be fine," said Max. "Now tell me what happened when you were arrested."

Von Grunewald smiled. "The police were quite interested in the smallest details of my life it seems. They questioned me extensively about every place I've been and every person I've seen in the last six months. In addition, they seemed to have very poor memories. They kept asking me the same questions repeatedly."

"That had nothing to do with their memories," Max explained. "It had everything to do with yours. They were testing you to see if your story stayed consistent."

"I see. A clever ruse."

"So you were able to satisfy them in the end?"

"Well, perhaps not entirely, I'm afraid. They decided not to charge me with any crime, but the police lieutenant Darwin warned me against leaving the city."

A taxi chugged past, blowing its horn and temporarily interrupting the conversation.

"That's punishment enough," muttered Max.

"Ah. We are approaching Times Square. This next street is 42nd. Many of the best Broadway theaters are along here."

"The Great White Way," said Allison, peering out at the profusion of traffic, people, lights and tightly spaced buildings. Bright colored billboards announced various shows and attractions with sensational pictures and garish lettering.

"We just passed the Knickerbocker Theater and then the Casino Theater back on 39th and over there's the Liberty Theater, playing Little Nelly Kelly. That's a George M. Cohan show. Our Belle is playing over at the 44th Street Theater I believe, and let's see. What else?"

Max was getting impatient. "This is all very interesting, but what about Lieutenant Darwin?"

"Lieutenant Darwin? He seemed a reasonable fellow, and he was most interested when I told him I had retained you to look into the case. He knew all about your involvement in that case in New Jersey a few months ago. The one where the young couple was found dead in the girl's bed in a locked room. He seemed quite interested that you were here."

"Great. Now I've got another police detective grumbling about interference."

"Not at all," Von Grunewald assured him. "In fact, he wants to meet you. I had to promise I'd deliver you to police headquarters tomorrow afternoon at 2:00."

"To take your place in the cells?"

"No, no. He said he just wants to compare notes with you."

"That's very reassuring," said Max. "Of course at the moment I have no notes to compare."

John Reisinger

Chapter 5
Hell in a Dress

After a hot and restless night of sleep occasionally interrupted by horns and sirens, Allison and Max arose early the next morning and ate at a small delicatessen just down the street. They sat at a small table eating bagels with lox and creamed cheese, a dish that was in short supply back in St Michaels.

"So I suppose you're off to grill suspects, Max?"

"I'm off to 3rd Avenue to talk to Helen Arness. Von Grunewald arranged it."

"A nice little chat with Hell in a Dress? That should be fun."

"A million laughs, I'm sure. Do you want to come with me?"

Allison frowned. "As entertaining as that would no doubt be, I don't think it's a good idea. From what I've heard, other women are the bane of Miss Dress's life, so having one show up when she's being questioned might not be quite the thing to encourage candor."

"Yes. I suppose you're right."

"Besides, I'm taking a stroll up to 52nd Street and nose around."

"What's up there?" said Max.

"Blind tigers; lots of them. Actually, up here they just call them 'speaks'. Remember when he took us past the area yesterday? Von Grunewald said the greatest concentration of speaks in the whole town was along 52nd Street between 5th and 6th Avenues. I'm going to take a look for myself and see if I can get an article out of it. The hayburners can wait."

"It looks like we each have a busy day ahead. Now you be careful out on the streets."

"Careful? I'm not the one about to be delivered to the police, my dear. What sort of game is Lieutenant Darwin playing do you suppose?"

Max shook his head. "It's hard to say since I've never met the man, but you can bet it isn't social. My guess is that he just wants to ask me about our meeting with Connelly, but it might be more."

"Like what?"

"Well, it occurred to me that if I were in the lieutenant's shoes and my prime suspect had hired an investigator, I'd want to know what that investigator knew."

Allison nodded as she took another bite from her bagel. "Granted, but you haven't found out anything yet. You couldn't possibly have access to any information the police don't already have."

"On the contrary. I have one thing the police will never have. I've had several confidential and informal discussions with Von Grunewald about the case and his role in it."

"Sure, but that's confidential information. You can't tell the police about it, can you?"

"Not intentionally, but Darwin might figure that if he gets me gabbing, I might let something slip. It would be worth a try. From what I can see, he's not exactly swimming in leads. Take a look at this." Max handed Allison the New York Post he had picked up on their way into the deli. Allison began to read.

NO ARRESTS YET IN CONNELLY CASE

Police continue to question acquaintances, servants,
tradespeople
Palm Beach Police contacted

Police continue their wide-ranging investigation
into the mysterious death of Ellsworth Connelly today.
Inquiries have been made of Connelly's wide circle of
friends, including contacts in Palm Beach and
Maryland. Ex German naval officer Gunther Von
Grunewald, a close friend of Connelly's ex wife, was
questioned extensively yesterday, but released when he
was able to provide a reasonable account of his
movements since the crime. The Post has learned that
Von Grunewald has retained the services of an out of
state private investigator to find evidence to clear him
of the crime, a move some have regarded as suspicious
since no one else associated with Mr. Connelly has done
the same.

Allison almost dropped the paper. "Max, how does
the New York Post know about you?"

"Obviously someone told them. My money would be
on the police."

"The police? Why?"

"To put more pressure on Von Grunewald. Look at
the last line. '..a move some have regarded as
suspicious...' Now exactly who do you suppose they're
talking about, since nobody in New York knew about it
but Von Grunewald and the police?"

"Whew. The police are pretty devious up here."

"They play for keeps."

The address on 32nd street was an old brownstone
that had seen better days. On either side of the front
stairs of most houses were large stone urns that had

once contained flowers, but now grew only weeds. On the building Helen Arness called home, however, Max noticed fresh and well-tended flowers. On a row of buzzers by the front door the name of the tenants were written in pencil on paper labels; all except the name Arness. That one was typed.

"A very particular woman," Max muttered to himself, "and very concerned with keeping up appearances."

He rang the bell and a slight, thin woman with chestnut hair answered the door.

"Mrs. Connelly?"

The woman looked as if she had just bitten into a banana and discovered it was actually a pickle.

"Helen Arness," she said reprovingly.

"Of course. I'm Max Hurlock. Thank you for seeing me."

She opened the door wider and Max was admitted to a spacious ground floor apartment decorated in an elaborate way that was almost Victorian.

Helen Arness motioned Max to an overstuffed chair by heavy red velvet drapes.

She got right down to business. "Hurlock. Is that an Irish name?"

Max was unfazed. "No, it's an American name. Now Miss Arness..."

"My ex-husband was Irish."

"I see."

"I don't like the Irish."

"Uh huh. Now, Miss Arness.."

"Just what is your background, Mr. Hurlock?"

Normally this sort of inquisition would have provoked a humorous answer from Max, but something told him that Helen Arness was not someone who enjoyed a good laugh.

"I investigate to try to find the truth. I've had some success in doing so in other cases and Mr. Von Grunewald retained me to investigate the death of Ellsworth Connelly."

She continued to look at him suspiciously.

"You were involved in that terrible Taylor-Bradwell business in New Jersey a few months ago, weren't you?"

"I was involved in investigating the crime, but I assure you I had no part in committing it. Can we talk about Ellsworth Connelly now?"

For a moment, she looked as if she was about to throw Max out, but her expression softened slightly.

"I was married to Ellsworth Connelly for about two years. I helped to make that man what he was, financially that is, and then I was cast out in the street."

"You say you helped him get ahead financially?"

"When we married, Ellsworth was working as a clerk in a stockbroker's office. But Ellsworth had a remarkable talent for two things: women and card games. He was absolutely phenomenal at bridge and related games such as whist, not just as a player, but also as a tactician. At the time, many society people were interested in learning the game and I encouraged Ellsworth to give lessons. I had a few friends on the fringes of society and I would play weekly bridge games with them while casually mentioning that my husband was a well-known expert and might be persuaded to give lessons. It was my idea to use our savings to set ourselves up in a fashionable hotel at Palm Beach in the winter and associate with the people who came down for the season. Ellsworth's gift of gab coupled with his card knowledge made him very popular and soon his reputation grew to such an extent that he was giving lessons to relatives of the Astors. All the while he was playing for money as well, and would win thousands in a single night."

"He made his fortune from cards?"

"He founded his fortune from cards. He invested the excess in stocks through information obtained from the broker he worked with. Soon, his money was growing from the cards games, lessons, and investments."

"It sounds like you helped him out quite a bit, Miss Arness," said Max. "If I may ask, what happened that led to the divorce?"

"What happened was the emergence of Ellsworth's other great talent; his way with women," she said bitterly. "He gave private lessons to young women in their homes and liked their company. We started fighting about it and finally the inevitable happened."

"The divorce?"

"Not at first. We separated. The divorce was only a few years ago. That was Ellsworth's idea. He begged me not to divorce him even though we were separated."

"Why?"

"He didn't say, but I imagine being married protected him from having to marry any of his floozies. In any event, I finally got fed up and divorced him several years ago. We agreed to split the money."

"And you believe you deserve part of money he made since then?"

"Mr. Hurlock, every penny that man made had its start in the early days when I set him up and guided him. Without me he'd be living in a cold water walk up in the Village or Soho. For that I deserve half of everything he ever made since then."

"And that was a point of contention between you?"

"Yes. All Ellsworth wanted to do was to keep the money to throw away on his little flapper friends. Well, Mr. Hurlock, I wasn't going to stand for that. In fact, I have retained an attorney to research the terms of the divorce decree to find a way I can claim what is rightfully mine."

"How often did you see Ellsworth?"

"We ran into each other from time to time. He was always gallant towards me in public; trying to impress whatever young bearcat he was with, no doubt."

"Including married women?" Max asked.

"It was all the same to Ellsworth. He was more interested in other things than in what a woman wore on her finger."

"Could there be a jealous husband in the picture?"

"Several, you can bet. Tony Mortimer for one. Then there was Martin Forsythe and Frank Talbot. Ellsworth was seen around town with each of their different wives at one time or another. Any one of their husbands could have put a bullet through Ellsworth's head and been glad of it."

"Do you know of anyone who threatened Ellsworth?"

Helen shook her head. "I heard something about Martin Forsythe banging on Ellsworth's door in a rage months ago, but I'm not aware of anything specific. I don't try to keep up with all of my ex-husband's misadventures. Frankly, I find them revolting."

She sat back in the chair and sighed. "Do you want a cup of tea, Mr. Hurlock?"

Max was startled by this sudden change of direction. "Er, no thank you. Miss Arness."

She looked at him sharply. "Gunther said you solved that case in New Jersey when the police were stumped. Is that true?"

"He exaggerates, I'm afraid. I just helped the police out a bit. That's all."

Helen raised an eyebrow. "False modesty makes me ill. I tend to believe Gunther's version."

"Right now I'm concerned with this crime." Max was anxious to direct the conversation in a more productive direction. "How long have you been seeing Mr. Von Grunewald?"

"Oh, I suppose a year or so, although I've known him for several years. We met at some social function or other. He's a gentleman, which is more than I can say for my ex-husband. You know, Mr. Hurlock, you seem to be a gentleman as well. I was expecting one of those dreadful private detectives; the ones who wear cheap suits, say 'ain't' all the time, and who peep in keyholes looking for signs of infidelity in divorce cases. You seem, well, normal."

"I'll take that as a compliment," said Max, blushing slightly. "Now what can you tell me about the party at the Waldorf the night Connelly was shot?"

Helen Arness made a dismissive gesture. "Gunther already told you what happened. It was all most unpleasant. Oh, I suppose I started it by making a cutting remark to Ellsworth's latest strumpet, but for heaven's sakes, he can't expect to flaunt these women in front of me and have me just smile and say 'Isn't that nice?'. Anyway, that woman and I had some words and Ellsworth stepped in to berate me. Then Gunther stepped in to berate him. Then they had words and I had to get Gunther out of there before the whole situation became even worse."

Max consulted his notes from his conversation with Von Grunewald. "As you departed did you say to Mr. Connelly 'You bastard. Someday you'll pay.'?"

For the first time, Helen Arness looked startled and unsure of herself. "Well, yes I think I did say something like that, but I wasn't threatening him."

Now it was Max's turn to look skeptical.

"I wasn't," she insisted. "I was only talking about the money. I had an attorney and someday I'd make him pay me what he owes. That was all I meant."

She huddled as if cold and stared at the floor. "It was just the money. That was all I meant."

John Reisinger

Chapter 6
Speaks Street

"Hello, toots. Can I buy you a drink?" The man was reasonably well dressed, but clearly intoxicated as he stood unsteadily in Allison's path. She was on 49th Street on her way to 52nd Street. Along the street stood a mix of shops and brown and gray stone residences

"A bit early for that sort of thing isn't it?" she asked.

"Early?" The man fumbled with a pocket watch, looked at it and frowned. "This thing must be broken. It says 11:35 and it isn't even dark out."

"So where's a good speakeasy around here? 52nd Street?" Allison asked, figuring the man was probably something of an authority on the subject.

"Oh, there's lots of 'em right around here. There's the Cafe Caruso over there and Tony Soma's on the other side. Then there's.."

"How about this place?" Allison had noticed what looked like a private club in a nearby brownstone.

"That's the Puncheon Club, but the regulars call it Jack and Charlie's. It just opened a little while ago. You want a drink there?"

Puncheon Club? Allison thought. Now isn't that a coincidence? "Would they let me in?"

"Well, they have to know you. I could take you there. They all know me."

"No doubt, but maybe a female friend would be better," said Allison, reasonably.

51

The man seemed to see the logic in this. "I suppose. Tell you what. Tell them you're a friend of Mrs. Parker. She's there almost every night, along with that Benchley guy."

"Mrs. Parker? Thanks." Allison left her new friend standing by the street lamp and made her way to the front door of Jack and Charlie's. She knocked discretely and a small panel opened.

"I'm a friend of Mrs. Parker's."

The door opened and Allison walked into a dimly lit room with a small stage on one end and small tables scattered about. A few patrons were sitting listlessly at the tables and a lone saxophone player was practicing on the stage. Not knowing the protocol, Allison warily approached the bar and ordered a soft drink. The bartender, who looked as if he could have doubled as the bouncer, looked at her curiously, but said nothing He moved over slowly and plopped a glass down in front of her along with a bottle of Clicquot Club. She poured a half glass and took a sip. She scanned the room once more. The saxophonist had left the stage and one of the patrons seemed to be asleep.

"Is it always this quiet?" she asked the bartender.

The bartender, who had picked up and started to read a newspaper after serving Allison the drink, looked at her. His desire to be left alone to read the sports pages in peace struggled momentarily with his eagerness to talk to a nice looking woman, and lost.

"Haven't been here before, have ya?"

Allison smiled. "I guess it shows. I'm from out of town and I was just curious."

The bartender adopted his wiser-older-man-guiding-the-naïve-young-girl demeanor. "Well, you've come to the right place if you want to see a good speak. This place is a hangout for half the big names in New York; movie stars, bankers, politicians, writers; you name it."

Allison nodded as she looked around. "So where are they?"

"Well, this is the slow time of day. People don't just come here for a snort; they come for the atmosphere. It's part of New York nightlife now. Used to be, they'd go to one of them lobster palaces and make a night of it. Then with Prohibition, those places had to stop serving wine and beer, not to mention the hard stuff, so people started thinking the fancy places weren't worth it, and the fancy places couldn't make enough money on just the food to stay in business. So the speaks started to spring up to fill the gap and here we are. You should come by here at night, long about 9 or later. I'm working until 11 tonight. What do you say you and me take in some of the sights afterwards?"

Allison took another sip of her ginger ale. "Oh, thank you, but I really won't have the time. (or the inclination, she thought) Though I might stop back for a little while tonight." She put down her glass and stood up to leave.

The bartender looked disappointed. "Suit yourself, I guess. Say, how did you get in here, anyway?"

"Oh, I'm an old friend of Mrs. Parker."

The bartender looked surprised. "Mrs. Parker, you say? Are you sure?"

"Of course. Why do you ask?"

"Oh, nothing. It's just that you're so... well, that is Mrs. Parker is so.."

"So what?"

The bartender frowned in thought for a moment, then smiled slyly. "Oh, nothing; nothing at all. Maybe I'll see you tonight."

"Maybe. Thank you for the information."

The Detective Bureau of the New York City Police was in police headquarters on Centre Street near Chinatown and City Hall. Max took a taxi and arrived at the time Von Grunewald had arranged. When he walked in the front door, Max thought had never seen so many police in one place. A bewildering array of people came and went through rooms full of people at desks. Some talked on the telephone, some interviewed suspects, some typed reports and some hollered across the room, all under a thin haze of cigarette smoke that somewhat softened the glare of the overhead lights.

Max braced himself for his meeting with a no doubt suspicious and hostile Detective Darwin. His first glimpse was not encouraging. A uniformed officer introduced himself as Detective Anderson, escorted him to a small office on the second floor and told him to wait until Detective Darwin was through with a phone call.

"No," boomed a voice through the door. "I don't want to hear that crap. You find him. That's what you're being paid for. I'm not having the whole case get gummed up waiting around for you. Am I making myself clear? Good! Now cut the bushwa and get going!"

Waiting outside the door, the uniformed officer turned to Max. "You're lucky. It sounds like he's in a good mood today."

Before Max could reply, the office door flew open and a large red faced man filled the opening. "Anderson! It's 2 o'clock. Where the hell's that Hurlock guy?"

"Right here, lieutenant," said the officer.

The sputtering Darwin noticed Max. To Max's amazement, Darwin's manner changed abruptly. He smiled broadly and extended his hand.

"Mr. Hurlock! I'm Harold Darwin. I'm so glad you could make it. Come on in. Can I have someone get you some coffee?"

"Maybe later," said Max.

The door closed behind them and Darwin shook Max's hand again. "Mr. Hurlock. Can I call you Max?"

"Sure."

"Well Max, I asked Von Grunewald to ask you to stop by so we could have a little chat."

Max sat down and looked at Darwin warily. "Fine by me. What about?"

Darwin looked surprised. "Why the Connelly case, of course. I understand you're investigating it too."

"That's right," said Max, "as I'm sure Von Grunewald told you, but.."

"But what?"

"Look, can I call you Harold?"

"Of course."

"Look, Harold, I get the impression you're the kind of guy who values frank talk."

Darwin nodded.

"Well, I've been involved with a few murder cases, and the local police usually regard me the way a picnicker regards ants. So if you're acting like my best pal for some special reason, I'd be curious to know what it is. It might be easier on both of us."

Darwin smiled. "Ha! You are a smart guy, and I mean that in a positive sense. I guess the friendly act didn't fool you. All right, Max, I'll level with you." He pushed his chair back and put his feet up on his desk.

"We cops are a pretty close knit bunch, especially around New York and Jersey. I've known Otto Pfeiffer down in Moorestown for years. Otto told me about what you did in the Taylor-Bradwell business they had down there. Not only did you crack the case, but what's more, you didn't hog the credit. Otto appreciated that, since it didn't make him look bad."

Max shrugged. "I don't have to run for office or make the mayor happy. If my client is satisfied, that's enough for me. He writes my checks."

"A very sensible attitude," Darwin said, nodding. "Us working stiffs appreciate that. The fact is, I think you can be a big help in this case. We can always use another brain on the job, especially one as sharp as yours."

"Otto Pfeiffer didn't think so at the time."

"Of course not. He figured you for some hotshot glory hog who'd only get in the way then loudly claim that he had solved the case. You wouldn't be the first. He knows better now, and so do I."

"Now you're the one being sensible," said Max. "You know how much we can help each other at no risk to you."

"Exactly," said Darwin, leaning forward in his chair. "I give you full cooperation, including sharing evidence, and you keep me fully informed of your findings, and then bow out gracefully when the culprit is found."

"Fine," said Max. "What do you say we start with a visit to the scene of the crime?"

"You read my mind." Darwin picked up a phone and dialed a number. "Anderson! I need a car."

Anderson appeared in the doorway. "Sir, I'm sorry, but there's a Mr. Forsythe on the telephone and he insists on talking to you."

"Forsythe?" Darwin turned to Max. "He's one of our suspects. About a year ago, he tried to beat the crap out of Connelly for messing with his wife, but Connelly kept ducking him until he calmed down. Maybe he's calling to confess and save us all a lot of trouble. Let's find out."

Max couldn't hear the other end of the ensuing conversation, but he was sure it wasn't a confession. Darwin almost winced at the tirade that was being directed at him. Finally, Mr. Forsythe paused for breath and Darwin answered smoothly.

"Now, Mr. Forsythe, I certainly can appreciate your concern with a police officer showing up at your home, and I can also understand your desire to keep your neighbors from forming any unpleasant conclusions, but we have a murder case we have to investigate. I'll tell you what. If we have to question you further, we'll send a plain clothes detective. Fair enough?"

The voice at the other end seemed calmer.

"Now, along those lines, Mr. Forsythe," Darwin continued, "we are asking a private investigator to make inquiries about the case to help us out. His name is Hurlock, and he may want to talk with you and possibly your wife as well. I promise he will not wear a uniform."

The voice on the other end became agitated again. Darwin was unfazed.

"Well, if you'd prefer the attentions of our uniformed officers... What was that? I knew you'd understand. Thank you for your cooperation."

Darwin hung up the phone and grinned at Max. "I guess you gathered that Mr. Forsythe doesn't want police showing up at his front door. He needs to keep up appearances, it seems. I understand he has a number of clients who would look askance at any hint of wrongdoing."

Max nodded. "But he agreed to see me?"

"On one condition; he reserves the right to throw you out on your ear at any time if he doesn't like you. Seems fair to me."

"So I have to rely on my charm? Great."

Darwin chuckled. "I wouldn't worry about it. Forsythe isn't really a serious suspect in my book. He's arrogant and hot-tempered, but his wife ended her fling with Connelly a year ago. If Forsythe was going to do something drastic, he would have done it long before this. He's not the kind of a guy to wait a year to do anything. Now where's that car?"

"This is a messy case," said Darwin as they drove across uptown. "We got suspects coming out our ears. The guy was chasing every woman in New York, married or not. So now we got both ex-lovers and their jealous husbands, not to mention people Connelly cleaned out of considerable amounts of cash in his little card games. As if that wasn't enough, Connelly's housekeeper got there right after the milkman and before we arrived. Turns out she messed up the crime scene a bit."

"That wasn't in the papers."

"No, and it better not be. We have to keep some things back in a big case like this to filter out bogus tips and confessions. Anyway, it seems Mr. Connelly had some woman's negligees in the spare bedroom, no doubt for the convenience of visiting lady friends. The housekeeper, a woman named Constance Tibbet gathered them up and hid them in the cellar, but we found them and she came clean. Seems she was trying to protect Connelly's reputation."

"A little late for that, I would think," said Max. "That's the part everyone talks about the most."

"Yeah. Look; the place is just down the block. There's a bunch of gawkers out there still. I don't know just what they expect to see."

The Connelly house was one of a number of spacious and comfortable brown stones along West 70th Street. Darwin and Max pushed past the idlers on the sidewalk and went up the five front steps. Darwin unlocked the front door and led Max into a cavernous reception room, just off the main hallway. Their footsteps echoed slightly on the stone floor.

"So what happened and when?" said Max.

"The chauffeur dropped off Connelly and Mandy Jewell around 1 AM. The next morning the milkman found that front door open and poked his head in and saw Connelly sitting on that chair near the hall door of the reception room. The milkman ran out and contacted the local cop on the beat and he called me."

"Wait a minute. Then when did the housekeeper get here?"

"We're not sure. She claims she went straight to the kitchen and didn't look in the front reception room at all until she heard the milkman slam the front door on his way out. She then came in and found the body for herself."

"And then ran upstairs and disposed of the negligees?"

"That's the way it looks, but I'm keeping an open mind. It seems a little too dependent on precise timing for my liking. She might just as well have taken them a day or so earlier."

"This is the chair where he was found?"

Darwin nodded.

Max squatted down behind the chair examining the wall. "This is the bullet hole I take it?"

Darwin nodded again and Max asked him to sit on the chair. Darwin sat while Max continued to explore the wall behind.

"You have the bullet?" Max asked.

"Yeah. It looks like a .45. Maybe army issue."

Max continued to look around the bullet hole. "Uh huh. Any shell casing?"

"We did find the shell casing; a .45, but no gun."

Now Max was looking at the stone floor around the chair. "Connelly was left handed, you know."

"You can tell that from looking at the floor?"

59

"No, I knew that from meeting him," said Max.

"So he was left handed. Does that mean anything?"

"Did you notice this chip in the floor? It would be on Connelly's left."

Darwin nodded. "Yeah, I noticed, and I know what you're thinking. If he shot himself, the falling pistol could have made that chip. Trouble is, we didn't find a gun. Besides, the chip is too far away. It's a good foot beyond his reach. Now do you mind telling me what you're getting at?"

"I'm not sure yet, except that I don't think we can rule out suicide just yet. Remember I met Connelly, so I know he was about your height. When you sat in the chair I could tell that the height of the bullet hole was about the same as the height of your forehead, indicating the pistol was fired from the same height as well. That would be consistent with suicide, as would the chip in the floor."

"But the chip is beyond where he would have dropped the gun," Darwin protested.

"Harold, when I was in the navy I had to qualify with the standard issue .45. The thing I remember most is how much it kicked. I often wondered what would have happened if I had relaxed my grip the instant that I fired. The thing probably would have jumped several feet. That would make it land just about where there was a chip in the floor if Connelly had shot himself. As for the lack of a gun on the scene, we have to consider the possibility that the protective housekeeper might have removed that just as she did with the negligees. Let's look at the rest of the place."

The rest of the house looked like the typical bachelor residence, if a good bit bigger and more luxurious. Only the presence of a well-appointed card room on the second floor gave any hint of anything unusual about the house's occupant.

They climbed the stairs to Connelly's third floor bedroom. Once again, the room seemed like the bedroom of any reasonably well off person. A large bed dominated a spacious room with several chairs and a small writing desk on one side and a large end table on the other. On the table were a glass containing false teeth and a small stand holding a toupee.

"I suppose this is how our Don Juan kept himself looking youthful."

"Yeah. He was 48," Darwin agreed. "Of course his money was what really made him attractive to the ladies."

"I didn't see this mentioned in the papers either."

"No, we're keeping the details quiet as much as we can," said Darwin

Max, who had been bending down inspecting the night table straightened up and nodded. "Well, I don't think Connelly committed suicide. It looks like he was murdered and murdered by someone he knew and trusted. What's more, it was probably not by a woman."

John Reisinger

Chapter 7
A Night at the Puncheon Club

Darwin stood with his mouth open. "Geez. No wonder they call you Sherlock Hurlock. You're guessing, right?"

"It's not a guess. It's a hypothesis, a scenario that fits the known facts so far, and is subject to modification when more facts are found. I don't believe in guesses any more than I believe in horoscopes. Whenever I propose a hypothesis, it's based on the evidence and on logic. I'm not always right, but I never guess."

"So spill it. Why do you say he was murdered by someone he knew, but not a woman?"

"There are no signs of a forced entry, so the killer either had a key or was let in by Connelly himself. Either way it would have to be someone he knew and trusted, especially since it happened so early in the morning."

"All right. We had an idea that was the case as well, but why not a woman? He certainly knew a bunch of them and a lot of them would have a motive."

"That's even more simple. Connelly lived for the ladies and was very conscious of his appearance. He would never have entertained, or even met a lady without first securing his toupee and false teeth, but here they are sitting on his night table untouched."

"But why only women? Why would he have let anyone see him in that condition?"

"That's good point Harold, and I thought of it myself. I have an idea about that, but it's too early to even put it in the hypothesis, so I'll save it until we know more."

"Meanwhile, we can rule out suicide?"

Max shook his head. "At this point we can't rule out anything. We don't have enough facts to be sure."

Max turned to go, then suddenly looked at the table again.

"Did you notice how clean the top of this table is?"

Darwin looked at the table. "Of course it's clean. The man had a housekeeper, remember? If she didn't at least keep his bedroom clean he'd have fired her. What would a clean tabletop mean to you, anyway?"

"It means I may have to adjust my theory."

"Ah, Mr. Hurlock," said the desk clerk at the Wolcott, "there's a message for you."

Max opened the envelope and found a telegram from Von Grunewald.

MAX:
ALL ARRANGEMENTS MADE WITH WOLCOTT-STOP-WILL MOVE YOU TO SUITE ON THURSDAY-STOP-WILL CALL TONIGHT-STOP
VON GRUNEWALD

"Two more nights in our little room?" he mumbled. "Well, at least we'll have something bigger after that."

He found Allison napping on the bed when he opened the door to their room.

"I'm awake," she said, without moving or opening her eyes. "I just thought I'd get a little rest, not that there's much else I can do in this place. Maybe a spot of tennis."

Max sat down heavily in the lone chair. "Don't despair, my love. We're getting a suite on Thursday."

Allison opened her eyes and sat up. "My hero; you've saved the day."

"Actually, it was Von Grunewald. I was too busy with Lieutenant Darwin."

Allison looked apprehensive. "Ooh. How did that go? At least he didn't put you in jail, apparently."

"Actually, we're the best of pals, at least at the moment. It seems his friend Otto Pfeiffer told him about the Taylor-Bradwell case, and Darwin is smart enough to want me working with him rather than against him. He's agreed to give me access to all the evidence as long as I share my findings in a discrete way."

"Well, you're nothing if not discrete, so that shouldn't be a problem. It looks like you've rung the bell with this one Max. Imagine, a police detective who thinks you're the cat's meow."

"Well, I do have a natural boyish charm."

"I'd be careful about turning loose any boyish charm on the police. It could get you arrested."

"No thanks. I've been arrested and wouldn't recommend it."

"So did you learn anything about the case from your new detective pal?"

"Not a lot from him directly, but he took me to Connelly's place to view the scene of the crime."

"How exciting! Did you find any smoking guns behind the curtains?"

Max smiled. "Nothing so dramatic, but the angle of the bullet seems to indicate either murder or suicide."

"Well, that narrows it down. I suppose that means we can eliminate the possibility of murder by Martian death ray."

Max ignored the remark. "I did see something interesting, though. Upstairs by Connelly's bed was a glass of water containing his false teeth."

"Interesting? I'd call it revolting."

"The glass was still sitting on a polished oak table and there was a white ring left by condensation on the glass."

"Well, it is hot and humid, and a glass of cool water would produce condensation."

"Right," said Max, "but there was no coaster under the glass. That's why there was a ring. Now if Connelly was in the habit of placing his teeth in a glass of water on that table with no coaster, there would have been rings all over the top, but the top was clean and shiny, which indicates the glass was put there by someone else that night."

"By the killer?"

"Well, maybe by someone who wanted it to look like Connelly got out of bed to let the killer in. I don't really know yet. Anyway, Von Grunewald is calling tonight, probably for a progress report. Why don't we grab dinner at that place down the street? Unless you have other plans, of course."

"As a matter of fact, I do."

"You don't mean.."

That's right. We're going to visit a blind tiger."

Although it was well past nine and the streets were dark, the noise of the city continued just as loudly as when Max and Allison stepped off the train. The air was still warm and muggy, and the stone fronts of the buildings felt warm to the touch.

"I'll never complain about the squawking of the ducks back home again," said Max just after a police car sped past with its siren screaming.

"At least the riveting stopped for the night, even though the traffic noise is making up for it. So tell me again why we're going to this speakeasy?"

"I'm going to gather material for my article," Allison replied. "You're going to escort me."

"Oh, I'm just here to provide male companionship?"

"No, you're here to help me avoid other male companionship. Such as that bartender today."

"But you've already been there once."

"Yes, but it's completely different at night. Come on, Max, you might even enjoy it."

"And if I don't, does it matter?"

"Not in the least."

"I suppose the possibility of breaking the law hasn't occurred to you? I'm not sure being arrested for one crime while investigating another one is a good strategy."

"The crime is selling or drinking illegal alcohol; something we won't be doing. We're just observing and gathering material for my article and for your investigation. Now try to look shady; here we are."

"The Puncheon Club? So if this is a speakeasy; how do we get in?"

"The same way I got in today. I claim I'm a friend of Mrs. Parker."

"Who's she?"

"I have no idea, but it worked."

Sure enough, Max and Allison soon found themselves at a table listening to the saxophonist she had seen rehearsing that afternoon. A bored looking waitress took their soft drink orders and they were left to observe the crowd that surged around the place drinking, laughing, and at one table, singing.

"I guess it's New Year's eve every night in this place," said Max, shouting to be heard over the saxophone. "As long as the police don't raid the place, I guess we're all right."

Allison smiled and nodded as she made notes on a small pad she had carried in her purse.

Max looked around some more, marveling at the variety of people. They seemed dressed in everything from formal wear to everyday clothes and consisted of as many women as men. About half, were smoking as well as drinking, and it occurred to Max that if the reformers intended to reduce drinking and smoking, Prohibition was not going to do the job.

Over in a corner of the room, Max thought he saw a familiar face.

"Allison, I thought I saw someone I know. Excuse me. I'll be back in a few minutes."

Allison looked up from her notes briefly and waved him on.

The man Max had seen had his back to him now, so Max wasn't sure until he tapped him on the shoulder and the man tuned around.

"Detective Anderson! What are you doing here?"

"Keep it down, Mr. Hurlock," said Detective Anderson, obviously embarrassed. "These people don't know I'm with the police."

"I'm not surprised," said Max, "but what are you doing here?"

Anderson guided Max to a relatively quiet corner. "I'm on surveillance duty."

"On what?"

"Before Prohibition, we used to have men hang out in the local bars to pick up information and gossip about local crime. A lot of the crooks went there and talked in their beer. Now it's a lot harder because the speaks all operate as private clubs so it's harder to get a man inside. I'm young enough that they don't know I'm with the police, so I stake out the place every so often."

"Why don't the police just raid the place?" Max asked.

"Two reasons. We don't want to mess up a good source of information, and we can never know when there'll be a city councilman among the patrons."

"This is unbelievable," said Max. "Have you heard anything tonight?"

"Well, I was working my way over to that table on the right to see what I could overhear. That guy with the dark slicked down hair and the cigar sitting there with his pals is Waxy Gordon, one of Arnold Rothstein's's top lieutenents. Rothstein runs most of the bootlegging in Manhattan."

"I suppose even criminals need a night off once in a while."

"Anyway, speaks are the new melting pots. Respectable people and criminals all mixed together in a place that doesn't officially exist."

"Democracy in action, I guess. High society and high crimes all under one roof."

On the other side of the room, the bartender had noticed Allison come in and frowned when he saw she was with another man. Apparently she didn't have time for him, but she did for someone else. He had run into stuck up women before; women who thought they were too good for him. And that stuff about Mrs. Parker. What a lot of banana oil. A woman like that would never be pals with Mrs. Parker. Suddenly the bartender smiled. He knew how to teach Miss Stuck-Up a lesson.

Allison was busy taking in the scene and still buried in her notes and didn't notice the figure come up beside her.

"Good evening, Miss. I'm glad you came back."

Allison looked up to see the bartender standing by her and smiling slyly.

"Oh, hello. Yes. I'm enjoying it immensely just making a few notes."

"Well, that's great. Say, there's someone you should talk to. Come with me for a minute."

"No, I really.."

"Just two tables away. Someone who knows all about speaks and about New York. It'll be a big help in your notes." He indicated a young couple deep in conversation two tables away. They looked harmless enough, certainly not gangsters or underworld figures.

Allison hesitated. She didn't trust the bartender, but didn't want to pass up a possible good contact either. Besides, it was only two tables away and Max was just across the smoky room somewhere, so what was the harm? She could always just go back to her table if it didn't work out.

A moment later she was standing by the other table. The man was bookish looking and well dressed. The woman was attractive, with bobbed black hair and a stylish, if somewhat world-weary look. In front of them were a large number of empty glasses and bottles. The bartender cleared his throat and the couple looked up. The saxophone player was on a break, so the room was relatively quiet.

"Mrs. Parker, this lady says she's an old friend of yours." Leaving Allison standing alone, the bartender then retreated to the bar to watch the bloodshed. He knew that Dorothy Parker, former theater critic for Vanity Fair, had the most caustic sarcastic wit in New York. "You could do surgery with that woman's tongue," someone had told him once. Now that stuck up woman who claimed she was an old friend would get what she deserved. Mrs. Parker would fillet the young upstart for using her name under false pretenses. This would be fun to watch.

Allison, too, suddenly realized just who Mrs. Parker was. She had read several articles about the literary scene in New York in Harper's magazine at the county library. Now she stood alone facing a slightly inebriated Dorothy Parker like a small furry animal looking at a hungry cobra. Fighting the urge to say it was all a mistake and retreat, Allison stood her ground. She realized this could be very interesting- if she survived.

Dorothy Parker looked Allison up and down. Her eyes narrowed in an inquisitive and somewhat suspicious way as she held a half-empty glass in midair next to her face. "Refresh my memory, darling. Exactly where do we know each other from?" Her voice was throaty and slightly slurred.

"Well, Mrs. Parker," Allison replied, "the truth is, we never met."

Mrs. Parker raised an eyebrow. "Never met?" She turned to her companion. "Do you hear that, Mr. Benchley? We never met. Thank God! For a moment, I thought I was drunk already, and it's far too early. I intended to remain coherent for at least another hour."

She turned back to Allison. "Then where did that unpleasant man get such an extraordinary idea?"

"Actually, I told the doorman we were old friends to get in here tonight."

The couple looked at each other again and the man spoke. "Why didn't you just walk in? They usually let young women in with no questioned asked. Don't tell me you've never been to a speakeasy before."

"No. I'm from Maryland and I'm here with my husband. I'm researching a magazine article I'm writing, and..."

"Oh my God," Mrs. Parker interrupted. "Not another would-be writer! I suppose you want me to give you advice; to tell you the secrets of the trade. Is that's what's behind this masquerade, my little country mouse?"

Allison hesitated, fumbling for a response, then her self-defense reflexes kicked in. "Advice? Why? Are you some sort of writer?" She asked, innocently.

Mrs. Parker stiffened, but her companion laughed. "Hah! Your country mouse has claws, Mrs. Parker!"

Mrs. Parker was not amused. "I suppose they don't get Vanity Fair in the backwoods of Maryland. Well, here's some free advice anyway: if you have to ask someone how to write, you can't. Now run along back to the cotton fields."

"Thanks anyway," said Allison, "but I think I'd prefer advice from someone without quite as many empty liquor quotes bottles in front of them."

"I'd rather have a bottle in front of me," Mrs. Parker shot back, "than a frontal lobotomy."

Allison shook her head sadly.

"I must say, Mrs. Parker, this is a fine way to treat an old friend. You just see if I invite you to my house this Thanksgiving."

Allison turned on her heel and started to walk away.

"Wait! Don't go," came the voice of Mrs. Parker. She was laughing.

Allison turned warily.

"Come sit here a while. You're a breath of fresh air, and God knows this place could use it. Won't you join us?"

"That depends. Are you going to be nice to me?"

"My dear, I *was* being nice to you. You should see me when I'm being rotten."

"I'll settle for nice, then," said Allison, sitting down.

Mrs. Parker gave her a smile that was entirely free of sarcasm. "So tell me my dear, what sort of articles do you write?"

Back at the bar, the bartender threw his rag down in frustration.

Max was surprised when he returned and Allison was not at the table. Assuming she had gone to the ladies lounge, he sat down to await her return. From nearby he heard her laugh and turned around to see her sitting with two strangers. It looked like Allison was making some contacts of her own.

"..Oh, yes, I suppose Goucher is a good school," Mrs. Parker was saying, "but education can only get you so far. You need some judgment to go with it. Take that woman over there with the red hat. She can speak 18 languages and can't say no in any of them."

Allison laughed again. "Well, Mrs. Parker, as I said, I'm gathering material for a magazine article on New York speakeasies. What can you tell me about them?"

"Speakeasies provide women with the means to drink in public. That's an improvement as far as I'm concerned. I hate drinking at private parties. Three drinks and I'm under the table. Four drinks and I'm under the host." Mrs. Parker picked up her drink and downed it in one gulp.

Allison blushed. "I don't think I can use that quote."

"Don't fret, darling. There are places I can't use it myself."

"There seem to be a lot of different people here. Is it that way in all speakeasies?"

"This is pretty typical," said Benchley, "All sorts of folks show up here. Take that man in the brown suit over there. He was the chauffeur for that society fellow that was murdered a couple of weeks ago."

"You mean Ellsworth Connelly?"

"That's the name," said Benchley. "Anyway, the chauffeur is here most nights. I spoke with him a few nights ago and it seems he's counting on inheriting some of Connelly's considerable estate. The possibility of money has clearly gone to his head. Why, he practically has it spent already."

"Is that so?" said Allison, trying to hide her excitement.

"Money, money, money," sighed Mrs. Parker. "If you want to know what God thinks of money, just look at the sort of people he's given it to."

Back at the hotel several hours later, Max and Allison lay awake listening to the rumble of the city outside.

"So tell me who this woman was again?" Max asked. "It sounds like you had a pretty productive evening, You found out some important information about Connelly's chauffeur and you met that Parker woman."

"Dorothy Parker. She's one of the leading lights of New York's literati. Her theater reviews in Vanity Fair are legendary. She writes poetry and short stories as well. She's also known for her cutting wit, which she tried out on me. I pretended I had never heard of her, just to get back at her."

"I can see the headline now: New York writer meets St Michaels scribbler: no prisoners taken."

"Now, Max, she was really quite nice once she knew she couldn't bully me."

"Maybe, but I think I prefer people who are nice without having to be wrestled to the ground. So what else did you learn from your new old friend?"

"I got some great information on speakeasies and a lead to another one up town north a bit. Maybe that'll be my next stop. Of course the most valuable bit of information might be about Connelly's chauffeur."

"Yes, that's good to know since I'm interviewing him tomorrow morning. It gives him a motive. What do you have planned?"

"I'm starting my article in the morning and I'm weighing the idea of lunch with Mrs. Parker and her friends. She invited me to stop by. She and a bunch of like-minded folks she knows apparently eat at the Algonquin Hotel every day and talk about literary matters. It sounds thrilling."

"Then why don't you go?"

"I'm a little wary of a whole table of people like her. I think she just wants to show me off as a backwoods curiosity. Still, it's a great opportunity. I think I'll go."

"Sounds delightful," said Max. "Will you have a food taster assigned to you?"

"Well, Max; if they're like Mrs. Parker and Mr. Benchley, I don't think they'll be that bad, just a bit self-absorbed."

Max looked dubious. "Just make sure they don't absorb you while they're at it."

"Oh Max; don't be a worry-wart. This is my big chance to meet some real writers, people whose names are known all over. I'd never have this opportunity in St Michaels."

"All right. I know better than to argue when your mind is made up. Would you be available in the afternoon? I'm interviewing Mandy Jewell and I think a female presence might ease the strain a bit."

"Sure thing. It sounds like a hoot."

"Assuming you survive lunch, that is."

John Reisinger

Chapter 8
Mandy Jewell

The knocking on the front door of their room drowned out the other sounds of the city the next morning as Max lay on his side with an arm over the still sleeping Allison.

"Who is it?" croaked Max finally.

"Bellhop, Mr. Hurlock. The front desk has an important telephone call for you."

Max looked at the alarm clock and saw it was a little after six and still dark.

"I'll be right down."

Max's eyes were open by the time he picked up the black phone at the front desk.

"Max Hurlock."

"Max, what the hell were you doing at the Puncheon Club last night?" came the gruff voice of Lieutenant Darwin.

"The same thing Anderson was doing; investigating. Is that why you got me out of bed in the middle of the night?"

"Look, Max. If you expect police cooperation, I can't have you breaking the Prohibition laws."

Max was awake now. "We had no alcohol, as I'm sure Anderson told you, so what's the problem and what's the urgency?"

"You wife was seen laughing it up with that Dorothy Parker woman and that Benchley guy."

"Is that against the law in New York?"

"It should be. Those two are dangerous. Between them they know every newspaper reporter and magazine writer in the five boroughs. Anything your wife told them could become public knowledge by noon."

"So what?"

"So, I told you there were certain aspects of this case I don't want made public."

"Allison never divulges anything she shouldn't, so you can put your mind at ease. As for the Puncheon Club, if you're really concerned about ordinary citizens going there, raid the place. Just be careful. You'll probably bag a judge or two in the process. It might make prosecution a little awkward."

The other end of the phone was quiet for a moment.

"All right," Darwin said finally. "Just be careful."

The line went dead.

"I can see why Darwin and Pfeiffer are pals," Max mumbled as he shuffled back towards the room. "They both went to the same charm school."

Ellsworth Connelly's chauffeur, Bill Fulton, seemed remarkably cheerful for a man who had so recently become unemployed. Max found him seated in a big leather easy chair in his East Village apartment. Max looked around the place and was surprised to see how well it was appointed. The velvet drapes, Tiffany lamps and oil paintings looked as if they belonged in a much more luxurious home. Obviously Bill Fulton was a man with expensive tastes.

"Yeah it was a real shame about Mr. Connelly," the man was saying. "I worked for him for over four years and he was always good to me."

"Did Mr. Connelly help you pick out the furnishings in this place?"

The chauffeur looked around. "Not exactly. He used to redecorate his place from time to time and let me have the old stuff. Mr. Connelly was a generous man. He told me he was going to remember me in his will."

"Remember you in what way?"

Fulton looked surprised. "Why, with money, of course; lots of it. He appreciated how reliable I am, and how I can keep my mouth shut."

"I can see that," Max replied dryly. "So he promised you some bequest?"

"Not in so many words, but right after that business with Gwen Perkins I told him he'd better be careful or someone might do him in. He said not to worry; that if anything happened to him I'd be provided for."

"He wasn't more specific?"

"Well, he had to be careful what he said around the house, cause Constance was always around. The housekeeper, you know. She would keep an eye on him and listen in on his conversations. That was harmless enough I suppose, except she saw herself as his keeper. You know. She'd tut tut and tell him he shouldn't do this or he should do that, all for his own good of course. No wonder the man never wanted to get married. He already had someone to nag him."

"How did you get along with the housekeeper. Miss Tibbet?"

"Oh, I was polite with her, but I never really trusted her. It seemed to me she was jealous of the time Mr. Connelly spent with me every day."

"What was your normal routine?"

"Saying there was a normal routine is a stretch. Mr. Connelly was all over the place; New York, Maryland, Palm Beach, and even Europe every couple of years. But when he was in New York, he'd call me when he wanted to be picked up, usually late in the morning. He'd give card lessons in his home until around 11:30, then go to one of his clubs for lunch. Then he'd usually give private lessons in other people's homes in the afternoon. That was when he made his contacts with his married lady friends."

"Then what?"

Fulton shrugged. "Usually he'd meet some lady for dinner and then go to a show or entertain at home."

"Did you wait outside all this time?"

"Oh, no. Usually Mr. Connelly would send me home after dinner if he entertained at home. If he hosted a stakes card game, of course, he wouldn't need me anymore, and if he entertained a lady, well, then he hoped he wouldn't need me anymore that night, if you know what I mean."

The chauffeur winked.

"I know what you mean," Max replied with some distaste. "Then I take it Mr. Connelly was something of a lady's man?"

Fulton laughed. "Yeah, like the Pope is something of a Catholic. Mr. Connelly was always seeing a different woman. I'd say maybe a different one every several weeks. He'd pursue then relentlessly, with flowers, presents, jewelry, and constant attention. Then, just as suddenly, he'd lose interest and drop them. You needed a scorecard to keep up with him."

"How did he meet so many women?"

"I'm damned if I know. They'd suddenly appear, then just as suddenly they'd be gone. I think he just chatted them up whenever he ran into any woman. A couple of times when I was driving him somewhere, he'd see some woman walking down the street and tell me to pull over. He'd jump out of the car and introduce himself. The direct approach you might say."

Max shook his head. "Did that approach usually work?"

"Most of the time he got a polite rejection and once or twice he got his face slapped, but once in a while he was able to reel them in. Then after a few frantic weeks he'd drop them again just as suddenly."

"I suppose some of the women didn't take it well?"

"You said it. On more than one occasion I'd change the route I was driving to avoid passing by the home of one of his rejected loves. And the scenes! Whenever I saw a woman rapidly approaching Mr. Connelly, I'd cringe, thinking it might be an ex-girlfriend waiting to bawl him out. Some of them really were bitter, and used language no lady should use. That Gwen Perkins even attacked him with an umbrella last year. Mr. Connelly had to get a restraining order against her."

"Max noted the name. How about jealous boyfriends or husbands?"

"There were some of them, too. Mr. Connelly had an affair with Dianne Forsythe over a year ago, and then broke it off. A few days later, her husband, Martin Forsythe showed up demanding to see Mr. Connelly. I was waiting outside with the car and I saw the whole thing. Mr. Connelly wouldn't let him in and the man pounded on the door damning Mr. Connelly's eyes for almost twenty minutes before he finally left. Then Mr. Connelly came out as white as a sheet and told me to drive him to the country for the rest of the day."

"Did Martin Forsythe ever come back?"

"Not when I was there, but I'll tell you something; I hear that Forsythe also fools around a bit. Not as much as Mr. Connelly of course, but he's been known to sow a few wild oats, if you know what I mean. I don't think he would have killed Mr. Connelly because he had a few ladies on the side himself. It was all a show."

81

"How do you know this?"

Fulton shrugged. "I drive around town and I talk to people. You'd be surprised what people will tell a chauffeur."

"I see. Tell me about the night Mr. Connelly was killed."

Fulton leaned back in his chair and sighed.

"I drove Mr. Connelly and Mandy Jewell to the Waldorf around eight or so. Mandy's a bit younger than Mr. Connelly's usual women, and she's pretty smart, too, although she pretends not to be. He'd been seeing her for well over a month, a lot longer than the others. Anyway, I picked her up from her apartment down on 4th Street. There was some sort of benefit reception at the Waldorf and Mr. Connelly was meeting some friends there. He seemed cheerful and happy; nothing unusual. I was instructed to be back to pick them up at 11, but when I did he said they were going to Zeigfeld's Midnight Frolics and to pick him up there at one. So that's what I did. I drove him and Miss Jewell back to his house and waited outside for a few minutes."

"What were you waiting for?"

"The signal."

"The signal?"

"Right. Whenever Mr. Connelly brought a lady home, I stood by to see if she needed a ride back to her house. If she decided to stay the night, Mr. Connelly would signal me to leave by flashing the front porch light on and off."

"Did you get the signal that night?"

"It took a little longer than usual, maybe 20 minutes or so, but then I saw it and I went on home. When I left they were together and both alive. The next morning he was dead and she was still alive."

"So what do you think?" Max asked.

Fulton stood up from his chair, indicating he was through talking. "I think you should be talking to Mandy Jewell."

Allison stepped out of the taxi in front of the Algonquin Hotel on West 44th Street and looked at her watch. She was right on time. Allison hesitated before opening the front door. Did she really want to encounter an entire lunch group of people like Dorothy Parker? Well, maybe they wouldn't be so bad, and there was a lot of good article material to be had. Besides, where would she ever get a chance like this again?

She walked through the main lobby and into a large dining room lined with dark wood paneling and potted palms. Waiters scurried about frantically among scores of diners and several chandeliers lit the scene with warm light from overhead. The glowing bulbs reflected in the sheen of the wood paneling. In the center of the room was a large round table crowded with people talking and laughing. For a moment Allison stood transfixed. She had never seen so many literary people in one place, let alone people who apparently made a living at it. She was a long way from St Michaels.

"Ah, there she is," a throaty voice cut through the chatter of the crowd. "Allison, over here."

Dorothy Parker was motioning her to come sit down. As Allison walked towards the table, she noticed a few of the diners becoming aware of her presence and looking at her with curiosity.

"Listen everyone. This is Mrs. Allison Hurlock. She writes magazine articles. She wrote an article about the small town flapper for some publication called 'Modern Girls Magazine'. I'm sure you all read it. Now I want all you literary vultures to be nice to her. She's from Maryland, but I suppose she can't help that."

A roar of laughter from the people at the table met this statement. A few said welcome, a few turned back to their conversations, and a few sat staring at Allison.

"You know, she looks like Mary Miles Minter, the movie star," said one very portly bespectacled man to no one in particular.

"This gentleman is Alexander Woolcott, dear," said Mrs. Parker, speaking loudly to be heard above the din. "Don't feel too flattered by his movie name dropping. He's the drama critic for the Times. The only reason he goes to a movie is to eviscerate it in print."

"I've read some of your reviews," Allison volunteered. "I just love them."

"Ah, a woman of refined taste," said Woolcott, smiling affably.

"Just as I've always told you, many people from the hinterlands can read and write too," said a dark haired man to Mrs. Parker. He stood and extended his hand to Allison.

"Fulton Pierce Adams. I write a column for the Tribune under my pen name FPA. The column is called the Conning Tower. I think you're beautiful."

"Apparently you're conning even when off duty, Mr. Pierce," Allison replied.

"She got you there, FP," said another man, slapping FP's back.

"That's George Kaufmann," said Mrs. Parker. "He produced that play at the Frayze Theater. What was it again, George?"

"The Deep Tangled Wildwood."

"There really should be a law against a play with such a long name," said Mrs. Parker. "It doesn't please anyone but the sign painters." She looked down on the table.

"Allison, we all know you write. It isn't necessary to do it at lunch," said Mrs. Parker.

"I'm taking notes," Allison replied. "So I can remember who was here."

"I wouldn't rush into that, dear; you might not want to remember. I suppose you'll write an article about us to wow all the rustics down in Maryland? I'm sure it'll be just the thing they'll want to read while cleaning fish, or possibly wrapping them."

"Well, if I do write an article, maybe I'll call it 'Slights of the Round Table.'"

Mrs. Parker smiled approvingly. "Now you're catching on. Excuse me, I have to speak to Mr. Heywood Broun a moment. He's a sportswriter, but I suppose no one is perfect."

Allison sank back in her chair . "Whew. I really feel like an outsider here," she said, a little louder than she intended.

"An outsider? Try being the only Jew in Appleton, Wisconsin."

Allison turned to see a dark haired middle aged woman who had been sitting next to her quietly.

"I'm Edna Ferber. I'm from the hinterlands, too, but a bit further north."

Allison's eyes widened. "Edna Ferber? Didn't you write The Girls? I read that last year."

"That's right. You really are a literary person."

Allison smiled. "Just magazine articles for now. I'm working on one about speakeasies. I've already been to the Puncheon Club."

"Try the 300 Club on West 54th. It's worth seeing for the hostess alone."

Allison made a note. "Thanks. How about you? Are you working on a book now?"

"I'm just finishing up one called So Big, but I'm looking for my next project. I'm thinking of writing a book about a traveling showboat. You know; the kind that travel the rivers down south and entertain people by the riverbanks. You're from down that way. Have you ever seen one?"

Allison nodded. "Sure. We have one that stops by St Michaels; the Adams Floating Theater."

" That sounds like just what I'm looking for." Ferber pulled out a piece of paper and began writing. "Here's my address. The next time you see this floating theater, would you see if you could get a schedule and send it to me?

"Sure thing. Glad to help," said Allison.

"Thanks. Oh, don't look now, Mrs. Hurlock, but Robert Sherwood is trying to get your attention. He's another movie critic. The man is six foot six. Mrs. Parker says that when he walks down the street with her and Mr. Benchley they resemble a pipe organ."

Max paced up and down on the 4th Street sidewalk in Front of Mandy Jewell's red brick apartment building, pausing occasionally to pull out his pocket watch and wonder what had become of Allison. Finally, he saw her making her way through the pedestrians.

"Hey, Max. Sorry I'm late."

"Are you all right?"

"Couldn't be better. I just had the most marvelous lunch. I met a whole table of New York's best writers and playwrights. They all gather at a big round table in the Algonquin Hotel every day and fill the air was filled with witticisms and wisecracks."

"Must make it hard to eat lunch," was all Max could think of to say.

"You know, you're right. I can't even remember what I had to eat. Come to think of it, I'm not even sure I ate at all. It was that exciting. I met Heywood Broun, Edna Ferber, George Kaufman, Alexander Woolcock, .."

"It sounds great, Allison," said Max, "but I have to admit, I've never heard of any of these people."

"Well, they mostly operate out of New York and work for New York newspapers and magazines. To tell you the truth, the only ones I had heard about before were Mrs. Parker and Edna Ferber. Still, it was stimulating being with other writers, especially ones as famous as they are."

"But you said you never heard of..." Max was confused.

" Max, just because you and I haven't heard of them doesn't mean they aren't famous."

"It doesn't?"

"Of course not."

"I'm   really glad you cleared that up, Allison, but right now Mandy Jewell is expecting us. I'm afraid this conversation might not be as interesting as the ones at the round table."

Allison looked up at the apartment building and rubbed her hands together. "On the contrary, I think it should prove fascinating. Tally ho!"

The door to apartment seven had been painted blue some years in the past, but was now shedding large paint chips to reveal the muddy green color underneath. Max noticed the smell of boiled cabbage in the hallway and looked at Allison. Her winked nose told him she noticed it as well.

A woman with white-blonde hair opened the door and looked at them suspiciously. The blonde hair looked even lighter in contrast to the black dress and shawl the woman was wearing.

"Good afternoon, Miss Jewell. I'm Max Hurlock and this is my wife Allison. I called you yesterday." Mandy Jewell nodded and motioned them inside.

The apartment seemed to consist of a single hopelessly cluttered room. Mandy Jewell appeared to be not so much living in the room as camping out in it. Piles of clothes lay limply here and there, along with enough old newspapers to cover the walls. Considering the state of the streaked yellow wallpaper, newspapers would have been an improvement. The furniture consisted of several chairs and tables with a bookcase in one corner of the room and a parrot's cage in the other. The scene was punctuated by occasional shrill outbursts from the parrot.

Mandy Jewell motioned them to sit in the only two uncluttered chairs.

"You said you are working with the police, Mr. Hurlock?" Mandy Jewell had a high, almost squeaky voice.

Max nodded. "That's right. Detective Darwin and I are exchanging information to try to get to the bottom of this case. I asked Allison here to come along because I felt it would be less awkward for you."

Mandy looked at Allison. "I see."

"Miss Jewell, how long have you known Mr. Connelly?"

"I had been seeing Mr. Connelly for well over a month when he was murdered:"

"You say he was murdered. The police are considering the possibility of suicide."

"Then they are wrong. Ellsworth was murdered."

"Forgive me, Miss Jewell, but how can you be sure of that?"

Mandy Jewell leaned back in her chair and sighed. "Let me save you some trouble, Mr. Hurlock. Ellsworth and I were romantically involved. On more than one occasion I stayed over at his house. I even kept some toilet items and lingerie at his house in the spare bedroom, something I'm sure the police have found out about by now. You see, Ellsworth and I were in love. He had asked me to marry him."

Max maintained his neutral expression, but Allison couldn't help gasping slightly. Mandy Jewell looked at her.

"You may well express surprise, Mrs. Hurlock. Oh, I know Ellsworth had a history of being a Lothario and I know there were many more before me, but we had a degree of compatibility that he never found with the others. We had long and deep conversations about the mysteries and foibles of life. I think he was tired of all the shallow society types he knew and longed for a more down to earth partner, someone from a more humble background. My family was poor, and before I met Ellsworth, I was giving dance lessons to keep body and soul together. I never had the fancy advantages of Helen Arness. Maybe that's one of the things Ellsworth liked about me. He wanted to start over with a simpler and more unaffected girl. That's how I know Ellsworth would never have killed himself."

"When did he ask you to marry him?" Max asked.

"The night he was murdered."

Max and Allison glanced at each other but said nothing. By this time, Allison was forcing herself not to gasp.

"Could you tell me about that night?"

Ellsworth's chauffeur picked me up here around seven and took me to Ellsworth's house. From there we were going to the Waldorf and meeting Ellsworth's friends, Horace and Martha Porter. We sat in the drawing room talking of this and that when suddenly Ellsworth asked me to marry him. As you can imagine I was stunned. He said he was at the time of life when he wanted to settle down and that we were...well, it was rather private. Suffice to say, he asked and I accepted."

"Did you tell anyone?"

Mandy Jewell shook her head. "No. He wanted to keep it dark for a few days so he could arrange a reception to make a formal announcement. Of course I agreed and we set off for the Waldorf."

"Wait. Did the housekeeper or the chauffeur know anything about this?"

"No. He didn't tell them."

"Could either of them have overheard?"

She looked thoughtful. "I'm not sure. They were both in the kitchen at the time. The chauffeur had come in for a cup of coffee. I suppose it's possible one or both of them might have overheard. The chauffeur never said anything about it and the housekeeper went home shortly after we left."

"What happened next?"

"We went to the Waldorf and met the Porters. It was a lovely affair, with an orchestra, colored lights, and a delicious buffet. We were having a splendid time until we ran into his ex wife, Helen Arness. She's one of those wives who don't want their husband, but don't want anyone else to have him either. She said some rude things to me and I'm afraid I responded in kind. Finally, Ellsworth and her escort started arguing before calming down. I don't remember all that was said, but I did hear Helen Arness say that Ellsworth was going to pay."

"What did she mean by that?"

"I don't know. Ellsworth refused to discuss the incident for the rest of the evening. We went to

Ziegfeld's Midnight Frolics after that, then back home. We talked about the wedding and about the party he was going to plan to announce it."

Max knew there was one fact that didn't fit and he knew he had to get it resolved.

"Did you stay that night?"

Mandy Jewell frowned, as if puzzled. "You know, that was a strange thing. I was going to stay, but when I went to find my bed things, they were gone. There was no negligee and no toilet items. We both looked all over the spare bedroom, but to no avail, so I decided to return home. By this time the chauffeur had left, so I just called a taxi and went home. The next morning, I found out poor Ellsworth had been murdered."

Max made a note. "Anything else you can tell me?"

"Just one thing. I know who did it."

Chapter 9
Friends of the Deceased

One thing you had to say for Mandy Jewell, Max thought afterword; she sure knew how to stop a conversation dead in its tracks.

"It was that German, Gunther Von Grunewald," she continued after a suitable dramatic pause.

This time, Allison gasped in spite of herself.

"Von Grunewald? Why do you say.."

"About a week before he was murdered, Ellsworth had a meeting with Von Grunewald." Her words were gushing out now, as if she couldn't wait to get her thoughts and in to the open. "I had stayed over the previous night and was in the guest bedroom upstairs getting my things together when I heard voices from downstairs. At first I assumed Ellsworth was talking with the housekeeper, so I ignored it until the voices grew louder and I could tell it was two men."

"Connelly and Von Grunewald?"

"That's what it sounded like, but I went to the head of the staircase to be sure. I went down a few steps until I could see into the reception room and there they were. Von Grunewald had some sort of paper in his hands and Ellsworth was pacing back and forth extremely agitated."

"Could you tell what they were arguing about?"

"Not exactly, but I know Von Grunewald was looking for money and Ellsworth was refusing."

"Money for what?"

"I don't know, but I heard Ellsworth say that he'd paid out all the money he intended to and that Von Grunewald wasn't getting another penny. Finally, Von Grunewald folded up the paper he was holding and put it in his pocket. Then he said 'You're a wealthy man, Connelly. You have to pay what you owe and I intend to see to it that you do.'"

Another threat, Max thought. Connelly seemed to collect them the way some men collect stamps.

"I asked Ellsworth about it later, but he just said it was some business and I shouldn't worry about it. Of course I have a pretty good idea what it was all about."

"What was it about?"

"Von Grunewald was seeing Helen Arness, Ellsworth's ex-wife. The only problem was that, as far as I know, Van Grunewald is already married; I've heard him mention his wife several times. I think Helen Arness was blackmailing, or at least pressuring Von Grunewald into interceding for her with Ellsworth to get a bigger cut of his money than she got in the divorce settlement. The trouble was, they underestimated Ellsworth. He's pretty shrewd where women are concerned. I'm guessing he saw through the scheme and threatened to go to Von Grunewald's wife with the whole story. Von Grunewald couldn't face the scandal, so he came back after the night at the Waldorf and killed him. It all fits together."

"Did you tell the police any of this?"

"Of course. They said they'd check it out, but from the way they said it, I'm not holding my breath."

Max and Allison grabbed a double-decker bus to get back to the hotel, but didn't enjoy the view.

"You know," Max said, "just once it would be nice if someone would tell me everything they know instead of doing the dance of the seven veils. Von Grunewald has been holding out from the beginning, but now it seems the police have a damning bit of evidence against him and they hold it back as well."

Allison looked at the shops and people they were passing.

"Not only that, but Miss Jewell has been less than forthright."

"Why do you say that?"

Allison got out her small notebook and flipped it open.

"She claims to be a simple girl from a humble background, someone who presented Connelly with a refreshing change from the well-bred Helen Arness. The trouble is that her grammar was flawless, and she used words such as Lothario, foibles, suffice, unaffected, and splendid. I'd say Miss Jewell is solidly middle class at least, and is well educated to boot."

Max smiled. "Bravo! I thought the same thing. Of course there's also the matter of the books."

"The books?"

"Right. There was a large bookcase on one side of the room and it was fairly stuffed with the likes of Chaucer, Thackery, Plato, Plutarch, Swift, and what appeared to be the complete works of Shakespeare. She also had some books on mathematics and science in the mix, and not a magazine or a dime novel in sight. My guess is they're the remnants of a college education. What's more, I'm sure you noticed all the newspapers around the place. Every one I saw was opened to either the society or the financial pages."

"Very good," said Allison. "All that time straining your eyes squinting into the haze on the bay for the next landmark haven't been wasted. So we have a woman living in humble circumstances, but who is both educated and calculating. Then why the deception? Why pretend to be a simple and uneducated soul?"

Max frowned in thought. "Maybe to encourage people to underestimate her."

"I wouldn't make that mistake. Max, that woman is a manipulator. In the course of that interview she managed to exonerate herself, cast blame on Von Grunewald, and set herself up for a claim on the estate. Not bad for an hour's work."

"Yes; apparently she does work quickly."

"Are you going to ask Von Grunewald about his argument with Connelly?"

"Not yet. I'm betting that as far as he knows, nobody else heard that argument, so I'll keep it under my hat for now."

"What's next?"

"I'm off to see the Porters. They're the ones who were with Connelly and Mandy Jewell the night he was killed. Want to come along?"

"No, I think I'll go back to the hotel and get started on my article. I'll see you for dinner."

"Is your article going to be about the New York literary scene?"

Allison shook her head. "I may write something for a literary magazine, but I don't think the bigger ones would be interested. Outside of New York, not that many people have heard of the people I met or read the publications they write for. On the other hand, everyone has heard of speakeasies and they seem to hold a fascination for people, so I'm still writing about them, although I think I can mention the literary people in passing. I got some good leads on speakeasies today. I'll see you back at the hotel for dinner."

"I'm not sure I'll be back in time for any dinner. I may make another stop if I can. If you have any speakeasy plans, you may have to go on without me tonight. Just be careful."

"All right. I'll leave word at the front desk if I do."

"Listen Allison, I'm proud of you for going into that literary lion's den alone today. I'll bet you held them at bay, too."

She rose to get off the bus.

"I'm still alive and kicking, and I'm really inspired to start scribbling. When we get home I may even buy a round table for the kitchen."

"Well, Mr. Hurlock, we've known Ellsworth Connelly for about two years, ever since he gave us bridge lessons. We just sort of hit it off, as they say."

Max was sitting in the parlor of the Porter's house on 17th Street. Martha Porter sat petting a white cat while her husband smoked a cigarette and gestured wildly. Heavy velvet draperies and assorted tables of framed photos and knickknacks gave the room an almost Victorian air.

"The thing is, Ellsworth moved freely among the upper crust, and we couldn't. Oh, my business is doing well enough, but wealth by itself doesn't get you far in this town. You can be the richest man in New York and still not get invited to the dinners or the parties of people like the Astors or the Vanderbilts. You have to have made your money in the right way and have had it for a long time. I can't tell you how many newly made millionaires bang their heads against the wall of high society around here, only to come away disappointed."

Max nodded in sympathy. "New rich versus old rich, I suppose?"

"Exactly. But because of his card playing skill, Ellsworth knew just about everyone and was a celebrity of sorts among the well-heeled. As a result, he got invited to all sorts of affairs even though he wasn't old money. We knew Ellsworth and his wife Helen back when they were struggling. We've kept in touch with both of them, so I suppose he asked us along so he'd have someone he could talk to."

"So that's how you came to be with him at the Waldorf?"

"Exactly. "

'Tell me about the confrontation Mr. Connelly had with his ex-wife."

Martha Porter shook her head at the memory. "Oh, my stars. It was most unpleasant. Mr. Hurlock, we were amazed how fast the confrontation developed that night. One minute Ellsworth and Miss Jewell were laughing and chatting and the next minute Ellsworth's ex-wife appeared and the swords were drawn."

"Did either Mr. Connelly or Miss Jewell seem tense or preoccupied before that?" Max asked.

"Not a bit," Martha Porter replied. "They both seemed cheerful, and were obviously enjoying themselves. Then Helen spoke sharply to Miss Jewell and everything just broke loose. It was quite embarrassing."

"Yes, for a moment I thought I might have to restrain Ellsworth," Horace chimed in, "but it petered out as quickly as it began. We went to Zeigfeld's Midnight Frolics afterwards and pretty much forgot about it. Of course, it wasn't a patch on the time that Gwen Perkins attacked Ellsworth with an umbrella. By George, that was exciting, eh, Martha?"

His wife shook her head. "Dreadful. Mr. Connelly was a good friend, but sometimes his life seemed a little, well, too adventurous for us."

"What happened?"

Horace Porter leaned forward, relishing the chance to tell a good story.

"It was last fall, around the end of October. We met Ellsworth at Lindy's for lunch that day and we had just stepped out on Broadway to enjoy the crisp autumn air when this remarkable woman appeared. She was well dressed and proper looking, but had the devil in her eyes."

"Now, Horace, you're being dramatic," said Martha Porter. "Let's just say she was agitated."

"Agitated is right! She ignored us altogether and planted herself in front of Ellsworth then started berating him in some very coarse language. She implied his parents weren't married, for instance."

Max stifled a smile. "I understand. Go on."

"As near as we could tell, Ellsworth had been seeing this woman for a month or so, then stopped calling on her. Ellsworth often did things like that. He was a good fellow in many ways, but where women were concerned, he could be a bit of a cad. It became evident that Miss Perkins took a very dim view of such behavior. Well, this went on for maybe a minute, with the woman getting louder and more abusive and Ellsworth smiling grimly and trying to back away. Finally, to our astonishment, she produced an umbrella she was carrying and proceeded to beat Ellsworth with it."

"Disgraceful," said Martha, still petting the cat. "I thought she would kill the poor man. He was so surprised, she struck him on the head twice before he could react. His hat went flying and his forehead was bleeding. Finally, she ran away."

Horace Porter took up the narrative. "Turns out the woman had been threatening him for some days, so Ellsworth had to get a restraining order against her to avoid further unpleasantness. By Jove, that man does lead quite a life."

"You sound envious," said Martha.

"No chance of that. Just watching him made me tired."

"When Miss Perkins ran away, did she say anything?"

"Oh yes," said Martha, nodding. "I heard her quite distinctly. She said he was going to be sorry he had ever met her."

Horace chuckled. "To which Ellsworth replied; 'I already am!'".

"How about Martin Forsythe? Did Mr. Connelly ever mention him?"

Martha nodded. "Oh, yes. Ellsworth was quite concerned about Mr. Forsythe for a time. Mr. Forsythe has a hot temper and was quite upset with Ellsworth about a year ago, but it all blew over very quickly. Once Mrs. Forsythe convinced her husband the relationship had never been, well, a close one so to speak, Mr. Forsythe went from pursuing Ellsworth to simply ignoring him."

"Did this sort of thing happen often with Mr. Connelly?"

Horace Porter looked thoughtful. "Oh, not very often, but it has happened before on occasion. I suppose it's what you might call an occupational hazard when one lives as Ellsworth lived. The Martin Forsythe business was only the latest. I'd say there were at least two or three other angry husbands that have threatened Ellsworth in the past, but eventually they cooled down and relented. After all, being angry is one thing; acting on that anger is something else entirely. People think twice before doing anything drastic."

"Very true," said Max, snapping his notebook shut, "but even so, someone pulled that trigger."

Allison sat on a sofa on one side of the sumptuous lobby of the Wolcott Hotel, took out a pad of lined paper, uncapped her pen and began to write.

Blind Drunk at a Blind Tiger:
The Unexpected World of New York Speakeasies
By Allison Hurlock

A dozen or so rickety tables are scattered across a smoky and dimly lit room. A saxophone plays jazz in the background. On each table are at least one bottle of bootleg liquor and several glasses. At one table sits a respectable looking middle age couple, while at the next an organized crime boss sits with a several henchmen. At still another table, some well-known actors, writers and newspaper reporters chatter happily about the politician they noticed siting at yet another table. Throughout the hazy room, men and women are represented in almost equal numbers and no one seems to be concerned that what they are doing is forbidden by federal law. Welcome to the improbable world of the New York speakeasy.

She looked at what she had written. "So far so good. Now for a little background." She picked up the pen again.

Before 1920, New York was sprinkled with taverns and bars on almost every street corner. Though many were a little rough around the edges the bars quenched the city's constant thirst for beer, wine and spirits. With the coming of Prohibition, however, such establishments became illegal overnight and either converted to other uses or simply closed.

The city's thirst, however, was still there.

In keeping with both the spirit of free enterprise and an instinctive dislike of inconvenient laws, New Yorkers soon began slaking their thirst elsewhere. Secret and not so secret "private clubs" appeared and began to operate in as many places as the bars once did. Since the clubs were private, police and other unwelcome visitors could be kept out and illegal liquor served to the "club members". These speakeasies, also known as blind tigers, blind pigs, or simply speaks, probably serve as much liquor as the old bars they replaced, but are different in some significant and unexpected ways. For one thing, women were seldom seen in bars, but are enthusiastic patrons of the speaks. In fact, the whole atmosphere of many speakeasies is one of a great melting pot of different people whose only common attribute is a desire for alcohol-aided fun.

Allison nodded with satisfaction, then looked at the clock over the front desk and saw it was almost six. Max hadn't returned and she began to feel restless. The streets would be light for another hour or two, so she decided to scout out the location of the 300 Club on West 54th Street, the speakeasy Edna Ferber had recommended at lunch. She left word with the front desk and stepped out onto 31st Street to hail a taxi.

Chapter 10
Hello, suckers!

At Police headquarters, it was almost five o'clock. Detective Lieutenant Darwin looked up from his desk in surprise; his tie was loose and his sleeves were rolled up to the elbows. "Well, Mr. Hurlock. What brings you here?"

Max walked into Darwin's office and shut the door behind him. "The quest for truth," Max said as he sat down.

Darwin looked at him curiously. "We're all looking for the truth, Max."

"Are we? If so, then some are looking a little harder than others."

"What do you mean?"

"Why didn't you tell me that Von Grunewald had an argument about money with Connelly?"

Darwin smiled. "Oh, that."

"What do you mean, 'Oh, that'? Did that little fact somehow escape your attention when you said we'd share information?"

"I suppose Von Grunewald told you?"

"No, it was Mandy Jewell."

Darwin cocked his head. "Then shouldn't you be asking your friend Von Grunewald that question?"

"I intend to, but right now, I'm asking you."

Darwin pushed back his swivel chair and lit a cigarette. He slowly blew out a long stream of smoke before he replied, as if carefully weighing his answer.

"Maybe I just wanted to see how good a detective you were; to see if you'd find out on your own."

"I don't think so," said Max. "I think you wanted to see if Von Grunewald would tell me on his own, seeing as how he didn't think anyone else knew about it. You were trying to use me as a way of testing Von Grunewald's honesty."

Darwin shrugged. "It worked, didn't it? Now I know that Von Grunewald is covering up."

"You knew that before; when he didn't tell you about it."

"That's different. He could be innocent and still hold back from the police out of distrust. I've seen it a hundred times. When he holds back from the man he hires to find the truth, however, then I know that the truth is the last thing he wants you to find."

"So that's what all this 'work together' bushwa was about?" demanded Max. "It was nothing but a little experiment in criminology?"

Darwin smiled. "Just police work- nothing personal. We have to get the truth and that's not easy when people aren't willing to tell it."

"Especially if that includes the police," said Max. "Now I'm just a country boy from the shore, so I guess I'm not up on all these sophisticated New York investigation methods, so let me see if I have it this straight; I share with you everything I turn up and all my sources. In return, you withhold whatever you like and keep me in the dark when you feel like it, especially when it concerns my client. Have I missed anything?"

"Now, Max, it was nothing personal. I just had to find out if Von Grunewald was on the level."

"If you'd been honest with me, I would have found out soon enough," Max snapped. "As it is, you didn't find out anything except that Von Grunewald doesn't want to air all his dirty laundry when he's under investigation in a high profile murder case. Apparently he doesn't trust the police. Where do you suppose he got that extraordinary idea?"

"Listen, Hurlock; your boy has something to hide, and I'm going to find out what it is."

"Then I wish you the best of luck," Max said, heading for the door.

Darwin suddenly looked alarmed. "Now wait a minute, Max. Come back and sit down....please."

Max remained standing by the open door. "If you've got something else to say, you've got 30 seconds."

Darwin bit his lip, making an obvious effort to control himself, torn between the necessity to be soothing and the desire to tell a smart aleck amateur detective where to get off. Finally, the soothing side won.

"All right, all right. I was out of line. I guess I'm an old dog who sometimes falls back on the old tricks. I wouldn't blame you for walking away, but I'm asking you not to."

Max didn't reply. He took out his pocket watch and looked at it.

"Fifteen seconds left."

Darwin turned red. "Look, damn it. You know you're not going to get far without my help, and to be honest, I can still use your help as well. I say we try it again. At this point, we need each other. No more deception; I promise."

Max snapped his watch closed. "Five seconds to spare. Now I'd like to look at the crime scene photos."

From her trip to the Puncheon Club, Allison knew better than to order food at a speakeasy. As with the bootleg liquor served at these establishments, high prices combined with low quality was de rigueur for food as well. The cab driver recommended a deli at the corner of 54th Street about a block away from the 300 Club, so Allison went there to grab a bite before heading to the speakeasy. Solly's Deli was a small and crowded place, but warm and thick with the rich smell of meat, pickles, and several equally delicious-smelling items Allison could not quite identify. She ordered a pastrami sandwich, which came with the biggest pickle slice she had ever seen, and took it to a small booth by the window. She inhaled deeply then took a bite.

"Mmmmm," she said quietly. "I never had anything like this in St Michaels."

As she savored the sandwich, Allison noticed a woman about her own age at the next table reading a copy of the New York Tribune. The paper was opened to a page containing The Conning Tower, the column by Fulton Pierce Adams, one of the people she had met at lunch. Curious, Allison leaned over.

"Excuse me, are you reading The Conning Tower?"

The woman looked over as if startled. "No; this is the Herald."

Allison pointed to The Conning Tower. "I'm talking about that column."

The woman looked at the column and wrinkled her nose. "Oh. I never read that stuff. It's just a lot of ramblings from people who think they're clever. If I wanted a lot of half-baked snide opinions, I'd ask my husband."

Half-baked snide opinions? As she walked towards the 300 Club a few minutes later, Allison had to admit that based on her lunch, that wasn't a bad description.

The 300 Club was bigger than the Puncheon Club and better lit. Although still early, patrons had started to arrive. The doorman didn't seem to be too particular who he let in the door. As the people continued filling into the room, a tall woman in a red silk gown and carrying a cigarette in a long holder appeared on stage and strode up to the microphone. She looked around the room smiling and raised her arms in a welcoming gesture, her bracelets and rings glinting in the footlights.

"Hello, suckers!"

The room erupted in laughter as the patrons waved to the figure on the stage.

"Who's that?" Allison asked a woman standing next to her.

"You must be from out of town, honey," the woman replied. "Why, that there's the one and only Texas Guinan. You know; the movie actress. She's the hostess here, and one of the main attractions. Nobody can keep a party goin' like Texas."

"The show starts in five minutes," the woman on stage bellowed in a West Texas accent a cowboy would have envied, "and we have the prettiest girls in town dancing for your pleasure. Now I don't want you boys out there grabbing anything but the bottles. I used to shoot rattlesnakes back in Texas and I'll do it again!"

The crowd hooted and hollered with noisy enthusiasm.

"So everybody have a good time and remember to spend a lot of money."

"Honesty. Now that's an interesting approach," Allison remarked.

Texas Guinan strutted off of the stage to the applause of the crowd. Allison pushed through the crush of people to see if she could get an interview. A minute later, she was in a small group surrounding the hostess.

"Excuse me, Miss Guinan? Could I speak with you?"

Texas Guinan turned around and noticed Allison for the first time. She looked her up and down a moment. "Sure, honey, but first, let's see some more of those gams."

"See what?"

"The gams. You know; your legs. Hike up that skirt. Let's have a good look and see what you got."

Allison looked around at the circle of now leering men and drew herself up stiffly. "Certainly not!"

Guinan looked at her curiously. "Listen, honey, how do you expect to get hired as a dancer if you won't show off your legs? My girls don't dance in plus-fours, you know."

"I am not applying for a job as a dancer," Allison replied. "My name is Allison Hurlock. I'm a writer and I'd like to interview you."

"Not a dancer? Well shut my mouth. Seems a waste, what with a chassis like yours, but I reckon that's your business. All right; the rest of you get back to your tables and start spending money so I can pay the rent. I have to talk to this lady."

The men, looking disappointed, reluctantly drifted away.

"Sorry, honey, thought I saw some good show talent. So you're writing about me?"

"Well, about clubs, actually. I noticed you let pretty much anyone in?"

"Not anyone. You have to have money," Guinan laughed.

"Don't you have to worry about the police?"

"They don't bother us too much, although I have been arrested once or twice," she said, gesturing around the room. "See, we don't serve liquor, just ginger ale and glasses with ice in 'em. We call 'em set ups. Of course, if someone brings in a flask to go with it, what am I supposed to do; throw 'em out?"

The band had started playing louder and the house lights brightened. To the applause and whistles of the crowd, a double line of fan dancers started to snake their way on stage. Allison counted 40 women hiding behind 40 white feathered fans and wearing only bits of some shiny material that, if all put together, would barely have barely made an adequate dress for one of them.

"You better close your mouth, Miss Allison," Guinan said, chuckling. "Before some fly lands there."

"I'm sorry," said Allison, embarrassed. " Your customers must be pretty happy with this place."

"I show 'em a good time. We get a lot of bigwigs and celebrities in here. Why George Gerswin was playing the piano over there the other night."

"How about Ellsworth Connelly? Did he ever come in here?"

Guinan shook her head sadly. "It was a damn shame about him, wasn't it? Not that I was all that surprised."

Allison looked at her. "Not surprised?"

Guinan took a long drag on her cigarette. "He used to come in here every week or so. Had a new filly on his arm nearly every time. He wasn't the best looking man I ever saw, but he was smooth and he was rich and he wasn't attached. That's a pretty powerful combination around these parts."

Her words were temporarily drowned out by applause as one of the dancers accidentally dropped her fan to the delight of the crowd.

"Not a bad reaction. Maybe I'll have her keep it in the act."

"You were telling me about Ellsworth Connelly."

"Oh, yes. Well, about a week or two ago, he was in here with one of his ladies. I didn't catch her name, but she was tall and had jet black hair. Anyway, they were watching the show, just like everyone else, when suddenly they started bickering."

"Could you hear what it was about?"

"No; the band was playing and the girls were dancing. Anyway, they got louder and louder until Miss black hair gets up and stomps off. Well, by that time, they had gotten almost as loud as the band and people were staring. I was just as happy to see at least one of them hit the road."

"So did Connelly go after her?"

"No. He just sat there for the longest time with his head in his hands. I'm telling you, that man was despondent. He was crushed. It was really sad to see."

"Is that why you weren't surprised he was murdered?"

"Oh, I didn't say he was murdered. You mark my words, honey. Whatever happened in here was the last straw for that man, but he wasn't murdered. Oh, no. Ellsworth Connelly committed suicide. Now, land's sakes, child; you got your mouth hanging open again. You really ought to watch that."

Count Von Grunewald's townhouse was in the Yorkville section, a long time haven for German immigrants on the Upper East Side. Restaurants with Teutonic names featured sauerbraten and knockwurst along with potato dumplings and red cabbage. On Von Grunewald's street, however, the homes were spacious and the German influences were much less obvious.

Von Grunewald appeared in the entrance foyer and ushered Max into a well-appointed sitting room.

"You said on the phone there has been a new development," Von Grunewald began.

Max nodded. "Actually, it's an old development, but I just found out about it. You had a loud quarrel about money with Ellsworth Connelly just a few days before he was killed."

For just a moment, Von Grunewald looked startled, but he quickly recovered.

"Oh, that. It was just a little bickering between friends. It was nothing, really."

"Nothing? The police seem to think it was considerably more than nothing. Why didn't you tell me?"

Von Grunewald flicked an invisible speck from his sleeve and shrugged. "As I said, it was really of no interest. I didn't see how it could be important to the case."

"You didn't see how the prime suspect arguing with the victim over money just before the victim turns up dead might be important? I'd like to see what you think *would* be important."

"We were old friends and occasional business associates. We had such arguments from time to time."

"Let's stick to this last one. What was it about?"

Von Grunewald was quiet a moment. Then he grunted. "Well, I suppose it doesn't really matter, but he owed me money."

"From what?..a card game?"

"Not at all. It was a race horse."

"Did you say a race horse?"

"That is correct. You see, I have only known Ellsworth a few years, but I became an investor in Tigress, one of his racehorses, a 30% share to be precise. I waited for over a year, but Ellsworth claimed the horse isn't ready and he is holding it back from competition.

Of course, no racing means no possibility of prize money or of any return on my investment."

"But that's part of the risk, isn't it? There are no guarantees in horse racing. If the horse isn't ready.."

Von Grunewald nodded impatiently. "Yes, yes; as you say horse racing is risky and uncertain, and it does not do to race a horse before it is ready, but I have made inquiries on my own. Despite Ellsworth's assurances, it seems the horse is competitive and could easily be entered in a race. I invested a great deal of money in that horse on Ellsworth's word. I believe t became obvious Ellsworth took the money and bought an old plug instead of a true thoroughbred and pocketed the difference. When I confronted him, he denied it, but offered to returned a portion of my money, but I felt he should refund all of it as a man of honor."

"And he refused?"

"He denied the horse was slow and continued to offer to refund a portion of my investment as a gesture of good faith. I insisted on all of my money and.."

"And what?"

"And things deteriorated as they say. We shouted at each other a bit, then it was over. It was nothing, really. That is why I didn't tell you."

Max said nothing, then got up.

"I see. Well, that clears that up. Now I really have to be going."

Von Grunewald looked at him curiously. "You have no more questions, Max?"

"Not at the moment, but we'll talk again soon."

Chapter 11
Queen of the Automat

"Oh Max, this new room is wonderful!" Allison giggled, rolling on the bed the next morning.

Max looked around with approval. "Especially compared to that cracker box we've been staying in. It even has a sitting room and two windows."

"And look; there are chairs to sit on. No more using the bed as a chair. We can use it as the good lord intended," said Allison.

Max flopped on the bed next to her and kissed her on the neck. "That's exactly what I was just thinking."

"I didn't mean the Lord of Whoopee. Well, maybe not just yet, anyway, but check back with me tonight."

Max sighed. "It's a date. Meanwhile, I suppose duty calls. I have suspects to chase and you have speakeasies and unknown famous writers to pursue."

Allison settled deeper into the soft bed.

"Von Grunewald really came through for us, Max. He wasn't kidding when he said he'd get us a better place."

Max nodded. "Yes, you can rely on Von Grunewald...sometimes."

Allison sat up on the edge of the bed. "What do you mean. Is he holding back information again?"

"Worse than that. Now he's taken to outright lying. I suppose I should be surprised, but somehow I'm not."

"Me neither. There's something about him I can't quite put my finger on. Oh he's polite and charming, and what he says always seems so reasonable, but I get the impression he's what the English refer to as 'too clever by half'. Max, if Von Grunewald is lying to you, why not give him the bum's rush and head back to St Michaels? We don't need this. It's hard enough digging up the facts when the client is telling the truth, but almost impossible when he isn't."

"All very true," Max replied, "but I'm not ready to give up just yet. I'm going to let Von Grunewald think he has me fooled and see where it goes. It might get him to let his guard down and reveal something he doesn't want me to know."

"It sounds like you're still playing cat and mouse with a U-boat. Just make sure you don't get torpedoed along the way."

Max took out his pocket watch. "I have another interview in a half hour; the somewhat excitable Gwen Perkins."

"Isn't she the one who set about Connelly with an umbrella?"

"Yes, apparently she has a tendency to overreact."

"Oh, I don't know," said Allison. "In view of Mr. Connelly's behavior, I'd say she showed remarkable restraint."

Max smiled and put on his fedora as he made his way to the door. "I'll be back in an hour or two. If you're not planning on a night out with the local celebrities we can grab a bite at Lindy's."

The Horn and Hardart Automat stood under a vertical neon sign in Times Square, between 46th and 47th Street. Max pushed open the front door to find about 20 tables, half of which were occupied by diners. Billed as the modern way to dine, the restaurant was a strange blend of the mechanical and the gastronomic. Two of the walls were solidly lined with rows of glass fronted stainless steel doors about six inches high and a foot wide. Behind each of these doors, post office box style, was a pigeon hole containing a plate of food. The patrons selected their meal or side dish from a window, and inserted several nickels to open the door. There were no waiters visible, just a cashier's booth for making change. The occasional rattle of coins in slots augmented the low hum of conversation in the room.

"Well, it's efficient," Max remarked, "but it has all the atmosphere of a subway car." He looked in one of the windows and saw a plate holding a portion of meat loaf that was in turn wrapped in waxed paper. Past the plate he could see through the other, open end of the box. Behind the wall of boxes, several waitresses scurried back and forth from an unseen kitchen replenishing the boxes as needed with freshly cooked delights. Horn and Hardart's wasn't so much a restaurant as a food assembly line.

Max sat at a nearby table and looked at the clock. Gwen Perkins was scheduled for a break in the morning before the afternoon lunch crowd came in. Presently a door swung open in the back and a short but well built redheaded woman in her early 30s appeared. She was dressed in the white uniform of the food workers who kept the automat shelves replenished, complete with a hairnet and rubber soled shoes, and was attractive in an earthy way.

"You Mr. Hurlock?" the woman asked.

Max stood up and smiled.

"I thought so," the woman replied. "You're the only one in here without a plate in front of you. I'm Gwen Perkins."

"How do you do? Thank you for seeing me like this."

"Well if you can find out who did in Ellsworth, I'll be one happy girl."

"Oh, you cared for him?"

"Cared for him? Say, that guy was a two-timer and a liar. He chases me like I was the love of his life for a few weeks, then just gives me the icy mitt; dumps me like yesterday's hamburger. He was a rat. As far as I'm concerned, whoever bumped him off did the world a favor, at least the female half of it."

"Then why are you so anxious to find out who did it?"

"Because it'll get the police to leave me alone. They've been swarming around me like flies on a day old pie. They questioned me at least five times. They think maybe I had something to do with it. Can you beat that?"

"Well, you are the only one of Mr. Connelly's acquaintances to have actually assaulted him. That sort of thing trends to make law enforcement people suspicious."

Gwen Perkins waved a hand. "Aw, that was nothing. I was just sore because he dumped me so suddenly. One day it was 'dear wonderful Gwen' and the next it was 'Gwen who?'. Well, a girl gets a little peeved when a man treats her like that, so when I ran into him out on the street in broad daylight, ...well I just let fly."

Max nodded in sympathy. "I see. Well.."

"I know it looked suspicious, but I get a bit riled when I get dumped like that. I would have told his wife on him, but he was divorced, so I guess I was just frustrated. I wanted to raise a few lumps on the man, but I never would have killed him."

"Miss Perkins.."

She smiled and put her hand on Max's. "Please call me Gwen."

Max withdrew his hand from under hers and wrote a note. "All right, Gwen. How did you meet Mr. Connelly?"

Gwen Perkins slowly took out a pack of Camel cigarettes and lit one. She inhaled deeply and blew out a long sigh of smoke.

"I met him here, as a matter of fact," she began. "Oh, I know this place isn't exactly Delmonico's, but you'd be surprised the number of well off people who come in here from time to time. We get a lot of people from the theater district, since it's so close, but there's a lot of offices around here and it's a great place for busy business people. It's not the money, it's the speed. They can eat here in 10-15 minutes and be on their way."

"And Connelly stopped in one day?"

She nodded and took another puff. "Exactly. We girls that keep the shelves stocked also take turns busing tables. Believe me, the dirty dishes pile up fast in a place like this. It's not a bad job. The regulars even tip us sometimes. So anyway, one day there's this distinguished looking guy sitting right about where you're sitting now. He was just finishing a 35 cent pork chop platter. I asked if he was through with his plate and he looks up at me and smiles. We started talking and I'm telling you Max, he was the most charming man I've ever met in my life...no offense."

"None taken."

"He was so gallant and so considerate, I was just swept off my feet. He asked me to go out that very night. We went to a speakeasy called Freddy's Place over on 55th Street and we had a wonderful time. We talked and we danced to the jazz band they have there. Don't get me wrong. I've met men here before, quite a few in fact. The other girls sometimes call me the Queen of the Automat. The truth is, I haven't had much luck with

117

men. But Ellsworth really seemed different." She smiled at the memory.

"The next month was like a dream. He called on me; he took me out to all kinds of speakeasies and some fancy places; he sent flowers; and he sent gifts. It was like his whole life revolved around me and I loved it. Pretty soon I started dreaming of a life together."

"Marriage?"

"Well, why not? My first husband died in that terrible Spanish Flu outbreak in 1919 and left me with nothing. I've been with a succession of men since then, looking for someone to take me away from the Automat. I really thought Ellsworth was the one."

"So what happened?"

She ground out the cigarette in a stamped tin ashtray. "Nothing. That's the hell of it. We were going great guns and my head was in the clouds, and all of a sudden, he wasn't there anymore. He didn't call, he didn't send notes....nothing. At first I thought something had happened to him, or maybe he was sick. I went to his house, but he was never there. I called, but he never answered. I sent notes and they were ignored. Finally, I caught a glimpse of him on Broadway one day with another woman, and I knew the truth. I realized he had just gotten tired of me. I guess that's what hurt most of all, even more than the broken dreams; the shear coldness of it all. I felt betrayed. I felt used and, yes, angry."

Angry enough to kill? Max wondered, but he let her continue.

"You don't need to hear about my nights of lonely despair; the crying; the misery. Suffice to say, That man left a hole in my heart in the cruelest way possible. Then a few weeks later, I saw him on the street in front of Lindy's. He was so comfortable, so assured, so unencumbered, so damned unconcerned. In that moment, I just sort of saw red and I attacked him with my umbrella. I hit him again and again, letting out my anger and frustration at what he had done to me. The police have questioned me about it over and over again. I suppose the smart thing to do would be to express regret, but frankly, Max, I don't have any. He got what he deserved. I decided right then and there that any man who did that to me would pay."

A door in the wall opened a crack and a voice called Gwen Perkins back to her duties. She quickly scribbled her address on a paper napkin and handed it to Max.

"If you need any more information, here is where I live. It's in the East Village. I have to go."

Max sat for a long time thinking of the woman behind the wall of glass doors and wondering if she could have been mad enough to kill. The more he thought about it, the more possible it seemed.

Lindy's was crowded that night as Max and Allison arrived. They found a table near the back and lost themselves in the menu.

"Geez, what's with all these sandwiches?" Max grumbled. "They must have a sandwich named after half the people in New York. Whatever happened to a Ham on Rye?"

"I think that's a Charlie Chaplin."

"And what are all these other items? Babka? Borscht? Egg crème? Who eats this stuff?"

"Hush, Max. Next thing you know, you'll be asking for crabcakes."

"Say, maybe I should suggest that. A crabcake sandwich named the Max Hurlock. I'll bet it would be a big seller."

"Max, that's considered shellfish. And before you ask, they don't have pork chops either."

"Well, it looks like they have Italian food."

"What? Where do you see that?"

"Right here. Look..Pastrami."

"Max, why don't you go into Vaudeville as a comedian," Allison laughed. "Then they'd really name a sandwich after you."

"After today, it'll probably be on stale bread. I had another interview leading nowhere."

"Gwen Perkins?"

"Also known as the Queen of the Automat. She had pretty much the same story as all Connelly's ex lady friends. He swept her off her feet then dumped her on her backside. Apparently that was his standard routine."

"What a rat. Maybe you could narrow down the search by listing the people who didn't want to kill him."

"Sure, as soon as I find one."

"Is it possible that Gwen Perkins killed him?"

Max nodded. "Oh, I'd say it's very possible. She said he got what he deserved and talked about making him or any man pay for dumping her."

"And don't forget, she is the only suspect we know of who actually attacked Connelly physically."

"Oh, yes. I haven't forgotten that little incident. I'd say she's the strongest suspect we've got. There's only one thing I can't figure out, though."

"Why isn't she doing a better job of covering herself?" asked Allison.

"Exactly. You'd think she'd downplay her feelings and claim she'd gotten over her affair with Connelly, yet she admits to hating him and seems glad to see him dead. She might as well take out a newspaper advertisement that she has the strongest motive."

"She may be Queen of the Automat, but she's far from being the Queen of Crime I'd say," said Allison.

John Reisinger

Chapter 12
Some words with the Police

Early the next morning, a thin spear of sunlight squeezed through a gap in the curtains and fell across the bed in Max and Allison's room in the hotel. The strip of light fell across Max's arm as it draped across Allison's shoulder just below the tangle of her curly brown hair. Still half asleep, he grunted and pulled her closer. Allison responded by releasing a long contented sigh. A few minutes later, they both awoke. Allison sat up in bed and slowly stretched like a cat awakening from a nap.

"Aaaaah. It's amazing how much better you sleep when you don't have to worry about whacking your arm on the wall every time you turn over. I love this new room."

Max smiled. "I could tell. Last night was like being back in St Michaels on a rainy night. It was great."

"Yes, you did seem to be enjoying yourself. Thank goodness the bed doesn't squeak."

He leaned over and kissed her on the forehead. "Maybe it will tonight."

"We'll see. Meanwhile, the world awaits. We both have things to do; things that involve other people. I have to pick up some more speakeasy background and I suppose you have suspects to sort out."

He walked over to the window and looked down on the street below. "Actually, I plan to drop in on my very good pal Detective Darwin and compare notes."

"I thought you didn't trust him."

123

"All the more reason to keep in touch. The police are a worthy group of men, by and large, but they don't welcome competition. Still, if I darken his doorway occasionally, I'll be able to get a sense of where his investigation is heading, and possibly some tidbits of evidence I'd otherwise miss."

"Oh, I know that's the theory, but it can't be much fun for you."

Max smiled. "All in a day's work, my love; the eternal quest for truth and justice."

"Speaking of which, I've been thinking about the Automat Queen, Gwen Perkins."

"What about her?"

"Well, when you have your little tete a tete with the forces of law and order, you might want to find out if they ever checked her whereabouts on the night of the murder."

"The trouble with that," said Max, "is that the murder occurred when most good citizens are home in bed, Very few people have a good alibi for 2 AM on any night unless they were out on the town and had witnesses."

"Didn't you say she frequented the speakeasies?"

"As far as I can tell, only when she was out with a boy friend. Still, I'll ask. You never know."

"Oh, and while you're at it, you might want to see if the police know anything about the mysterious black haired woman Texas Guinan told me about."

"That's on my list. See you tonight."

When Max was gone, Allison decided to make use of another of the small luxuries afforded by their new room and work at the desk. She spent some time going over her notes from the previous nights and then began to write.

Blind Drunk in a Blind Tiger
The unexpected world of New York speakeasies
(continued)
People who have never been to a speakeasy might easily assume they are just clandestine barrooms, but they offer far more than the old neighborhood taverns. One of the unexpected aspects of New York speakeasies, for instance, is the entertainment they provide. While the old "lobster palaces" sometimes featured demure violin music, and the entertainment in barrooms was limited to occasional drunken barbershop singing, the "speaks" are fast becoming the place to go in New York for entertainment. The acts include singers, revue dancers, comedians, and all types of jazz musicians. There are even reports that vaudeville theaters are suffering from the competition. It may be a coincidence, but many official sources such as the police and the newspapers sometimes refer to the speakeasies as "resorts". Women especially, have found a new place to relax and have fun in the speakeasies.

She leaned back in her chair and looked over what she had written. She really ought to mention Texas Guinan and her 40 girl revue.

"I wonder if I could be sued for mentioning the names and addresses of some of these places?" she wondered out loud. "After all, they're supposed to be secret, even though everyone seems to know where they are. I suppose the police would be the most annoyed if I exposed names and addresses, since they would then have a harder time ignoring them."

Her thoughts were interrupted by a knock on the door.

"Max can't be back already," she said, as she twisted the knob.

To her surprise, no one was there. She stepped out into the hallway and looked up and down. A door to the stairway at the end of the hall was closing. She hurried to the door and poked her head into the stairwell. She heard footsteps on the stairs then another door opening several floors below. Looking around, she could see that whoever had been rushing down the stairwell was now long gone.

"Practical jokers? I suppose in New York anything is possible. Hello, what's this?"

Several treads down, her eye was caught by the faint glimmer of a woman's earring. Allison picked it up and noticed it was still warm.

"That's the trouble with these screw-on jobs," she remarked. "They fall off too easily."

As she got back to the room and went to latch the door she noticed a small piece of folded paper on the floor. She picked it up, slowly unfolded it, and read a typewritten message.

Allison's eyes widened.

"Well, Max. You wanted some clues. It looks like you just got a doozy."

Detective Darwin seemed to be in an expansive mood when Max walked in. He even stood up and shook Max's hand.

"Good to see ya, Max," He said, offering a cigarette that Max refused with the wave of his hand. "I was just wondering how you were getting on."

"Well, as a matter of fact.."

"That's great, Max; really great. So tell me; what have you learned about the Connelly case?"

"I think the proper question," said Max, "is what have we learned about the Connelly case?"

Darwin feigned surprise. "We? Oh, you mean us? Well, there's not much to tell. We're just plodding along, you know..following leads.."

"Have you turned up anything on a black haired woman Connelly was seen with at Texas Guinan's 300 Club on West 54th about a week ago?"

Darwin looked surprised. "Black haired? No we never heard anything like that. We'll check it out. As I say, we're just plodding along."

Max leaned across the desk. "You have the country's biggest police force and a sensational high society murder case on your hands and you're just plodding along?"

"All right," Darwin grumbled. "I'll level with you. We've got 20 men on the case and all we've got is nothing; nothing we can use at least. Oh, we've got suspects all right, plenty of them. Anybody that couldn't turn up a suspect in this case couldn't find a hooker at a convention hotel. The problem is narrowing them down. Between the ex-girlfriends, the husbands of the ex-girlfriends, the people Connelly beat at cards, several assorted business partners like your friend Von Grunewald, and other people he had business dealings with, we need a damned score card program to keep 'em all straight."

Max nodded. "I'm having the same trouble. So far I've talked to Von Grunewald, Helen Arness the angry ex-wife, Mandy Jewell the latest girlfriend, Bill Fulton the money hungry chauffeur, Connelly's friends the Porters, and violent ex-girlfriend Gwen Perkins. Other than the Porters, they all either hated Connelly or stood to gain from his death."

"You haven't talked to Constance Tibbet the housekeeper?"

"She's next on my list."

"How about the Forsythes?"

"Not yet. What can you tell me about them?"

Darwin leaned back in his chair and lit another Lucky Strike.

"Dianne Forsythe had a brief affair with Connelly well over a year ago as you know. Martin Forsythe went after Connelly, probably to thrash him good. Connelly made himself scarce and the whole thing blew over as far as we could tell. It seems that if Martin Forsythe had intended to kill Connelly, he would have done it long before this."

"Fulton said Martin Forsythe is something of a woman chaser himself."

"Just occasionally," said Darwin. "He doesn't hold a candle to Connelly. We checked it out."

"So you've eliminated Martin Forsythe as a suspect?"

"We haven't eliminated anybody yet. We can't afford to. All the same, Martin Forsythe seems pretty far down the list."

"And Constance Tibbet?"

"She's a bit more interesting as a suspect. From all accounts Connelly treated her badly; low pay, long hours, no appreciation. If on top of all that she suspected he was changing his will to the chauffeur's benefit, well, you figure it out."

"Maybe," said Max, "but that sounds pretty speculative."

"Oh, there's more. You know how she hid the nightgowns and the toilet articles before the police arrived, of course. Everyone assumes it was to protect Connelly's reputation, but I'm thinking it might just as well have been to make herself look good."

"Yes, I see what you mean," said Max, nodding slowly. "Then she would appear to be the faithful servant, loyal even after death. No one would suspect such a person of murder. I'm impressed. You do have a devious mind."

Darwin grinned. "I deal with devious people. So what have you found out?"

"Helen Arness certainly had the motive and the ill will to do in her ex-husband. If resentment were water, she'd be Niagara Falls. That would explain why Connelly didn't bother with his toupee or false teeth when he let her in that night."

"Good," said Darwin. "Plus, we did some checking and found that your friend Von Grunewald dropped her off at her place around 12:30, so she had plenty of time to get over to Connelly's and give him a little lead valentine. How about Miss Jewell?"

"Mandy Jewell doesn't have a motive if she's telling the truth about Connelly's marriage proposal, but I suspect she isn't. I don't figure Connelly for the marrying type; not with the bachelor life he was so obviously enjoying. If he was about to ditch her, suddenly she has a motive too."

"She's not much of a suspect," said Darwin. "I figure that if Connelly was about to ditch her, it wouldn't have been on the same night he took her to that shindig at the Waldorf. It's more likely he would have just stopped calling on her; that was his usual routine. If he had died a few days later, I'd say she's a suspect, but not the same night."

"Based on what you know," said Max.

"Of course."

"I've found that it's often what we don't know that causes the problems."

"Maybe. How about the chauffeur, Max?"

"Bill Fulton. Now there's an interesting study. He was practically a conspirator with Connelly in his conquests. They had secret signals and almost worked as a team. Plus, to hear him tell it, Fulton was a big beneficiary if Connelly were to die. If that's true, or even if Fulton only thought it was true, he had a powerful motive."

"Not to mention plenty of opportunity," Darwin agreed. "We questioned him several times and searched his rooms, but there's nothing we can hang our hat on just yet. Now how about Gwen Perkins?"

"I suppose you've questioned her, and checked her whereabouts?"

"Several times. She strikes me as a hard-nosed little cookie. She's pretty sour on men in general and determined to take it out of their hide if she doesn't like the way they're treating her. Of course you know she attacked Connelly with an umbrella. Brother! I'm telling you, Max, I wouldn't want to cross that one. Still, I don't think she did it."

Max was surprised. "Why? You just told me several reasons to think she did do it."

"Oh, she's feisty and full of fight, but attacking a man with an umbrella and shooting him in the head are two very different things."

Max frowned. "But certainly not mutually exclusive. Have you searched her place yet?"

"Not yet. We wanted to hit the better suspects first. We'll probably get there tomorrow, but I doubt we'll find anything.'

"How about your questioning?" asked Max.

"Same story. A lot of pent up anger, but not a lot of real evidence."

Max nodded, then Darwin spoke again.

"I noticed you left out Von Grunewald."

"That's right. I think it's your turn to do the talking. What did he tell you about his argument with Connelly?"

"He's a cool one, that guy. He doesn't get rattled easily." Darwin remarked noncommittally.

"Crouching underwater in a submarine while a tin can drops depth charges on your head will do that to you," said Max. "So what do you know about the argument?"

"Well, we did some digging and found Von Grunewald had several business deals with Connelly over the last few years. Mostly he'd lend Connelly money for a business venture of some kind. They invested in race horses mostly."

"What about the argument?"

"As near as we can tell it was about one of the hayburners, name of Tigress. It seems Connelly got a big investment from Von Grunnewald by being, shall we say, optimistic about the horse's speed. We figured Connelly took Von Grunewald's money for a racehorse and bought a nag instead, pocketing the difference. Von Grunewald found out somehow and demanded his money back. Connelly refused, thereby giving Von Grunewald a gold plated motive."

"That's the story he told me as well," said Max, "only it's a lie."

"What, so you're a racing expert now?"

"Not exactly." Max told Darwin about his visit to the Hawkins Pride Farm and the blazing speed of Tigress.

"Maybe it was another horse?" Darwin asked hopefully.

"He told us both it was Tigress."

"Does he know you're on to him?"

"No," said Max. "I thought it best not to let on and see where it might lead."

"Now you're thinking like a cop," Darwin said, with obvious approval.

"I'll take that as a compliment."

"Well," said Darwin finally, "it looks like your friend Von Grunewald just moved up a notch on my suspect list."

"He was already pretty far up on mine," Max replied. "Anyway, I'd like to look at your file on the case, including crime scene photos."

Darwin looked dubious.

"Well, I dunno. Civilians usually can't be allowed to review case files when an investigation is in progress."

"Nuts to that,'" Max snapped. "This civilian is helping with your investigation in case you've forgotten."

Darwin held up his hand. "All right, all right. You're welcome to look through whatever we have. There's an empty interrogation room next door. I'll have someone get the file."

The only furniture in the small interrogation room consisted of three battered metal chairs and a metal table spotted with cigarette burns. Everything was painted gray, making Max feel as if he was back in the navy. In spite of the shabbiness of the furniture, the overhead light was a strong fluorescent that hummed slightly as it shown down on the file in Max's hands. The file was almost an inch thick, and contained interviews, photos, and lists of evidence. Max had seen the crime scene photos before, so he concentrated on the police interviews and the inventories of objects associated with the crime. As he went down the list of objects found at the crime scene, he stopped.

"Wait a minute. What happened to.."

Max shuffled through the file until he found the photos. He examined two of them carefully, then looked at the lists again. There was no doubt about it.

Max picked up a photo and a list of evidence and knocked on Darwin's door.

"Harold, I need you to check something."

Detective Darwin looked up and frowned. "Sure Max. Maybe I could get you a cup of Java while I'm at it."

"I'm serious, Harold. Take a look at this list of objects found at the scene.'

Darwin gave the list a cursory glance then shrugged. "Yeah, so what?"

"Notice the list of correspondence found on the table from that morning's mail.'

Darwin looked again. "Yeah; there were six letters he had been reading. One was from his tailor, one was.."

"All right," Max interrupted. "Connelly received six letters that day and was apparently reading them, or perhaps had read them earlier in that same room. Now look at this crime scene photo. Do you see the letters?"

"Yeah, sure. They're right on the table in plain view, just as the list says. Six letters."

"Now look at the envelopes on the other side of the table. How many do you see?"

Darwin squinted at the photo. "What the hell? There are seven envelopes. How come there's an extra envelope?"

"The proper question," said Max, "is where is the seventh letter and who sent it?"

"Hey, Andy!"

Detective Anderson appeared in the doorway.

"Where's the box of evidence from Connelly's house?"

"I'll get it for you. I have it nearby."

'Darwin rummaged through the evidence box and came up with a packet of envelopes from the crime scene.

"Here we are. Damned if there aren't seven, just as you said, Max. Now to match them up with the letters."

Like a man playing Solitaire, Darwin laboriously laid out the envelopes and laid corresponding letters on each of them until only one envelope remained uncovered.

"Here's the extra one," he said.

Max looked at the remaining envelope. "Hmm. No return address; New York postmark; plain white paper. It doesn't tell us much."

"It tells us Connelly got a letter that the killer removed from the room afterwards."

"Unless the housekeeper removed it," added Max.

"Well, you're talking to her next," Darwin remarked. "You can ask her. Maybe she'll confess."

"How did she strike you when your boys talked to her?"

"She didn't seem like a killer, more like a strict maiden aunt I had once. She didn't approve of Connelly's habits, ..or his taste in women. Even so, she was protective of his reputation-she admitted hiding the nightgowns to discourage Mandy Jewell from spending the night. Still, we didn't find anything to connect her directly with the killing."

Max rose and opened the office door.

"Well, I'm going to see her in a little while. I'll let you know if she says anything startling. Thanks for the use of the hall, Harold."

As Max was leaving the building, Allison appeared in the doorway.

"Max; I'm glad I caught you."

"Allison. What in the world.."

"Someone shoved this under our door about an hour ago. There was no address and no envelope; just this. I thought I should get it to you right away."

"First we have an envelope without a letter and now a letter without an envelope," he remarked. Max took the folded paper from her and read the typed message.

YOU ARE LOOKING IN THE WRONG PLACE.
CONNELLY WAS MURDERED BECAUSE OF A HORSE.
A FRIEND

John Reisinger

Chapter 13
Constance Tibbet recalls

As usual, it was Allison who broke the stunned silence.

"It seems like someone wants to help you find your way."

"Or maybe find their way. That's what concerns me," Max replied grimly.

"You think it's a red herring to throw you off the track?"

"It's certainly possible. Maybe. Still, I think maybe I'll make a call to our horse training friend Mr. Hawkins back in Maryland."

He looked at his pocket watch. "I have to get going. I have an appointment to talk to Constance Tibbet, the housekeeper. I'll give Hawkins a call later."

"Can I help?"

Max thought a moment.

"Say, maybe you could call Hawkins and get a feel for what's going on with Tigress, or any other of Connelly's horses."

"Sure. He keeps the books. He'd know if there's any hugger mugger going on."

"Good. I'd be particularly interested if Von Grunewald's name pops up."

"Consider it done, Max. I'll have some time today. I'm only going to the library to do some speakeasy research. Do you need anything else?"

"Well, since you'll be uptown north anyway, maybe you could meet me and help me with an interview."

"Sure. Where and when?"

"How about three o'clock on a park bench at 72nd Street and Fifth. That'll be handy to the Forsythe's place."

"I'll be there, but there's one thing I don't understand."

"Only one? I can think of at least a half dozen things about this case that have me stumped at the moment."

"What I mean is, if that letter you got today is the real McCoy, who could have sent it? Who could possibly know about the motive other than the killer?"

"A good question. I only wish I had a good answer to match it. Well, the more we shake the trees, the more likely it is that something will fall out."

Constance Tibbet sat rigid and straight backed with her hands folded tightly in her lap. Her expression was sour, regarding Max with disapproval, but then Constance Tibbet seemed to look at pretty much everything with disapproval.

"Scandalous, that's what it was, Mr. Hurlock; simply scandalous," she said, pursing her lips and shaking her head. "All those hussies swarming around Mr. Connelly like so many bees after a honey pot. Why, they were practically lined up at his door. I've never seen the like. Young women behaving that way- older women as well. Some of them even left nightclothes and personal items at the house just to make it easier to spend the night. I don't wonder that poor Mr. Connelly was murdered. With all those brazen women fighting over him, why, he never stood a chance."

They were in the card room on the second floor of Connelly's townhouse, the place Connelly gave lessons and held high stakes card games. The room was richly appointed, with a cut glass chandelier, gold framed paintings, and leather upholstered chairs around a velvet covered oak card table. Although large and airy, the room was stifling hot, a condition made worse by the tightly closed windows. Constance Tibbet, however, seemed to be quite cool in an old fashioned high-necked dress that made her look as if she could have been the model for Grant Woods's American Gothic painting. In her presence, the furniture seemed to stand at attention in a precise geometric arrangement. Even flowers in a vase had been cut to precisely even heights.

She was younger than Max had expected, maybe 40 or so, and had a face that would have been pleasant if she had allowed it to be. Her sandy brown hair was pulled back in a severe bun that accentuated her features in an unflattering way.

Max discretely wiped a bead of sweat from his upper lip and nodded his head sympathetically.

"But I thought Mr. Connelly was generally the pursuer in his relationships?"

She shook her head in a way that suggested a teacher correcting a child that had just said the moon was made of green cheese.

"Men always think that, Mr. Hurlock, and that's just what a certain type of woman wants them to think. Oh, I'm sure Mr. Connelly often made the first contact, but only after being lured into doing so. Why some of these women were practically flappers, with their short dresses and bobbed hair, and stockings rolled down to their calves. Some of the more brazen ones even applied rouge to their exposed knees. Why, poor Mr. Connelly was just putty in their hands."

In spite of himself, Max raised a skeptical eyebrow, a gesture that thankfully went unnoticed.

"I have no doubt that the police will find that one of Mr. Connelly's pursuers killed him out of jealous frustration."

"Any idea which one?"

"Take your pick. Any one of them was capable of such a thing."

"Did you ever try to warn him?"

"Oh yes; on several occasions. I explained how important it was to find a levelheaded and practical woman; not these immoral gold diggers, but he was oblivious to reason."

"Is that why you hid the nightgowns and toilet articles?"

Her eyes flashed anger for a second, then went back to their usual coldness.

"I acted in his best interest."

"Even when it was against his wishes?"

"Someone had to take him in hand. He was fortunate I was there to look out for him."

"Tell me about the chauffeur, Bill Fulton."

She sniffed as if she were suddenly passed downwind from a stockyard.

"An unpleasant little man, and a bad influence on Mr. Connelly. He actually encouraged Mr. Connelly in his disgusting escapades. What's worse, he even tried to worm his way into Mr. Connelly's will. He buttered up Mr. Connelly to such an extent that for a while it seemed Mr. Connelly would actually leave him a substantial bequest."

"But he didn't leave Fulton anything?"

"The will hasn't been read yet, Mr. Hurlock, but I can safely say there will be nothing there for Mr. Fulton."

Max looked at her with narrowed eyes. "Did you have anything to do with that, Miss Tibbet?"

For the first time, she smiled slightly. It was a cold smile of self-satisfied triumph.

"I have worked for Mr. Connelly for over five years, and I have always considered it my duty to look out for him. Mr. Connelly was a wonderful man, but he was easily led astray by people who did not have his best interests at heart."

"As you do?"

"Exactly."

"Where were you the night he was killed?"

"I was visiting my sister. She lives just a few blocks north of here. I left around 8 and returned at 8 the next morning."

She could have easily and quickly returned anytime during the night, Max realized. The question was; did she?

"I should have realized something was wrong when I discovered the front door was unlocked," she continued, "but Mr. Connelly was often forgetful that way, especially after a late night out. I didn't discover him until almost 8:30."

"Did you visit his room the morning you discovered his body?"

"His room? Well, no. Usually I work my way up, tidying up the house each day. Obviously, I never got that far after discovering him in the reception room."

"Did he usually keep his dentures in a glass of water on the oak side table in his room?"

"Oak side table? Why, no. It was too close to the bed and he was afraid he might knock the glass over if he left them there. He kept them on the top of the bureau. It also had a marble top, so there would be no bother with coasters or water rings."

Max looked over his notes.

"I suppose you are familiar with the women Mr. Connelly saw?"

There was that disapproving look again.

"I saw most of them when he brought them to the house, I sometimes cooked dinner for them and cleaned up after them in the guest bedroom, but I certainly never became friendly with them."

I can believe that, Max thought.

"Then maybe you can identify the black haired woman he was recently seen with at the 300 Club?"

For the first time, Constance Tibbet looked rattled. Her eyes widened and she became even stiffer than usual."

"B..black haired woman you say?"

"Yes. She was with him and engaged in deep conversation apparently."

Her lips tightened, and Max noticed her foot was tapping rapidly on the thick carpet. Her eyes shifted sideways, as if searching for an answer..or for time. Finally, she looked at Max with a cold and neutral gaze.

"With the number of woman Mr. Connelly saw, I'm sure it is quite likely he pursued at least one that had black hair, but I'm afraid I can't help you beyond that."

Max stepped out on the street with a sense of relief, both from the heat of the closed room and the coldness of Contsance Tibbet.

"Max! Over here!"

Max looked across the street and saw Von Grunewald standing next to his green Buick. He was wearing a white suit and a straw hat.

"Have you had lunch yet? I thought we could grab a bite of sauerbraten over in Yorkville."

Max walked across the street. "How did you know I was here?"

"I called for you at the hotel and your lovely wife was kind enough to tell me where you were. Oh, and she says to tell you she has made the call you talked about, but found little that was of interest."

"I see. Thanks. Well, it is after one and I haven't had a bite, so lead on."

"*Wunderbar.*"

Dei Lorelei restaurant was a small storefront sort of a place on West 86th Street. Inside, the air was dark and cool. Ornate beer steins hung on the walls, along with pictures of Rhine castles and people in lederhosen. Von Grunewald led Max to a table covered with a blue and white checked tablecloth.

"Nice place," said Max noncommittally.

"Yorkville is the heart of the German community in New York, although there are a lot of others here, too. This place has the best German food in the city."

"And that's good?" Max asked, looking at the menu with a good deal of trepidation.

"Of course! Don't you like German food?"

"I don't know. I guess I've never been attracted to a cuisine where the best dish is called wurst."

"Very funny, but I think you'll appreciate some of these dishes. Surely you like sauerkraut?"

"I suppose so, although during the war we called it Liberty Cabbage."

"Well, there are a great many wonderful dishes. Look, here's Leberkaese, that's sausage loaf."

"Sounds wonderful," Max said hesitantly.

"And look, they have Schweinebraten, Jaeger Schnitzel, Kassler Rippchen.."

Max looked at the menu. "Uh..how about this; Eisbein?"

"That's pig's knuckles."

"Oh. Well, how about this one; Suelze?"

"Head cheese."

Max closed the menu. "Maybe I'll stick to a sausage and sauerkraut. Somehow I'm not as hungry as I thought."

"*Sehr gut*! Some Bratwurst is just the thing."

After they ordered, Von Grunewald got down to business.

"Max, I have been thinking about our last meeting. I know I have not been entirely candid with you up until now, but I want to assure you that I am not attempting to deceive, nor am I concealing anything of substance. The fact is, Max, I am a private person. Exposing details of my life is not easy for me, so I'm afraid I sometimes withhold information with which I am not comfortable."

Max nodded in a non-committed way.

"The point is, I have not meant to deceive you. You must have trust in me that I am trying to help you in good faith. You may ask me anything and I will try to answer."

Max looked at Von Grunewald skeptically. "Why the change of heart?"

Von Grunewald shrugged. "Max, you must understand. I am a suspect in this crime, possibly the best suspect the police have. Sometimes I am tempted to hold back information that might reflect badly on me."

Max frowned. "Avoiding self-incrimination is fine when you're talking to the police; that's your right as a citizen. But I'm not a judge or jury. I'm the guy who's very possibly going to keep you out of the electric chair, but only if I have all the facts."

"Yes, yes. Of course. I understand."

"So are you going to tell me what you've left out?"

"You already know. I argued with Connelly about money."

"Because of a racehorse named Tigress."

"Yes."

"A racehorse that was not nearly as fast as Connelly had led you to believe."

"Yes; that is correct. Ah, look. Our food has arrived."

The waitress had materialized beside them with two steaming plates. She placed the first one in front of Max, who eyed it warily. A huge Bratwurst sausage lay on the plate like a beached whale. Beside it was a steaming heap of brownish yellow sauerkraut, and beside that was a smaller heap of some pale colored wet things that were about the size of a pencil eraser.

"That is Spaetzle," said Von Grunewald. "It's a basic German side dish.

Max sniffed it. "So what is it; pig's intestines?"

Von Grunewald looked hurt. "No; it is simply a type of small macaroni. Try it, Max. You will enjoy it, I promise you."

Max took a fork full of the sauerkraut. "It's not the Spaetzle I'm worried about; it's the baloney."

Allison hailed a taxi near the hotel and headed up to the New York Public Library to do some research. She had been to the main branch of the Enoch Pratt Library in Baltimore several times, and even the Library of Congress, but nothing prepared her for the marble vastness of the New York library. The first thing she noticed, besides the way her footsteps echoed on the terrazzo floors, was the almost total absence of books anywhere near the entrances and on much of the first floor, a rather odd feature for a library. Once she got upstairs to the main reading room, however, the sheer scale of the place and the number of people studiously pursuing knowledge awed her. For a moment she wondered how many times the Talbot County Public

Library could fit into the space, but gave it up as too ridiculous to contemplate. Soon she was seated at one of the tables with a file of newspapers.

Her idea had been to look for articles about New York speakeasies to provide some background to her blind tiger article. She didn't have far to look. On most days several articles appeared detailing the latest raids and the embarrassing lists of well-known people caught up in them. The letters to the editor were revealing as well. From her informal survey, it seemed as if most people were opposed to Prohibition, but wanted it to continue as long as it didn't apply to them.

"It's just as Mark Twain said," she said out loud. "Nothing so needs reforming as other people's habits."

"I beg your pardon?"

Allison looked around to see a heavy set older woman sitting behind her reading a stack of magazines.

"Oh, sorry. I was just reading about speakeasies."

"Oh, those." The woman spoke as if Allison had been discussing diarrhea. "I know all about speakeasies from firsthand experience. I live right across the street from one. People coming and going at all hours; jazz music playing; drunks staggering down the street. It's an abomination."

"Did you complain to the police?"

The lady snorted. "The police know all about it. They're being paid off by the owners."

Allsion was shocked. "Do all speakeasies pay off officials?"

"Some do. The others use an alarm system to warn them of raids. They have hidden compartments for the liquor and bottles of fruit juice or teapots to make it all look innocent. When they get raided, the police don't find any evidence to bring charges. It's easy to tell a place like that, you know. You look at the tables. The

146

joints that depend on deception instead of payoffs will have all the booze served in teacups to make everything look innocent in case of a raid."

"You seem to be an authority," said Allison.

"Honey, I'm just an ordinary person, but I can see what's going on. That's more than I can say for those fancy public figures that can't even see that Prohibition has caused more crime, more drinking and more disrespect for the law than all the saloons it got rid of. Take that article you're reading. Look at the quote on the bottom of the next page."

Allison turned the page. At the bottom was a quote from the famous evangelist Billy Sunday. (Allison was always amazed to think that it was his real name.) Sunday had been an enthusiastic supporter of Prohibition, and the article quoted what he had said when the law was first passed;

The reign of tears is over. The slums will soon be a memory. We will turn our prisons into factories and our jails into storehouses and corncribs. Men will walk upright now, women will smile and children will laugh. Hell will be forever for rent.

"Well," said Allison. "His sermons may be divinely inspired, but I can't say as much for his predictions."

John Reisinger

Chapter 14
The Central Park Menagerie

Max sat on a bench in Central Park watching the traffic along Fifth Avenue and admiring the upscale apartment buildings on the other side. He had another hour until his four o'clock appointment with Martin Forsythe.

He looked at his watch. "Where is Allison? She promised to meet me here ten minutes ago."

"Max!"

"Oh, there you are, Allison. Did you get lost?"

She sat down on the bench next to him and exhaled loudly.

"Max, when you said to meet you on a park bench at 79th Street and Fifth Avenue, you might have considered that there are at least 20 such benches in the area, and that the streets are teeming with men in dark suits and fedora hats."

"I guess my instructions were somewhat lacking in precision."

"Oh, by the way, I did talk to Mr. Hawkins about Connelly's race horses. It seems Connelly was in the habit of changing the horses' names when it suited him. The Tigress we saw, in fact, was the second to have that name. The first one was a plug who couldn't outrun my Aunt Minnie."

"So that means Von Grunewald might have been telling the truth."

"Maybe. Or maybe he just knows how to find a good cover."

"Well, that's possible."

"Now tell me how your day is going."

He briefly told her of his talks with Detective Darwin and Constance Tibbet.

"So there was an extra, unmarked envelope at the murder scene," said Allison. "Well, I don't see the point of sending a man an empty envelope, so I'd say the killer took whatever was in the envelope away with him."

Max nodded. "That's most likely, but there's another possibility. Constance Tibbet was very protective of Connelly. She freely admitted hiding the nightgowns. She wanted to protect him even in death. Maybe she took whatever was in that envelope away before she called the police."

"That's very interesting about the protective Miss Tibbet," Allison said. "Maybe she wasn't so much protective of him as she was making it hard for his lovers so she could have a shot. She wouldn't be the first housekeeper to be romantically interested in her employer. Her reaction when you asked about the black haired woman was revealing, too."

"Yes, and there was one other quirk I noticed," said Max. "Whenever she talked about Connelly's girlfriends, she talked about them chasing him. To hear her tell it, they were always the aggressor."

"That's not so strange. If she had designs on Connelly, she had to deny he was interested in other women."

"Right, but when she talked about the black haired woman, she referred to her as a woman Connelly pursued."

Allison frowned. "That's odd. Maybe it was just a slip of the tongue.'

"Maybe."

"So what's next, Max?"

"I'm meeting Martin Forsythe at the Central Park Menagerie nearby. He agreed to prevent the police from showing up at his office or his home. It seems he has some clients who might look askance at something like that. If you have time, maybe you could observe discretely. You're good at reading people and you can get lost in the crowd."

"Why not?" Allison replied. "First a blind tiger, and now a zoo."

The Central Park Menagerie was at the south end of Central Park, near the sea lion pool. Max arrived early and sat on a bench inconspicuously. Presently, a stocky, well dressed middle-aged man sat down at a nearby bench and rested his hands easily on his walking stick. He didn't seem to be interested in the sea lions, but kept looking back and forth. Max introduced himself.

"Good day, Mr. Hurlock," said Forsythe. "Thank you for meeting me here. I was afraid having someone from the police come to my home might prove embarrassing."

"Of course. This is a good a place as any."

"Splendid. I'll be glad to tell you anything you need to know, but I'm a little confused. How are you involved in this matter?"

"A fair question, Mr. Forsythe," Max replied. "The fact is, I am assisting the police. You knew Connelly, had reason to dislike him, and are known to have laid siege to his house demanding satisfaction at one point. That makes you someone of great interest. If I can find out what happened, it could clear you and save you a lot of police interrogation and trouble."

"That makes sense, but why you? What makes you better than the police?"

"I have a different perspective. They're under public scrutiny and are hounded by the press. I can work in the clear, so to speak. And frankly, I've enjoyed some success in such matters in other cases."

"You mean the Taylor-Bradwell case?" Forsythe laughed. "You see? Two can play this detective game. I never meet anyone without doing a little checking. I have a great many contacts and I can find out a great deal when I want to. It's just a matter of asking the right questions of the right people."

"Maybe you should be investigating, then."

"Me? I daresay I could come up with a few wrinkles the police would never think of, but no thanks. They've got a tough one on their hands, especially with all the publicity. I prefer to work in a discrete manner, not in the headlines. That's why I'm talking to you here and not at my home or in some grimy police station. So no gumshoe work for me. I'll stick to my real estate business."

"So what was your relationship with Ellsworth Connelly?"

Forsythe smiled. "Like so many others, I now wish I had never met the man. He chased every woman in town, counting on his oily charm and his money to attract them. God knows it wasn't physical attraction, what with his big nose and false teeth; money and flattery did the trick. Well, that's his business of course. If he wanted to make a fool of himself and others, it was no concern of mine until he tried it on Dianne. I was away a lot, and Dianne was naïve. People like Connelly prey on women in such circumstances, and he started calling on Dianne and taking her to lunch occasionally. It was plain he was just softening her up for the kill as it were. Things had gotten as far as their meeting at night at his townhouse when I got wind of it and put a stop to it."

"What were your intentions when you went to Connelly's house and demanded to see him?"

"I won't lie to you. I was going to thrash him at first, teach him to stay away from married women, but he had the good sense to not be among those present. The next few days when I came round, I had calmed down. Oh, I still wanted to confront him, but just to make it clear that he was to stay away from Dianne forever. But the moment passed and I pretty much forgot about it. I finally came to the conclusion that Connelly was more to be pitied than resented. It seems to me his reputation may have been exaggerated. Of course, with Connelly, it's hard to know where truth ends and legend begins. Why if he had done all the things people say, he'd have to be twins."

"I hope this isn't too personal, Mr. Forsythe, but I have to ask this. Have you ever been, well, in the habit of seeing other women?"

Forsythe frowned. "That's exactly what I mean about truth and fiction. People love gossip, whether true or not. Of course I have to meet women occasionally in my business, but that's where it ends. Still, you can't stop tongues from wagging. Someone will see me acting pleasant to a female client and think the worst. It amazes me how creative people can be when speculating on the actions of others. Why, they even accused me of seeing a waitress at one point. It's outrageous, but I suppose it's human nature."

"The night Mr. Connelly died..."

Forsythe chuckled. "Now it's the old 'where were you on the night of', is it? I just love detective stories; even real life ones. It's no secret. I was called out of town by one of my clients in Albany. I left about midnight. My wife Dianne can verify that. The doorman may have seen me as well, though I'm not certain."

"That would give you plenty of time to..."

"I suppose it would have, but so what? This city is full of women and men who have every reason to kill Ellsworth Connelly. As far as I'm concerned, Dianne made a foolish mistake, but it's over with no real harm done. I made a foolish mistake as well, losing my temper, but that's over too."

"You're quite correct; there are plenty of people who had reason to want Connelly dead," Max continued, "but very few of them actually were seen threatening him the way you did."

"Very few you know about, you mean," Forsythe replied. " I wouldn't be surprised if there were dozens more. Besides, as a detective you should know that confronting a man in broad daylight is a far cry from sneaking around his home in the dead of night and killing him in cold blood."

Max nodded. "A fair point, I admit, but what you did at least shows someone willing to act on his grievances."

Forsythe nodded. "Mr. Hurlock, I can well understand why you and the police would take an interest in any man who had lost his temper the way I did, but it seems to me you're missing the most important point."

"What's that, Mr. Forsythe?"

"The incident took place over a year ago. If I were angry enough to murder Mr. Connelly, I would have done it then. Why would I have waited so long? The simple answer is that I wouldn't, and neither would anyone else. No, Mr. Hurlock, if you want to know who killed Connelly, look to the present; to someone who has a motive right now. For heaven's sakes, there must be any number of jilted girlfriends, angry business associates and aggrieved husbands walking around the city whose bad experiences with Connelly are far fresher than mine."

"I'm just discussing possibilities, Mr. Forsythe."

Forsythe smiled again. "Of course. In your place I'd do the same, but I like to think that I'd realize when I'm on the wrong scent."

John Reisinger

Chapter 15
Connections

Max and Allison walked in and out of the lengthening shadows from the tall buildings lining Fifth Avenue as they made their way south towards their hotel. The progress was slow because Allison insisted on stopping to inspect store windows, so they had time to discuss the case. The noise from the traffic, though still loud, seemed less intense than it had in the more confined spaces of streets that were not as wide.

"All right, let's see," Max began. We have Von Grunewald, who has been lying to me and who was apparently involved in some sort of money dispute with Connelly..."

"Not to mention having a more than passing interest in Connelly's bitter ex-wife," Allison added, her head turning to look at another store window.

"Right. Next we have Helen Arness, AKA Hell in a Dress; angry ex-wife who argued with Connelly the night he was killed and said he would pay."

"And Mandy Jewell, the smart manipulator who acts dumb and claims Connelly wanted to marry her. If he said he wouldn't that night, she might have gotten mad enough to do something drastic. Plus she was the last person known to be with him before he turned up dead."

"Then there's Bill Fulton the chauffeur. He expects to get a big bequest, maybe big enough to kill for."

"Don't forget Gwen Perkins, the Automat Queen," Allison added. "She felt angry and betrayed by

Connelly's rejection of her. She even assaulted him with an umbrella and vowed to make him sorry."

"Of course there's also the Porters, but they were friends with no motive."

"No known motive," Allison corrected him.

"Martin Forsythe was definitely angry enough to do something unpleasant to Connelly at one time, but that was over a year ago as well. The question is, is he still that angry and if so, why would he wait so long? He doesn't seem like the type to wait very long for anything."

"And finally," Allison said, "there's Constance Tibbet, the faithful and protective housekeeper."

"She certainly didn't shrink from taking matters in hand where Connelly was concerned," said Max, "but I don't see that she had any motive to kill him."

"Let's see, that's seven suspects with known motives and another three with no motive apparent."

A bus roared by, temporarily drowning out any attempt at communication.

"I have a list of several more spurned women," said Max, "but they go back even farther, so I doubt they are in the running. I'm at a dead end at this point.""

"So what do you do now, Max?"

"I look for the missing piece or event."

"You mean a loose end of some sort?"

"Not exactly. It's like this: When I was first starting out, I had an assignment to check out the condition of an old building in Baltimore prior to a sale. The place was in a good location, but the owner had been sitting on it for years, refusing to sell. He had some sort of sentimental attachment to it or something: he said he was going to fix it up one day. Anyway, suddenly the owner agreed to sell, just like that. Nobody could believe it, since he had always been so stubborn. Well, I was curious, so I did some checking. It turned out the man was in his 80s and had just had a mild heart attack. That was what convinced him the place wasn't worth the trouble any more. That was what I call the precipitating event. You know; the catalyst that makes something seemingly unrelated happen."

"So you think there's a precipitating event that brought about Connelly's murder?"

"I'm sure of it. Something set off one of our suspects, something I haven't discovered yet. When I do, everything will fit together."

"That's my Max. Well, in the meantime, I've still got my blind tiger article to research. I'm heading up to one on the upper west side tomorrow. There's a really tiny place up there. It'll give some balance, since I've been to some big ones."

"The upper west side? That's where Constance Tibbet's sister lives. I have the address here somewhere. Yes; here it is. Is there any chance you could stop by and talk to her; just to see if Constance Tibbet's story of visiting her the night of the murder checks out?"

Allison shrugged. "Let me see the address. Oh, what's the use? I can't figure out proximity from street addresses; the numbers are all willy nilly. I'll check our street atlas and see how close it is to where I'm going. If it's not too far, I'll swing by and talk to her. If she's anywhere near as cold as her sister, I should be able to stay cool all the way home."

They finally arrived back at the Wolcott at nine o'clock and walked into the now familiar gold rococo lobby and asked for messages. The desk clerk handed Max an envelope.

"Hey, here's a letter from Chip Carswell at the Star-Democrat. It seems the Prohibition agents caught up with the Merkle brothers."

"The ones with the happy pigs?" Allison asked.

"Who else? It seems an agent was driving through on his way to Tilghman Island for some fishing when he smelled the sour mash. He wasn't sure where it was coming from, so he wandered around the back roads until the smell was almost overpowering and found the Merkles cooking up a fresh batch. Now the Merkle boys are under arrest and trying to raise bail, but worst of all, their still got seized. Poor Duffy and P.J."

"Poor pigs," said Allison. "Their diet is going to be a lot less fun."

Up in the suite a few minutes later, Max flopped in the soft chair and kicked off his shoes while simultaneously taking off his hat and tossing it on the bed.

"Well, today was a busy day and tomorrow promises to be the same," Max said. "I suggest we make it an early night and hit the hay."

"Well, ..eventually."

"I thought you were tired."

"Not that tired."

A short time later, Max and Allison lay sprawled on the bed entangled in the sheets and sleeping contentedly. The sounds of the city came in the open window as a gentle summer rain started pattering against the windowsills.

Around midnight, however, Max awoke and got out of bed. He sat for a few minutes looking out the window at the lights of the city. Allison, sensing his absence, sat up in bed and rubbed her eyes.

"Max? Are you all right?"

He turned to her.

"Sorry. I didn't mean to wake you. I just started thinking about the case."

"In your sleep?"

"Afraid so. Although for a while I was dreaming I was floating in the clouds surrounded by drunken pigs, slow racehorses and blind tigers."

"The sleep of reason produces monsters."

"Anyway, I suddenly started thinking about connections."

"Connections?"

"There have been a lot of unusual connections in this case; meeting Connelly at the horse farm just weeks before he was murdered;, Von Grunewald and his nephew on my ship;, Detective Darwin comparing notes about me with Detective Pfeiffer, Connelly running into his ex-wife at the Waldorf;, the information you picked up at the speakeasies.."

"Not to mention my meeting several literary lions without even trying."

"Exactly. Anyway, it got me thinking about connections and it made me think that the key to this case might lie with another connection, one we haven't discovered yet."

"You mean someone who might know someone else?"

"Maybe. Or someone who might have a reason to kill Connelly that we never thought of."

"There seems to be no shortage of reasons to kill Connelly. We have them in spades."

"That we do. And we might have the killer and his obvious motive right under our noses. Still, I keep wondering about that missing connection."

"So how do you find this connection, assuming it actually exists?"

He looked out the window again.

"Just keep digging and be alert in case it turns up, I suppose."

Allison yawned and stretched dramatically. "That sounds grand. In the meantime, however, I'd suggest you connect yourself with this bed so you're not asleep on your feet tomorrow."

The speakeasy on West 75th Street was the smallest one yet. There was no sign and nothing to distinguish it from the rows of brownstones marching monotonously along the street. One of the patrons at the 300 Club had suggested the place as an example of a small and secret speak, sort of the opposite of Texas Guinan's showy establishment.

The address on the slip of paper proved to be a basement apartment with an entrance under the stair that led to the building's first floor. After passing the place several times, Allison knocked on an unmarked door with chipped paint. The door had a small sliding panel that Allison expected to open at any moment, but the place seemed to be deserted.

"A little early, ain't cha?"

Allison looked around and saw a pleasant looking middle aged woman standing on the sidewalk with a sack of groceries.

"That place don't open until at least nine or so. Even then you got to have you a password."

Allison mounted the three stone steps back up to sidewalk level.

"I've never been here, but I'm doing research for an article."

"You a writer?"

"I try to be. Do you live around here?"

"Well sure I do. You don't think I'd be lugging these groceries any farther than I have to do ya?"

"No. Of course not. So I guess you know all about this place?"

The woman laughed. "Enough to know I don't want any part of it. It's owned by some gangster and his henchmen run the place. They get their booze from some local 'leggers'. It used to be the apartment for the building super, so it only holds maybe a dozen customers."

"I see. Do they have entertainment?"

"Only if you consider watching some drunk get the bum's rush entertaining. You're thinking of the higher class speakeasies downtown. This one's more of what they call a gin joint. On one end you got places like the 21 Club and on the other end you got places like this joint."

"Does it have a name?"

"Not really, though folks around here call it Bill's Juice Joint."

"Who's Bill?"

"He's the super that used to live there before it got sold to the speakeasy boys. We sort of named it in his honor. We all liked old Bill."

"Is Bill's ever raided?"

"Not yet. I figure they grease the right palms, if you know what I mean. Other people say it's because they're too small to bother with. Even so, I wouldn't be surprised to see Izzy and Moe to drop by any night now."

"Who are they?"

"Geez, honey. You must be from out of town. Izzy and Moe are the best Prohibition agents around. They use trickery, disguises, and I don't know what all to get into places like this to shut them down. They get written up in all the papers. Listen; I gotta go. My rhubarb is starting to wilt."

Allison watched the woman go, then looked down at the shabby door, then decided she had gotten enough information.

Max walked in the door of police headquarters and asked for Detective Darwin. He was only slightly disappointed to find Darwin out on a case, so he talked to Detecive Anderson instead. At Max's request, Anderson once again supplied the case files, including the dossiers on the people associated with the case. Max spent the next two hours going through the files looking for some connection he had missed; some link between people or some hidden motive he had no yet considered.

He found nothing.

Max pushed himself away from the table in the interrogation room and considered his next move. The only connection he had uncovered that the police had apparently missed was the ill feeling between the chauffeur Bill Fulton, and the housekeeper, Constance Tibbet. Fulton said Connelly had promised to "take care of him" if anything happened to him. But what if Constance Tibbet overheard and decided to take some action to protect herself? She seemed to know all about Connelly's will.? What if she was afraid he was about to change it to favor her hated rival? And if that was the case, how would he ever prove it?

"Hey, Detective Anderson!"

Anderson stuck his head in the door.

"When is Connelly's will going to be read?"

Anderson looked at his watch. "In about a half hour."

"What?"

"I thought you knew. That's where Darwin went. It's just a few blocks away. Let me write down the address."

Max stepped out of the building and started down the street.

"That's one connection I almost missed."

Allison had no trouble finding the address of Constance Tibbet's sister, Charity, and soon stood in front of a modest but well-kept brownstone with flower boxes in the windows. A few children played in the almost empty street and a cat dozed on a windowsill. She pulled the bell knob and heard a chime ring faintly in a first floor apartment. The door opened. and a tall thin woman appeared.

"Are you Charity Tibbet?"

The woman smiled warmly. "Why, yes I am."

Allison introduced herself, explained her business, and was ushered inside a small but neat apartment decorated with prints of famous oil paintings. Charity Tibbet seemed nothing like her sister. She was fashionably dressed, outgoing and friendly.

What Allison noticed most, however, was her thick black hair.

After verifying that Constance had visited her sister the night of the murder, Allison began to gently probe in another area.

"Did you ever meet Mr. Connelly?"

Charity smiled again. "Oh, yes. I called for Constance one day and he introduced himself. What a charming man. He was so gallant, like something from a play."

"Was that the only time you saw him?"

Here Charity's smile faded somewhat. "No, I met him for lunch several times and at several night clubs. As I said, he was very dashing."

"Did Constance know about it?"

"Not at first. It seemed so trivial and harmless, at least to me."

"How did she react when she did find out?"

"Rather badly, I'm afraid. My sister is somewhat protective of both Mr. Connelly and of me. She became very angry and even cursed, something I had never heard her do before. It was very unpleasant. She said Mr. Connelly had a habit of trifling with woman's affections and said he would ruin me in the end if I didn't stay away. She made me promise to stop seeing him at once."

"Did you?"

"Not at first, but I did become more aware of Mr. Connelly's tendencies and started noticing how he was slowly but surely pushing me in a direction I didn't care to go. So considering everything my sister had told me, I did tell him I would not be seeing him again."

"How did he react?"

"He didn't take the news very well. We were at the 300 Club. That's actually a speakeasy, but it bills itself as a nightclub. I told him I wouldn't be seeing him again and he seemed crushed. He kept asking if it was something he did and if he could do anything to make me change my mind. I suppose he didn't know how to act when the shoe was on the other foot. He got louder, forcing me to get more emphatic. We were starting to create a scene, so I bid him goodbye and left. He was still seated at the table when I hailed a cab to go home. He seemed quite distraught."

"I suppose he was very downhearted," Allison suggested.

"I would have called it dejected. The man seemed crushed; so much so that for a moment I weakened and considered giving him another chance. But in the end I remembered what Constance had told me and assumed his despondency was all for show. I felt very bad about it but felt it had to be done."

"What did you think when you heard he was dead?"

She was silent a moment, inwardly reliving the memory. When she finally answered, Charity Tibbet's voice was so quiet almost inaudible.

"I thought he had killed himself."

Chapter 16
Heirs

The law office of Ketterman and Horn was on the fifth floor of the Flatiron Building. Max rushed past the potted palms and glass of the lobby and found a conference room lined with mahogany paneling and framed portraits of the firm's founders. Inside, a dour faced lawyer sat at the head of a long table and around that table sat Helen Arness, Gunther Von Grunewald, Mandy Jewell, Constance Tibbet, Bill Fulton, Detective Darwin, and several others Max assumed were relatives of Connelly.

Max had arrived too late to witness the actual reading, but was just in time to see its effects. The room was buzzing with angry conversations.

"You witch! You got to him, didn't you?" Bill Fulton snapped at Constance Tibbet.

"Certainly not," she responded. "He merely had better sense than you gave him credit for. You've just been counting chickens that were never going to hatch."

"This isn't over yet," Helen Arness said between gritted teeth to a man Max assumed must be her attorney. "I want you to prepare a lawsuit against his estate. I told him he'd pay and by God, he will. Just because he's dead doesn't mean he can escape."

"Don't bother suing a dead man," Mandy Jewell growled. "You had your chance and lost it. I'm the one he wanted to marry. A share of the estate should go to me."

"My dear," Helen Arness said in a voice dripping with sarcasm, "I'm afraid you gave him far more than he'll ever give you. I do hope you enjoyed it."

The angry bickering filled the room as the lawyer at the head of the table waved his arms and vainly pleaded for calm. In the midst of the confusion, Von Grunewald noticed Max and motioned him to a seat next to him.

"Max. I'm glad you could make it."

"It was dumb luck. Nobody told me about it."

Von Grunewald looked surprised. "No? I thought I did. Oh well; here you are anyway."

"So what happened? I take it most of these people didn't get what they wanted."

"That includes me, I'm afraid. As far as I'm concerned, Ellsworth Connelly owes me for the horse he swindled me on."

"How about the others?"

"Well, Connelly left most of his estate to some charities and scholarships. Several relatives, a brother and some nephews, aunts and uncles received $5,000 each, and Constance Tibbet got $3,000. The chauffeur, Mr. Fulton received $500, while Helen Arness and Mandy Jewell didn't get a cent."

"So almost everybody is unhappy."

"Not really," Von Grunewald said. "Miss Tibbet seems perfectly happy. Her bequest while modest, is adequate for her needs, and she seems to be delighted that the others didn't get what they wanted. I don't know what the term is in English, but in Germany we called that *Schadenfreude*; being happy at the misfortune of other people."

Max nodded. "We don't have the word, but we sure have the feeling, and Constance Tibbet seems to have it in spades. Do you think there's anything to the chauffeur's accusation that she fixed the will?"

Von Grunewald frowned thoughtfully. "I don't know. She seemed to me to be a person who tried to exercise a certain, shall we say, influence on Connelly. I have also noticed her making a point of dusting or rearranging things in the room when I was meeting with him, obviously listening. I can well imagine her bending his ear, as I believe the expression goes."

"So she may not have dictated or physically altered the will, but she put certain ideas in his head about it?"

"Yes, I think it is certainly possible. The woman seemed to think it her mission in life to guide Connelly's actions."

Bill Fulton was banging on the table now and pointing a finger at Constance Tibbet.

"You cheated me out of what was rightfully mine. You turned Mr. Connelly against me. I'll sue! By God I'll make you pay for what you did to me!"

"Oh, hush up," she spat back. "You're making a fool of yourself."

"Both of you hush up," was Helen Arness's contribution to the flow of reason. "When my attorney gets through there won't be anything left for you two to squabble over anyway."

Detective Darwin, who was sitting across from Max smiled and leaned over to him. "Well, Max, that's that. I came here to see if there were any bombshells. You know, Connelly leaving everything to Diane Forsythe or Martha Porter, or some other woman, but none of his lady friends were even mentioned. As for the rest of these mugs, if any of them killed Connelly for the money they were wasting their time."

"Yes, but that doesn't rule it out. After all, no one knew for sure what was in the will until today."

"True, but at least if money was the motive, nobody here committed the perfect crime."

"Nobody?" said Max. "I'd say Constance Tibbet certainly accomplished all she set out to do and did it in a way that did not expose her to punishment."

"Yeah, yeah, but she didn't kill him."

"Are you sure about that?" Max asked cryptically.

Allison brought her notebook and writing pad to the lounge in the hotel lobby and found a comfortable lounge chair beneath a mirror framed with gilt cherubs. She sat down and continued with her speakeasy article, writing about the sleazy gin joints.

There are estimated to be thousands of speakeasies in Manhattan alone, a figure that constantly changes, growing larger almost daily. Most people have heard of the larger and more glamorous places like the 21 Club, but at the other end of the scale are many more "gin joints", small hole-in-the-wall places that huddle hidden in the shadows in almost every neighborhood. There are no signs outside of such places and no well-heeled or famous clientele within. Entertainment is a distraction and an expensive luxury at a gin joint. These places are devoted solely to drinking; not happy, sophisticated and lively social drinking, but dreary, hollow eyed, drown-your-troubles drinking.

She put her pencil behind her ear for safekeeping and looked at the page she had just written.

"...hollow eyed, drown your troubles drinking?" she mumbled. "That may be laying it on a bit thick. I've made the places sound downright depressing. But then, from what I've seen, that's just what they are. Besides the ugly fact is that lurid prose sells articles. Now let's see.."

Like vampires, patrons of such places only appear at night, seeking cover in darkness and anonymity. Shadowy figures appear before sliding peepholes in shabby doorways muttering cryptic passwords to gain admission to the dank inner sanctum of inebriation.

She looked at the latest paragraph and frowned.

"Vampires? Inner sanctum of inebriation? Did I actually just write that? I'm just not hitting on all sixes; it sounds like a dime novel written by a temperance crusader. Lurid is one thing. This borders of morbid hysteria. I need something fresh."

She started writing again, then looked up. What about Izzy and Moe, those colorful prohibition agents that woman had mentioned? Their story would jazz up the article and give a view from the enforcement side. She went to the front desk and asked for a telephone to call the Prohibition enforcement office. To her surprise, the supervisor agreed to let her interview the pair tomorrow.

"Now we're cooking with gas," she said, as she went back to her writing.

As she laboriously tried to rewrite the last paragraph in a way that was vivid without being too wild eyed, she looked up and saw Max enter the front door.

"Max," she cried. "Thank goodness. You're just in time to save me from a creative breakdown. I've stopped writing prose and started writing slush."

"I don't believe that for a minute," Max assured her. "You only write two ways: good and better."

She stood up and kissed him. "Flattery will get you everywhere."

"That's what I'm counting on," he replied.

"Well, you don't look very happy about it."

173

"Oh, that. I just came from the reading of Ellsworth Connelly's will."

"That must have been cheerful; sort of like a séance, only with prizes given out.."

"As cheerful as any gathering that includes Helen Arness, Mandy Jewell, Tom Fulton and Constance Tibbet."

"Now that sounds like a merry band. I don't suppose they were strewing flowers in your path."

"They were too busy trying to stab each other in the back. Nobody got the big bequest they were all expecting, and they're all blaming each other."

"How sad. Now I suppose they'll have to get jobs."

"Well, Miss Tibbet did all right; not enough to be wealthy, mind you, but enough to keep body and soul together if she lives modestly. Maybe she'll move in with her sister."

"Speaking of which," said Allison. "I spoke with Miss Charity Tibbet today."

"Oh, of course. I almost forgot. Did she verify Constance Tibbet's visit the night of the murder?"

"Oh yes. No problem there, and I found out another bit of information that may interest you."

"Well, don't keep me in suspense. What is it?"

"Not so fast," said Allison. "First I need for some gallant young man to come along and take me to dinner."

"As soon as you tell me. I'm as hungry as you are."

"How about Arthur's up on 40th?" I'm in the mood for chicken."

"Fine, fine. Just tell me about Charity Tibbet. What did you find out?"

"Oh, just one little thing."

"Yes?"

"It seems that our Miss Charity Tibbet is the mystery woman with the black hair."

"No."

Allison held up her hand in a two-fingered salute. "Scout's honor."

Max scratched his chin absent-mindedly. "So Constance Tibbet's sister was involved with Connelly as well. I'll bet that stuck in the housekeeper's craw."

"I'm sure. That would explain why she referred to Connelly pursuing instead of being the innocent victim."

"And for a woman like Constance Tibbet, who always had to be in control, and who probably wanted to snare Connelly for herself, that would be intolerable."

"But wait. Charity handed him his hat the night they went to the 300 Club," Allison reminded him. "She told me. At that point, whatever went on between them ended."

"So it appears, but I wonder if Constance knew about that? It was only a few days before Connelly was killed, and Constance didn't see her sister every day. Suppose Charity hadn't told her yet. What if she thought they were still at it? What if she blew her stack and decided to take matters into her own hands?"

Allison nodded. "It's certainly possible. She had lots of reasons. Killing Connelly would protect her inheritance before he could maybe change his mind, and it would protect her sister from getting despoiled and abandoned by him. Pretty strong motives."

"Right," said Max. "And don't forget she has admitted tampering with evidence. That might very well include ditching the murder weapon."

"And she's one of the few people he might have met with without bothering to put in his false teeth."

"It all fits,' said Max. "Of course proving all this is another matter."

175

John Reisinger

Chapter 17
Words on pages

The phone at the front desk of the Wolcott rang very early the next morning and Max was called downstairs to speak with Harold Darwin. The New York detective was in one of his gruff moods.

"Max, are you holding out on me?" he demanded as soon as Max picked up the phone. "By God, you'd better not be pulling any monkey business, or I'll.."

"Good morning to you too," said Max. "And since you didn't tell me about the will reading, I'd say you have no room to complain about anyone else holding out."

"Say, I saw your little coffee klatch with Von Grunewald at that will reading. What did he tell you?"

"You must be a great detective," Max remarked. "You have such a deliciously suspicious mind."

"Never mind that. You're supposed to share information. What did he tell you?"

"Put your suspicious mind at ease; you're liable to strain something. He was merely filling me in on what had happened so far, seeing as how a certain NYC police detective had forgotten to tell me there even was a reading so I got there late."

"That's all?" Darwin still sounded suspicious.

"You got me," Max admitted. "He confessed everything, but he asked me not to tell you."

"Wise guy.." Darwin muttered. "All right, Max, but if he does spill any beans, you'd better come clean about it."

"And you'd better stop mixing your metaphors. Look, I haven't had breakfast yet, so if you have no more accusations.."

"All right, but the Commissioner's on my butt every damned day. I've got to crack this case or it'll crack me, so if you're..'

"I'm not. Don't worry."

"And if you find out anything.."

"Then I'll be singing out like a canary. Don't worry. I have to go now."

"Fine," Darwin growled. "Just keep me informed."

The line went dead.

Allison had arrived downstairs and was now leaning against a column looking at him.

"Our good friend detective Darwin," Max explained. "The perfect way to start the day."

"Maybe if you're a masochist. Is he still suspicious?"

"Extremely, but I don't take it personally. He's suspicious of everybody."

"So you're off to tackle La Tibbet once again?"

"Yes. I'm afraid I have to tilt at that particular windmill one more time. How about you?"

"I have an interview with a couple of rather colorful Prohibition agents this morning."

"Sounds interesting. Then what?"

"Well, unless you need me, I think I'll drop in on the round table for lunch."

"The round table at that hotel? The one with all the writers and critics sinking their fangs into each other? I thought you were lucky to escape the first time."

"All very true, but I have to have a chat with them. You see, I was reading this while you were on the phone."

She showed him a copy of the New York Herald folded over to Fulton Pierce Adams's The Conning Tower column.

Max skimmed the article.

"Oh, it's a collection of new poems by that Dorothy Parker woman you met. What about it?"

"Look at the third one."

Max looked.

The Country Mouse

Small and meek, you can barely hear her squeak,
The country mouse comes to the city
Searching for sophistication, overcoming
consternation,
Finding all the city mice so suave and witty

She is writing on her pad "This doesn't seem so bad
and will titillate my hometown mice and rats."
But do be careful dear, while you're staying here ,
for the equally sophisticated cats

"So? What about it?"

"Max, she's talking about me! She even called me a country mouse the first time I met her. And she chided me for writing on a pad when we were at the round table."

"Well, maybe." Max was unsure if this was true and didn't quite see how it was a problem if it was. "I just don't see.."

"She's mocking me! 'Look out for sophisticated cats' indeed. She was just being nice to observe me and my country bumpkin ways long enough to get some material out of it."

"Living in St Michaels doesn't make you a country bumpkin."

"Living on the other side of the Hudson does to these people."

"Allison, do you really care what those people think? Aren't they just a bunch of..."

"They are a bunch of serious writers, writers who write for big audiences. They're leaders of public opinion who write things people quote. People care what they think about everything. They're what I'd like to be someday. That's why I'm so mad they're mocking me. They're telling me I'm not up to their standards."

"I don't know, Allison. Besides, if this woman is the literary star you say she is, maybe it's an honor to be the inspiration for one of her...."

"Honor? Since when is it an honor to be the butt of a joke? I'm going to see her and give her a piece of my mind."

"Uh, I'm not really sure that's such a good idea. You've seen her in action."

"But she hasn't seen me in action."

Max sighed. "Look, if you want to confront the woman with the most vicious tongue in New York, I can't stop you, but promise me you'll at least consider the possibility that the poem was meant as a compliment, or...."

"Or what?"

"Or maybe she wrote it weeks ago and it didn't have anything to do with you."

Allison's face fell. "Oh, Max; do you think so?"

"I don't believe it. You're disappointed. A minute ago you were outraged about being mocked."

"Well, yes," she conceded, "but being ignored is worse."

The house on 70th Street was cooler than Max remembered, as was Constance Tibbet.

"Mr. Hurlock, I have spoken to you and I have spoken to the Police several times. I have nothing more I can tell you."

"Oh, I think you have," Max said sternly. "You can start by telling me why you never mentioned that your sister Charity was involved with Connelly."

Her face became even more rigid. "I don't have anything to say about that, and I'll thank you to leave immediately."

"Suit yourself," Max said with a shrug of the shoulders, " but if I leave here, I'm heading straight to Police headquarters to see Detective Darwin. I'm sure he'll be only too glad to come by and continue the questioning, that is, if he doesn't decide to take you downtown to avoid the bother."

For the first time, her self-confidence seemed to weaken. "Downtown? For what?"

"Miss Tibbet, you're about to go from being the star witness to being the chief suspect, and take it from me, you won't enjoy it nearly as much."

She looked shocked. "Me? Why would they suspect me?"

"For starters, you had a sister in the clutches of a man you knew was probably going to simply despoil her then toss her aside like all the others, and you had to stop that from happening at all costs. Oh, I'm sure you tried to talk her out of seeing him, but the Connelly charm was stronger than your control and you knew where it was heading because you'd seen it so many times before."

"But I.."

"It had to be hard watching your sister getting lured into Connelly's web. You had to protect her. You had to stop Connelly at all costs. So the night he went to the Waldorf, you hid the nightgowns so Mandy Jewell wouldn't stay the night and you'd have a clear field to kill Connelly. You went to your sister's house for a visit but she must not have told you she wasn't seeing him any longer. You returned and shot him."

"My God, you can't believe that?" she stuttered.

"Can you give me a good reason not to?"

She dropped her feather duster to the floor and sat heavily in an armchair. "It isn't true. I would never harm Mr. Connelly. I looked out for him. I...I loved him."

"You what?"

"I was concerned about Charity, it's true, but that was over. She had ended the relationship a few days before. I don't expect you to understand, Mr. Hurlock, but I wanted what was best for my sister, and I wanted what was best for Mr. Connelly. I knew that he needed me to straighten out his life and bring out his better qualities. I love Charity, but she would only have encouraged him in his wanton ways. I was the one who should have him. It was best for everyone."

Max looked at her suspiciously. "Now let me get this straight. You were in love with Connelly and purposely discouraged other women, including your sister from seeing him so you could have him?"

"It was for his own good," she insisted.

"And his constant womanizing didn't concern you?"

"Of course it was a concern, Mr. Hurlock. I'm not blind, you know, but marriage to a strong woman who has his best interests at heart would have transformed the man. We would have been very happy."

Max shook his head slowly. Constance Tibbet probably wasn't a killer. Under her stern exterior, she was a naïve romantic clinging to the doomed belief that she could single handedly change Connelly's entire life solely with good intentions. How many women chained themselves to a life with worthless men because of that same woolen-headed mindset? Max suddenly felt like an intruder. He wanted to leave, but there was one more thing he needed to find out.

"Miss Tibbet, you hid the nightgowns and toilet articles to keep Miss Jewell from spending the night, didn't you?."

"I hid them to protect Mr. Connelly."

"To protect Mr. Connelly. Of course," said Max, "but did you remove anything else?"

She looked up in apparent bewilderment. "Anything else? What do you mean?"

"I mean, did you find a gun in the room when you found Mr. Connelly that morning?"

"A gun? Why, no. I never saw a gun."

"I see. And the front door was unlocked when you arrived?"

"Yes. I said that. The front door was unlocked, but the inner vestibule door was locked. Usually both doors were. I thought nothing of it since Mr. Connelly often forgot to lock the doors after a night out. He sometimes got above himself when the champagne flowed a little too freely, you understand."

"Of course. Now one more question; what was his relationship with Mr. Von Grunewald?"

Constance Tibbet frowned again, but it was a frown of uneasiness. "I never trusted that one. Oh, he was all good manners and formality, but I could see through that. I'm not surprised the man was a U-boat captain during the Great War. He has an edge of ruthlessness and cunning that makes me nervous. I can well imagine him sending a ship to the bottom without a second thought. Whenever he was here, I kept an eye on him for Mr. Connelly's sake. Mr.Connelly thought I was just being overly suspicious, but I still don't trust the man."

"Anything specific?"

She pursed her lips again. Clearly she was regaining her usual stiff composure.

"Whenever he was here, and it was at least twice that I know of, all he talked about was money. He talked about having money, making money, and most of all, how much he said Mr. Connelly owed him."

"You mean they had some kind of financial arrangement?"

She looked at him suspiciously. "Mr. Hurlock, are you an honorable man?"

"I like to think so. What are you driving at?"

She paused, as if trying to make up her mind.

"I have something to show you, Mr. Hurlock, but on one condition."

"What's that?"

"You must promise not to tell the police about it."

"I'm afraid I can't promise that. Withholding evidence is against the law. I investigate crimes, but I draw the line at committing them."

"This isn't evidence, Mr. Hurlock."

"I'm not sure the police would agree. If you have anything that could throw light on this case, I'd advise you to produce it. Otherwise you'll be withholding evidence."

She considered this for a moment.

"All right. I'll let you be the judge. I'll show you, but if you agree it's not really evidence, you won't mention it to anyone."

"Fair enough."

She went into another room and returned a minute later with a piece of paper in her hand.

"Mr. Connelly was secretive about his financial dealings, but one night he left a paper on his night table. I thought it might be important, so I copied the information while he was asleep."

Max looked at the paper.

"This looks like notes for a contract of some sort."

"That's exactly what it is. In 1921, Mr. Von Grunewald agreed to pay one half the cost of a racehorse. Mr. Connelly was to repay him with all of the prize money the horse won in 1923."

Max looked up from the paper.

"It doesn't say the name of the horse."

"No. As I understood it, the exact amount would be finalized once a horse was selected and mutually agreed on. So what do you think? Is this evidence or not?"

Max nodded. "I think I'll wait a bit before telling the police about this. I think because we only have your word that it's a true copy of Connelly's notes a judge might consider it hearsay and therefore inadmissible in court. There's no law against withholding hearsay."

"Thank you. I wouldn't want it known that I snooped on Mr. Connelly.'

"But I reserve the right to change my mind if I get additional information."

"Of course."

"So how much prize money have Connelly's horses won so far this year?"

"I believe Persimmon won $2,400, Redbud won $600, and Tigress hasn't been raced yet."

"So if the horse was Persimmon, Von Grunewald did pretty well, but if it was Tigress.."

"He would have been very unhappy with Mr. Connelly."

Constance Tibbet, Max thought ruefully, seemed to have a gift for understatement.

The New York Prohibition office had a jumbled, scraped together look, as if it had been set up one day and was due to be closed the next. A row of mismatched file cabinets lined one wall and small empty desks filled several small rooms. A bored looking receptionist took time out from doing her nails to explain that the agents were all out except for Izzy and Moe who had stayed behind to talk to her.

Allison was surprised to see two middle aged men who looked more like short order cooks than government law enforcement agents. Neither was as tall as she was and both looked as if a flight of stairs would exhaust them. The only aspect of their appearance that even remotely hinted they were Prohibition agents was the fact they were built like beer barrels.

"Howya doin'? I'm Izzy Einstein and this is my partner Moe Smith." Einstein said. "Whatcha want to know?"

"I'm writing an article about speakeasies and I want to know about the enforcement side. I understand you use disguises to infiltrate speakeasies."

Izzy smiled, resembling nothing so much as an overweight elf. "Aw, yeah. We do lots of disguises. One time I was a southern colonel, a butcher, and one time Moe and me was husband and wife. I got served a drink in sympathy on account of Moe made such an ugly woman. One time I got this football uniform and smeared mud all over it. Then I went into this place and told 'em I needed a drink to recover from a tough game. I got the drink and said 'Dere's sad news here; you're busted!'"

"But how come the other agents don't make as many arrests as you two?" Allison asked.

Izzy frowned. "Less enthusiasm?"

"Yeah," said Moe, "not to mention the fact that most of 'em are taking payoffs to look the other way."

"The thing is," said Izzy, "we get paid to do a job and that's what we do. Anyway, I wouldn't want to have to explain bribes to my Rabbi."

"Besides," said Moe, "we're havin' too much fun this way."

"Where does the liquor come from in the places you raid?"

Izzy smiled. "Just about everywhere; local stills, moonshiners from out of state, even local breweries. Some of the mob boys bought up some local breweries and make booze on the sly. Others make 'medicinal' alcohol by the case."

"What about liquor from other countries?" Allison asked. "How does that work?"

"Well, a lot of it comes over the border from Canada. Whiskey mostly. Pretty good quality. Some of it comes from Europe and the Caribbean. They send it on ships that wait out at sea beyond the twelve mile limit and offload to speedy rumrunners at night for the run ashore. Then there's a local agent who arranges to store the stuff in a warehouse somewhere until it can be hauled to a speak."

"How about rum? Where does that come from?"

"Mostly the Caribbean. Cuba's probably the biggest supplier," said Moe.

"It's pretty good quality, too," said Izzy. "Remember a few months ago Moe? We busted dis place that had a dozen cases of Cuban overproof; straight off the boat."

"Overproof?"

"Well, most rum is around 70-80 proof. But overproof rum is 151. That stuff'll take paint off."

"Then why do they use it?"

"There's a few cocktails that call for it, but the real advantage if you're a speak is the fact that it's twice the alcohol content."

"Yeah," said Moe. "And that means you can cut it and still have plenty of good kick for cocktails. It's sort of like a liquor in concentrated form and that means dey can smuggle in less of it."

"So there's less chance of getting caught," said Allison.

"You got it," said Izzy, lighting a cigarette. "One of the yeggs we collared said it came from some warehouse." He reached over to a nearby table and pulled out a map.

"Problem was, we only cover to the river; the East River I mean. See?" He indicated a spot on the map with a meaty finger. "This warehouse was right about here. Well, that's over in Brooklyn, so we couldn't touch it. So we gave the information to the Prohibition boys over there."

Allison looked carefully at the map and wrote the street name down on a slip of paper.

"And what did the police in Brooklyn do?"

Izzy snickered. "Whadddaya think dey did? Bupkis."

"Bup..?"

"Nothin'. They never touched the place. Say, just what kind of an article are you doing anyway?"

"Well, to tell you the truth," said Allison. "I'm here with my husband, Max. He's investigating the murder of Ellsworth Connelly."

Izzy let out a low whistle. "We heard tell of that Connelly guy. What a shame."

"Do you know if he was involved in speakeasies or rumrunning?" Allison asked.

Moe shrugged. "We heard rumors, but nothing we could sink our teeth into. Someone said he might be connected to that warehouse in Brooklyn."

"I'll tell you one thing, though," Izzy volunteered. "If he did want to smuggle rum, that warehouse was a good set up for it."

"A good set up? What do you mean?"

"The warehouse was right on the river, just off the main ship channels. A boat could be in and out of there without anybody noticing."

"But what does that have to do with Mr. Connelly?" Allison asked.

"Well, I read in the papers he had dis big yacht down in Florida. He'd take the train down in the winter and cruise around, then take the boat up to New York in the spring. Then he'd pay a captain to run it back to Florida so it'd be waiting for him next winter."

"So how does that make a good setup for smuggling illegal liquor?"

"Well, let's just say one of his ports of call while he's cruising is Cuba, or maybe Puerto Rico. He loads up on something compact like the overproof we were just talking about and takes it back with him to New York. He was a well-known yacht guy, so the Coast Guard wouldn't touch him. He'd drop it off to a shore agent at a riverfront warehouse, then do it again next year."

"Just one trip a year?" said Allison. "Why would he bother?"

"Because with a 50 foot boat he could probably carry enough overproof to clear at least $50,000 on that one run. Maybe more."

John Reisinger

Chapter 18
Detective Darwin considers

Max phoned Von Grunewald, but he was out, so Max went to police headquarters to go over his notes and see if there was anything in the file of Constance Tibbet's interrogations to support what she had told him.

Detective Darwin was out, so Max was undisturbed as he went through the records. As he looked, the word "connection" pushed its way into his mind once more. Normally he disdained intuition, preferring logic and evidence, but he couldn't get the idea out of his head. Somewhere there was some connection between people or events that he had missed, or maybe it was staring him in the face unrecognized.

He looked at the photos again and saw Ellsworth Connelly sitting in the chair in his reception room as if waiting for a guest. The photo was black and white, but there was no mistaking the ugly black blotch on his forehead or the dark splatter on the wall behind him. Max shuffled through the photos again, this time with a magnifying glass trying to see if there was some detail he might have missed. There were the letters, and there were the envelopes...no sign of a murder weapon. Connelly sat slumped in the chair with his hands at his side. Max ran the magnifying glass over the photo and stopped. He adjusted the glass. He was right.

Just then Detective Darwin appeared in the doorway.

"They said you were in here. Got anything to tell me?" he said with his usual lack of formalities.

191

"I'm not sure," said Max. "Take a look at this."

Darwin looked. "So what am I looking for?"

"It's a little hard to see, but look at his left hand. It's in a fist, a very tight fist."

"So? If someone was about to shoot me in the head, I might be a little tense too."

"Right," Max agreed, "but at least this seems to prove that Ellsworth Connelly didn't kill himself. He was left handed and that would have been the hand in which he held the gun."

"How do you know he was left handed?"

"When I met him in Maryland I noticed his watch was on his right wrist and deducted he was left handed. He confirmed it. So if he killed himself with a point blank shot to the head, he wouldn't have been conscious long enough to drop the gun and then make a fist."

"I suppose so, but of course it could also be just rigor mortis."

"No," Max answered emphatically. "Rigor Mortis causes stiffening several hours after death, but the only way muscles or tendons can actually contract is if the body starts to dry out, and that takes days."

Darwin looked at him. "Jeez; what do you do in your spare time down in Maryland?"

"Anyway," Max continued, "I was pretty sure it wasn't suicide. This just confirms it."

"So you didn't learn anything new?"

Max scratched his chin thoughtfully. "I'm not sure. Of course, I don't want to get carried away with speculation, but the tightly clenched fist might indicate Connelly wasn't taken by surprise. He was facing someone who was threatening to kill him and he knew it."

"Yeah, maybe." Darwin blew out another cloud of Lucky smoke. "What else ya got?"

Max pushed the photo away and leaned back in his chair. " I spoke with Constance Tibbet again. What she told me pretty much agrees with what she told your boys, except she has a pretty low opinion of Von Grunewald."

"Nothing unusual there."

"She seems to think he had some sort of financial arrangement with Connelly that might be a motive for murder."

Darwin casually lit another Lucky Strike with a wooden match. "So what do you think?"

"I'm still gathering the facts. How about the NYPD? You want to let me in on how you're doing?"

Darwin sat down and sighed, coughing slightly in his own smoke.

"I still got guys digging and running down leads. The trouble with cases like this is that too many people know about them."

"Too many?"

"You take your average murder in New York. Some guy gets bumped off in an alley somewhere or maybe in his kitchen. We talk to a few friends, or maybe the wife, and presto; we make an arrest. Most of the time it's a bootlegger in a territory dispute, or a husband-wife argument that got out of hand, or just some dumb argument by even dumber people. We solve the case and move on. The thing is, nobody outside of the stiff's acquaintances knows what's going on, and that makes it easy. Nobody gives us advice, nobody looks over our shoulder, and most of all, nobody tries to help."

"Now wait a minute.." Max began to protest, but Darwin held up his hand.

"I don't mean guys like you; guys that know what they're talking about. I mean all the mugs out there that have nothing better to do than to hook onto a big time case. It just gums up the works and wastes our time. Hell, yesterday we even got a confession from some palooka in Queens. Claims he killed Connelly because the voices in his head told him to."

"I suppose it's possible, isn't it?"

"No, it isn't; not in this case, anyway. Turns out the guy was in Bellevue at the time Connelly was killed. They should have kept him."

"I may be joining him soon," Max remarked. "Do you have a file of background of the people interviewed?"

"Natch, but it's pretty boring stuff. You know; hometowns, relatives, employment records, a rough record of their travels..that sort of thing."

"I know," said Max, "but I'd like to go through it anyway. You never know what might fit in somewhere."

"All I can say is I hope Von Grunewald is paying you by the hour."

Allison arrived early at the Algonquin and was disappointed to find the round table empty.

"Lucky for them," she muttered to herself. "But once they get here, they're going to see what a country mouse can do. I'll teach them to look down on Allison Hurlock. I'm just as good as any of them."

As she stood contemplating the room, a waiter approached.

"Are you here for lunch, Miss?" The waiter was in his fifties, with a lined face and watery eyes.

"Er..yes. I'm waiting for someone."

"Could I show you to a nice booth by the window?"

"No, I was thinking of sitting here."

The waiter looked at the round table, then back at her. He seemed distressed. "Oh, you don't want to sit there, Miss. That table's reserved. You see, every day the literary and theater people show up and that's their table. You wouldn't want to be subjected to that."

Allison looked at him curiously. "Subjected to what? What do you mean?"

"Oh, it's none of my business of course, and I don't want to intrude, but, well, just between you and me, those people are in their own world, and I'm afraid they're not very nice to people outside of it. The thing is, I've seen them and waited that table a lot, and I don't think they realize just how small that world is."

"Small?" Allison was fascinated by this outsider's view of the Round Table.

"They're all so very clever, aren't they?" the waiter continued. "Everything has to have a punch line. They call this the Algonquin Round Table, but it's also known as the Vicious Circle. They spend the whole time trying to top each other on who can be the most witty. Nothing is ever serious. When I first started working here, the hotel had a special waiter named Luigi assigned just to this table. For a while everyone at the table called it the Luigi Board. Nobody ever asked Luigi what he thought. That's the way it is with those folks. Everything's a joke; usually at someone else's expense."

Allison frowned. "Yes, I suppose that's true."

Now that the ice was broken, the waiter seemed anxious to tell all to Allison. It was obviously something he'd thought about a lot.

"The thing is, they think what they say is something special, something wonderful and important, but in the end it's just words. Soon spoken and soon forgotten."

Allison looked at him thoughtfully. "You seem to have a talent with words yourself. That was very well put."

"Well, I'm afraid I've spoken out of turn," the waiter continued, blushing slightly. "Of course you can be seated there if you want. The rest'll start coming in here any minute. I just thought you didn't seem like one of them. I know people, you see. After a while you get a sense about people in this job. I can tell you have a kind heart, and I guess I was just trying to keep you away from people that don't. I'm sorry."

The waiter scurried away.

Allison stood watching him go, then looked at the table again.

"What am I doing?" she said out loud. "He's right. I'm not like them...and I don't want to be!"

With that, she turned on her heel and walked back out of the front door.

Max looked through the background files for over an hour, making notes. He then called Von Grunewald again. Von Grunewald was still out, so Max went to East 52nd Street and the offices of the Jockey Club. A tall man with a pencil thin moustache greeted him.

"Why, yes, Mr. Hurlock. It's always great to meet someone from Maryland. That's real horse breeding country down there. They appreciate their thoroughbreds."

"Thank you," said Max. "I'm trying to find out some information on a horse named Tigress owned by the late Ellsworth Connelly."

"Oh, yes. Poor Mr. Connelly. He was a respected owner and he will be missed."

"Did you know him?"

"Why yes. I met him once when he came here to look at the Stud Book."

"To look at the what?"

"The Stud Book. It's a registry the Jockey Club keeps of horse breeding and lineage to help keep the bloodlines straight and provide a resource for breeders."

"Oh, of course,' said Max a little dubiously. "What was his interest in the Stud Book?"

"As I said, Mr. Connelly was a respected owner of thoroughbreds. He was researching a horse he anticipated buying."

"Now we're getting somewhere. Was the horse's name Tigress?"

"Tigress? No, that wasn't it. As I recall, the horse was Cyclone."

"How long ago was this?"

"Oh, it's been at least a year or two now."

"Did he end up buying Cyclone?"

"I don't know, but I could check the Stud Book if you would like."

"If it wouldn't be too much trouble."

"No trouble at all. Follow me."

He led Max into a large room filled with filing cabinets.

"The original records are kept and processed at Lexington, Kentucky, but we keep copies here as well. Ah, here we are." He indicated a large loose leafed binder on a table and began leafing through it.

"Now let's see where Cyclone wound up. Hmmm. It looks like Cyclone was too young to race when Mr. Connelly considered buying her, but her practice runs look impressive. Hmmm. It looks like Mr. Connelly didn't buy Cyclone after all."

"So who owns her now?"

"The CV Partnership in New York."

"Do they have an address?"

"Just a post office box and there's a notation here that the box is no longer in that name."

"How about Tigress?"

Pages rustled for a few seconds.

"Owned by Ellsworth Connelly... kept at Hawkins Pride Farm...No record of racing..."

"Nothing unusual?"

"Not really. He bought the horse and I suppose it's being raced now."

"I happen to know it isn't being raced," said Max, "even though its practice times have been good. Can you think of any reason for that?"

"Oh, I couldn't say for sure, but the horse is a two year old, maybe a little more. They are more prone to injury when they race than the older horses, so maybe Mr. Connelly was just being cautious; protecting his investment as it were."

Max snapped his fingers. "Of course. That's the reason Connelly didn't race Tigress. He had a partnership with Von Grunewald in which Von Grunewald received all the prize winnings this year. Why would Connelly want to race Tigress and risk injury just to enrich someone else? The smart thing to do would be to keep Tigress in training one more year. He probably kept telling Von Grunewald that the horse was slow just to put him off."

"I'm afraid I'm at a loss, Mr. Hurlock," the Jockey Club man said. "Who is this Von Grunewald gentleman?"

"Someone who told me a story I didn't believe, but it turns out he was probably telling the truth.""

"You mean you didn't go into the lions den after all?"

Max and Allison had met as they returned to the Wolcott and were now seated in the lobby idly watching a man at the front desk arguing about his bill as they compared notes.

"No. I had a very enlightening chat with a waiter, and it made me realize just how unimportant that poem really was. There was no real harm done. After all, even the formidable Mrs. Parker has to make a living, I suppose. Let her have her clever fun. It certainly doesn't hurt me. I did find out something interesting when I interviewed Izzy and Moe, the Prohibition agents. They think Connelly might have been running rum to a warehouse in Brooklyn. That might make the blind tiger and the puncheon tag fit together nicely."

"It sure would," said Max, "if it's true."

"Well, here's the address of the warehouse if you think it's worth pursuing. Anyway, what about you? Did you find out anything new?"

"Well, it seems Connelly was purposely holding Tigress back from racing because Von Grunewald would get any prize money and the horse could get injured. He probably made various thin excuses to Von Grunewald, claiming the horse was hopelessly slow and that's what the dispute was about."

"So Von Grunewald was telling the truth all along?"

"Well, at least about his financial deal with Connelly. In other areas he's been less than candid."

"Does that help clarify the case?"

"Hardly at all. It doesn't get me one step closer to the killer. I just think there's a connection somewhere that I've missed; a connection that will put everything together."

"That would be nice, but where will you find it?"

Max laughed softly. "If I knew that I'd be looking there right now. I did look through the police background files on the suspects. There was a lot of information there, but nothing significant...."

Max paused a moment, then smiled.

"Well, I did find one thing. It was more of a strange coincidence, really; the sort of thing that must happen a lot in a place like New York. If I read the file correctly,

Martin Forsythe's had a series of business meetings on 41st Street the second week of January. It was almost around the corner from the automat. Just think: two suspects working less than a block from each other."

"Odd, but hardly incriminating," Allison remarked. "So what do you think it means?"

"Probably nothing. It wasn't nearly as unlikely as Connelly meeting us in Maryland just a week before he died. It's just amazes me how many coincidences there are in such a big place."

"So where are you now?"

Max put his feet up on a nearby stool. "Well, as I see it, whoever killed Connelly had to be someone who planned the crime carefully. That's why we have the note, the extra letter to Connelly, and the planted clues such as the false teeth. That would seem to eliminate Gwen Perkins who is too direct and impulsive for such an elaborate crime. An impromptu assault with an umbrella is much more her style. I think we can eliminate Helen Arness as well. She wouldn't kill a man if there were any chance of getting the money she was after. And the Porters have no motive as far as I can see."

"But they've known him the longest," Allison interrupted. "Could there be some dark secret in his past that would give them a motive?"

"There's no sign of one. Besides, they seem like such nice people. Anyway, Constance Tibbet was too much in love with Connelly to kill him, but she is still covering up. Martin Forsythe might have been angry enough to kill Connelly a year ago, but with his arrogance and hot temper, it seems unlikely he'd wait so long. Of course Dianne Forsythe might have felt resentment at Connelly for the difficulties he had brought her, but there's still the fact that a year has passed."

"How about the chauffeur?"

"Fulton did have a powerful motive if he thought Connelly was about to cut him out of his will because of Constance Tibbet's influence. Mandy Jewell had no motive if she is telling the truth about Connelly wanting to marry her."

"But if he rejected her that night?"

"Then she goes to the top of the suspect list," said Max.

"Alongside Von Grunewald?"

"I'm afraid so. They seem to be heading up the hit parade at the moment. It's a good thing he's paying me in advance."

Excuse me, Mr. Hurlock, there's a phone call for you." They looked up to see the desk clerk standing by the sofa. "It's a Detective Darwin, sir."

Max and Allison looked at each other.

"The perfect ending to a perfect day," Max sighed as he walked to the phone..

"Max." The voice on the line was loud and abrupt. "I promised to keep you informed. Well, thank you for your help, but the case is over."

Max gasped. "Over? What do you mean?"

"We just arrested Gwen Perkins for the murder of Ellsworth Connelly."

John Reisinger

Chapter 19
Grilling Gwen Perkins

Max opened his mouth, but it was a few seconds before any sound came out.

"Gwen Perkins?" he stammered finally, "The Queen of the...I mean the woman from the automat? Why? When I talked to her she struck me as a little vindictive, but I didn't see anything that pointed to..."

"We found the murder weapon in her room," Darwin interrupted. "We've sent it for a ballistics check, but it's a .45 Colt and I'm betting the bullets will match the one that killed Connelly."

"What does she say about it?"

"She hasn't confessed yet, if that's what you mean; claims she has the gun for protection and it's never been fired. It's all an act, of course. She just needs a little time to realize the jig is up."

Max's mind was racing with this new and unexpected development.

"Say, Harold; I appreciate you telling me, and I guess this puts the lid on the case, but would you mind if I sat in when you question her?"

"Nix on that, Max. Against regulations, Besides interrogation is a game only a limited number can play. Tell you what, though. If you'd like, you can watch and listen. The interrogation room has a room next to it with a one way mirror. You better hurry, though. We start in about 15 minutes."

"I'll be there."

"Did I hear that right?" Allison was beside him with an amazed expression on her face. "Did they really arrest the Automat Queen?"

"I'm afraid so. It seems they found the murder weapon in her room. It looks pretty bad for Miss Perkins."

"Do you still think she didn't do it?"

Max shook his head. "I'm not sure what to think. It still doesn't add up."

"Well, you did say she was vindictive about anybody jilting her."

"Oh, she is. It's just that being vindictive isn't quite the same thing as being homicidal."

"It's not the same thing as being a shrinking violet either," Allison reminded him.

"No, I suppose not. ...Look, how about coming down to police headquarters with me to observe the interrogation of the Automat Queen?"

"Count me in. I've never met royalty before."

A few minutes later, they were approaching police headquarters.

"It doesn't make sense," Max insisted. "Gwen Perkins isn't a dumb Dora. Why would she keep the murder weapon in her room where it would just about convict her if someone found it?"

"Obviously, she thought no one would. That's the thing with murderers, Max. They never expect to get caught, so they take foolish chances. Good thing, too; otherwise they'd be a lot harder to catch."

"That's true, of course," Max admitted, "but why wouldn't she just dispose of it in a public trash can, or maybe in one of the trash bins behind the automat. They're probably emptied every day or two. Why leave it in her room?"

"Maybe your chum Detective Darwin will ask her."

Detective Darwin was just about to enter the interrogation room when they arrived.

"Ah, Max. And who is this?" Darwin's cigarette almost fell out of his mouth when he saw Allison.

"Oh, this is my wife Allison. Is it all right if she sits in as well?"

Darwin smiled roguishly. "I never refuse a lady. The more the merrier, as long as you stay in the other room."

The observation room was dark and smelled vaguely of sweat and cigarettes. On one wall was a panel of one way glass that permitted them to observe the interrogation room without being seen. Over the glass was a small speaker that was crackling softly.

"Cozy place," Allison observed. "Who is their decorator, I wonder? It makes our first room at the Wolcott look positively luxurious. They should bring all the suspects in here. They'd confess just to get out."

On the other side of the interrogation room a door opened and an officer led Gwen Perkins in and seated her at the single table. She looked dazed and tired. She sat alone for a minute, dully looking around the room. Finally, the door opened again and Detective Darwin walked in, along with Detective Anderson. They shuffled some papers for a few seconds, then Anderson spoke in a friendly manner. His voice sounded tinny over the speaker in the observation room.

"Cigarette?"

She shook her head as if it were an effort.

"How about a coffee or a glass of water?"

She shook her head again and Anderson got down to business.

"Now, Miss Perkins. We want to help you out of this mess, but you've got to help us. Tell us about the gun."

"If she believes that," Allison whispered, "she really is dumb."

Gwen Perkins looked up. "I told you. I've had that gun for at least two years. It's for protection. I'm a woman living alone in the city. I need to protect myself."

"That's what the police are for," Darwin shot back.

"By the time the police get there," Gwen Perkins replied, "the only thing left to do is draw a chalk outline around the body. No thanks. I'll take care of myself."

"You took care of Ellsworth Connelly pretty good, didn't ya?" Darwin demanded.

"No, I didn't."

"Look, Missy. You better come clean or you're headed straight to the chair!"

Allison turned to Max. "Well, Detective Darwin is certainly a charmer, isn't he?"

"It's an act," Max replied.

"An act?"

"Sure. It's a little psychological game called 'good cop, bad cop'. It must be Darwin's turn to be the bad cop. I imagine he's pretty good at it.". The bad cop threatens the witness and the good cop acts reasonable and sympathetic."

"So what is the point of all this amateur theater?"

"The witness turns to the good cop for comfort and protection and tells all."

"And this is admissible in court?"

"Shhh. Listen. She's telling them about the gun."

Anderson made a gesture to Darwin to settle down and turned back to Gwen Perkins.

"Now, Miss Perkins; you say you had the gun for protection, but it's a Colt .45. That's an awfully big and heavy gun for a woman, isn't it? The recoil alone would be enough to sprain a wrist.'

"I wouldn't know. I've never fired it."

"Oh for the love of...." Darwin began, but Anderson shushed him once more.

"But why would you choose such a gun in the first place?" Anderson raised an eyebrow to convey just a hint of suspicion.

My brother Jim was in the army during the war. He gave it to me. You can ask him. He lives in Albany.

"We will, and we're having the gun checked out. Meanwhile, tell us about your relationship with Ellsworth Connelly."

Gwen Perkins then recounted the same story she had told Max; the whirlwind courtship; the enthusiasm, and the abrupt betrayal. She ended with her umbrella attack on Connelly and her vow never to allow a man to mistreat her in the future.

"Well," said Darwin, "so that's why you killed him."

"I didn't kill him. I told you that."

Darwin leapt to his feet and started shouting. "Come off it. You had the perfect motive and you had the murder weapon. I've seen killers go to the chair who didn't have half as much evidence against them. How stupid do you think we are?"

Gwen Perkins looked Darwin in the eye.

"I assume that's a rhetorical question..?"

While Darwin exploded in simulated anger, Allison turned to Max.

"I like her. She'd fit right in at the round table,"

On the other side of the glass, Anderson was physically restraining Darwin, who looked as if he was on the edge of apoplexy. In spite of herself, Gwen Perkins was visibly rattled.

"Miss Perkins," Anderson began again in his role as the voice of reason, "I know this is all most unpleasant for you. We've been doing some checking into Mr. Connelly and I'm afraid what you've told us about his treatment of women is all too true. I can well understand that his actions were intolerable. I can even understand how you might have felt compelled to strike back at him in some way. As far as I can see, he certainly earned it."

He paused, but Gwen Perkins did not respond.

"And I think," Anderson continued, "that a jury would understand, too. People take a dim view of men who are cads, you know. Now I'm not promising you'll be let off completely, but I think we can avoid the chair or even a life sentence under the circumstances as long as you're honest about it and come clean."

"I have."

Anderson looked pained, but Darwin was on his feet once again. "All right; it's time we cut out beating around the bush. Your gun is being analyzed and within an hour they'll have the results. Now we all know what they'll find, don't we? They'll prove the gun has been fired recently and that the bullet matches the one that killed Connelly, so stop wasting our time!"

Anderson spoke in a voice deep with sympathy and concern.

"I'm afraid he's right, Miss Perkins. Once the test results on the gun come back, we'll have all the evidence necessary for a finding of murder in the first degree, and that means the chair. Now if you want to get a break, you've got to come clean and you've got to do it now. Please....for your sake. You're too young to die."

"Laying it on a bit thick, isn't he?" Allison remarked.

"Why not?" said Max, "If she confesses, it saves them all the trouble and mess of having to prove it in court. It's certainly worth a try."

In the interrogation room, Gwen Perkins sat silently looking at the floor.

Anderson gave a heavy sigh and rose to leave. Darwin snorted and followed. The door slammed and Gwen Perkins sat alone in the room softly crying.

Allison was sympathetic. "Those two should be ashamed of themselves treating a defenseless woman like that. New York's Finest indeed. Finest bullies is more like it.'

"Allison, that 'defenseless woman' is most probably a killer. Whatever they did to her isn't a fraction of what she did to Connelly."

"I thought you didn't think she did it."

"So far, the evidence seems to suggest otherwise."

They left the observation room and saw Anderson and Darwin smoking and drinking coffee.

"Well boys, ready to get out the rubber hose?" said Max cheerfully.

Darwin took a long drink of black coffee. "No need. Once we get the ballistics report, she'll fold like a cardboard bathtub. We'll just let her stew a while."

"So you think she's the one?" Max asked.

Anderson looked at him curiously. "We have motive, means and opportunity, plus pretty soon we'll have physical evidence connecting her with the murder weapon. We're having it checked for fingerprints, too."

"Well," said Max, "seeing as how it's her gun, I don't know who else's fingerprints you expect to find."

"That's the point."

"Detective Darwin?" came a voice from across the room,. "There's a phone call for you. It's about the Connelly case."

"Take a message," Darwin said irritably. "The case is closed. Who is it, anyway?"

"It's a Miss Arness."

Darwin looked at Max suspiciously. "Did you tell her..."

"No. We're not exactly the best of pals."

"Then how did she know..."

"She's a well-connected woman. I wouldn't be surprised if she didn't have some inside sources around here, Harold, but why don't you pick up the receiver and ask her yourself?"

"I will. Hello? This is Detective Darwin speaking. Yes? Who told you... I see. Well, yes it's true. We have her now. No, she hasn't confessed. We're waiting for some laboratory tests on the gun. Oh, an hour at the most; probably sooner. It all depends. Yes, if you wish. I... Yes, I see. Goodbye Miss Arness."

He placed the phone back in the cradle and exhaled. "Whew. Now that's a dame that plays for keeps."

"Hell in a dress," Allison murmured.

"So who told her?" Max asked.

"I'm not sure, but from the way she talked I'm guessing it was the commissioner, if not the mayor. That woman has some connections."

"Including connections to the crime?" Allison asked.

"Oh, no. We eliminated her as a suspect a week ago. She was on the other side of town at the time."

"Since we're not really sure exactly when the murder occurred, that seems to be a little imprecise," Max observed.

"It's close enough," Darwin snapped. "Besides, we got the Perkins dame red handed, so who cares?"

"A jury might be interested," said Max. "A good defense attorney might point out that when you're talking about motives, she might be right up there with the best. Besides, she had a run in with her ex-husband that very night and threatened to make him pay. On the other hand, I suppose there's no evidence she ever hit him with an umbrella."

Darwin turned to Allison. "Is he always this hard headed?"

She nodded. "Pretty much. You could use his head for a hammer sometimes. The thing is, though, he usually hits the right nail."

"Well this time he's hit his thumb. Gwen Perkins killed Ellsworth Connelly and that's all there is to it."

"Look," Max said in his reasonable voice, "I'm not saying you got the wrong person necessarily; I just think we might not have all the evidence yet. What else was in her place? I never saw it."

Darwin took out a piece of paper and scribbled on it. "Tell you what, Max. Here's a police pass for you to search Gwen Perkins's place yourself. Just show it to whatever cop is guarding the place against newspaper people. Then maybe you'll be satisfied. You know it's possible for a crime to get solved without your help."

"I didn't ask for that, Harold," Max replied. "I just wondered what else turned up in that search."

Darwin was starting to reply when a uniformed officer dropped a manila envelope on his desk.

"Ah. Here's the ballistics report," he said, rubbing his hands together. "Now we'll cut through the bushwa and settle this once and for all. Come to papa."

He pulled out a sheet of typed paper and read silently as a smile slowly spread across his face.

"All right, Sherlock Hurlock," he announced with a note of triumph. "You can bring on the jury you were talking about, and you can throw in Helen Arness for good measure. This is all I need. Only Gwen Perkins's prints were found, the gun has been fired recently, the extractor and firing pin marks on the shell casing found at the scene match the gun, and a bullet they fired from the gun matched the one that killed Connelly."

"Check and mate," said Allison.

Chapter 20
Loose ends

"Yes, Gunther, it was Gwen Perkins, apparently. The gun in her place turned out to be the murder weapon. So obviously that eliminates you as a suspect."

Von Grunewald's voice on the phone was equal parts happiness and relief. "Max, that's great. I am a free man at last. I don't know how to thank you."

"Don't thank me, Gunther. The NYPD cracked the case. I was just a bystander."

"Nonsense. I think your investigation kept the pressure on them until they had to solve the case in self-defense. At any rate, I'm in the clear now and that is what I wanted."

"Well anyway, she still denies everything, but she's locked up without bail until the trial. I think the evidence against her is pretty strong."

"Max, I want you and Allison to stay on as my guest for another week. Relax and see the sights of New York. You've earned it."

"No thanks, Gunther. To tell you the truth, we're anxious to get back home. I just need a couple of more days to tie up some loose ends."

"Of course, Max. As long as you like. This is *wunderbar!*"

Max hung up the phone and sat back in the easy chair in their room. Allison had gone to the city records office for more background material for her article and the room was about as quiet as a hotel room in downtown Manhattan ever gets.

Whenever he started to wonder if yesterday had been just a bad dream, all he had to do was look at the newspaper.

ARREST MADE IN CONNELLY MURDER
Gun Found in Subject's Rooms

Police today announced the arrest of Gwendolyn Marie Perkins, 32, for the murder of Ellsworth Connelly, wealthy card expert and man about town. Mr. Connelly was found shot to death in his West 70th Street home on July 10. Miss Perkins, an employee of the Horn and Hardart Automat, was a former acquaintance of Mr. Connelly. According to police, Miss Perkins had been romantically involved with Mr. Connelly, but had been rejected by him. The ill feelings generated by this rejection led her to seek revenge. Police found the gun used to kill Mr. Connelly in Miss Perkins's rooms. The suspect's fingerprints were found on the gun and the gun's bullets matched that used in the killing. Miss Perkins admits her resentment of Mr. Connelly, but denies killing him....

Max sighed, picked up his notes and ran his eyes over the pages. With all the people he talked to and all the investigation he had done, it was strangely unsettling to have the case ended so abruptly, but the facts seemed undeniable. In spite of all the theories of card cheating, business swindles, race horse deals, inheritances, rumrunning, or jealous husbands, it all came down to a simple case of the fury of a spurned woman. Well it wouldn't be the first time.

He put his notes aside and picked up a few handwritten pages of Allison's article on speakeasies. How did she manage to write with such perfect

214

penmanship? His own handwriting was so bad he wrote notes in block lettering so people would have a fighting chance of understanding them.

With the wide variety and number of speakeasies in New York, some locals have found they can serve a variety of functions. Of course there is the opportunity to buy illegal liquor, and there is also the dazzling variety of entertainment speakeasies offer. But ...the uses of speakeasies don't end with just booze and Jazz; people use them as meeting places, as settings for business dealings, places to meet new people, and even as places to meet people you might not want to be seen with. As hostess Texas Guinan told me recently, "Honey, my club is a place where you can hardly count the number of things you can do. You just have to use your imagination. Don't get stuck in conventional thinking."

Max smiled. Maybe old Texas had something. He was stuck in conventional thinking himself. Suspect plus motive plus murder weapon equals *guilt*. Case closed. Ipso facto, Q.E.D. No other explanations need apply. The problem was that Max couldn't get over the feeling that there was a lot more to the case. He was looking for a precipitating event, but still hadn't found it.

He sat back and his eye came to rest on a folded piece of paper by the lamp. He picked it up and saw the address of the Brooklyn warehouse Izzy and Moe had told Allison about. He looked at his watch. It was still morning; there was plenty of time. It just might tie in somehow.

Max took a cab to the Brooklyn address and looked around at the gray industrial area. "Nice place. It's like an alley only without the charm."

There were several warehouses along the street, but Max noticed one that was surrounded by a solid board fence, as if to ensure privacy. He casually walked back to the fence. The warehouse was a brick building with boarded up windows, squatting gray and silent by the East River amid a tangle of scraggly weeds and barely visible through a few gaps in the board fence.

A minute later, Max found a loose board and was inside the enclosure facing the old warehouse. A stray cat peeked around a corner, then disappeared into a patch of weeds. The warehouse was silent and Max tried the side door and found it locked.

Around the back he noticed a small barred window above eye level. Max pushed an old wooden barrel underneath and climbed up to have a look. The window was filthy, but Max was able to clean it somewhat with his handkerchief. He gazed into the dimly lit interior and waited for a minute to allow his eyes to adjust to the darkness. Inside the warehouse was a large open space except for what looked like a small office in a far corner. Pyramids of wooden crates were distributed across the floor.

There were no visible labels on the boxes, just a few numbers written in chalk, but as his eyes became more acclimated to the dimness, Max noticed one crate that was partly open, probably for inspection. Amid the fluffy excelsior packing the box, Max could clearly make out rows of tightly packed bottles, but bottles of what?

As he wondered how he could verify that the bottles contained bootleg liquor, he suddenly heard a rattling sound at the front doors. Someone was opening the lock. A bright dagger of light slithered across the floor as the doors to the warehouse swung open. Max huddled against the window frame to be less visible, but to still be able to see inside.

"All right. Back it in," came a voice.

The warehouse rumbled with the sound of a truck engine. A few seconds later, Max could smell the exhaust fumes through a crack in the window.

"A little more. Hold it. Right there."

A second man jumped down from the cab of the truck and pulled out a clipboard.

"All right. Is this lot 7?"

"Yeah. There's a chalk mark on the crate."

"That's 35 cases of lot 7 off to Benny's on 31st Street."

"We better check to make sure we got the right stuff. Remember when the lots got mixed up last week?"

"Yeah. The supplier stacked the boxes in the wrong place and the boss yelled at us...said we should have checked. Well. Let me open this crate to make sure this time."

He produced a small crowbar and pried open the corner of one of the crates then squatted down and peered inside.

"Yep. It's full of bottles of the finest El Castillo overproof rum, just like it's supposed to be. Let's get the truck loaded."

Max heard shuffling and grunts as the men started to load the crates into the truck. Each case that was taken from the stack and thumped into the truck brought the men closer to the window.

More boxes were removed. The pile was much smaller now. Finally, the men stopped with only about a dozen cases left.

"O.K. that's the 35 cases. Wait a minute and let me catch my breath."

Max quietly breathed a sigh of relief. He'd be able to get out after all.

The driver was wiping his forehead with the back of his coat sleeve and stretching.

"I'm getting too old for this crap. This stuff is heavy."

"Yeah, maybe we should deliver crates of marshmallows instead."

"If they made 'em illegal, maybe we could."

"Yeah, then we could...Hey; what's that?"

The driver had been looking around casually as he spoke, and suddenly his eyes strayed to the window and met Max's.

"There's somebody outside the window! Get him!"

Max jumped down from the barrel. In a second, he was streaking past the open warehouse door towards the only way out; the front gate. One of the men ran up behind and lunged at him and missed, and wound up sprawled on the ground. Meanwhile, the driver circled in front of Max to cut him off before he reached the gate.

"Hold it right there, buddy. We want to talk to you," the man hissed.

Max was just a few feet away now, and saw to his horror that the man blocking his escape was reaching inside his coat for his gun. Remembering his high school football days, Max neatly sidestepped and stiff armed the driver, who was thrown off balance and stumbled.

"Hey! Come back here!"

Max headed towards the gate of the fence. The men had closed the gate behind them when they came in, but Max was betting they hadn't bothered to lock it. Not only had they left the gate unlocked, but the men had left the open padlock hanging on the latch. Max slipped through the gate, closed it behind him, then snapped the lock shut.

Max knew the lock wouldn't hold his pursuers for long and he wouldn't have time to grab another cab. He ran a few hundred yards then slipped into the dark interior of a dirty looking garage, much to the surprise of a heavy set man in greasy coveralls wiping his hands with a rag.

"You here to pick up a car, mister?"

Max smiled. "No. Actually, I've had a slight disagreement with some gentlemen in that warehouse down the street and I thought I'd duck in here until the air clears."

The garage man looked out the window and squinted suspiciously. "What men? I don't see nobody." The garage man looked bewildered until he saw the truck rumble by.

"You mean those guys was after you?"

"Well, let's just say they want to talk to me and I have other plans. I found out they're bootleggers."

The garage man snickered. "Big deal. I run a garage and even I know they're bootleggers. That place became a booze warehouse a month after Prohibition started and has been drawin' bootleggers from all over ever since. You didn't have to go sneakin' around. I been here the whole time. I coulda told you all about it. I can see it all from here, but I mind my own business."

"Do you know who owns it?" Max asked.

"Some guy in Manhattan, I heard . That's all I know. It's a busy place, I can tell you that. They got trucks coming in and trucks going out all the time; boats, too."

"Boats?"

"Sure. They bring the stuff in from ships offshore, usually in small speedboats to get past the Coast Guard. Once in a while a barge or two. I even saw a big yacht there once."

Max's ears perked up. "A yacht? What kind of yacht?"

The garage man shrugged. "I'm an auto guy. I don't know from nothin' about boats. All I know is, it was big and had masts like a sailboat and lots of shiny wood and brass. I remember it because I wondered about it. I even walked down and took a closer look as the boat pulled away."

"When did you see the yacht?" said Max.

"I think it was around April of last year. Haven't seen it since, though."

He looked back towards a car he had been working on. "Look, I got a flivver that needs a new clutch up on the lift and it ain't gonna fix itself, if you know what I mean. I gotta go. Good luck with your snoopin'."

"Wait," said Max. "Did you see any writing or numbers on the boat that you can remember?"

"No, nothing like that. Just the name."

"The name? What was it?"

"Oh, it was some funny word. Let's see. Oh yeah; Finesse. That was it"

After her morning at the records office, Allison skipped lunch and strolled around Times Square, going from theater to theater looking at the posters and the ornate marquees. "I'll get Max to bring me back for a show tonight to get his mind off of things," she said. "The question is; which one?"

She was standing in front of the Liberty Theater reading the playbills for Little Nellie Kelly when she saw a familiar face. A little farther down the sidewalk was Dorothy Parker, along with a tall man she didn't recognize. As they drew closer, Mrs. Parker glanced over and saw Allison. She stopped and grabbed the man's arm.

"Now, Harold, here's a writer you could get at a bargain rate. It's probably all you can afford anyway. This is Allison Hurlock, a writer friend of mine. Allison, this is Harold Ross. He's a high school dropout who has this extraordinary idea about starting a sophisticated humor magazine. Only in New York."

"How do you do? So you're a writer, too?"

Allison blushed slightly. If Dorothy Parker considered you a writer, it was like Lionel Barrymore considering you an actor.

"Mrs. Parker is too kind," she began.

"Nobody's ever accused me of that before," said Mrs. Parker. "Well, Harold, I said she was a writer, not a good judge of character."

"I've been writing magazine articles mostly," Allison continued. "They've appeared in Modern Girls magazine, Home and Hearth, Today's World, and the Salisbury Literary Digest."

He seemed interested. "Salisbury in England?"

"No, Salisbury on Maryland's Eastern Shore."

"I see." Suddenly, Harold Ross seemed less interested. "Well, my magazine will not be edited for the old lady in Dubuque."

"Harold, I once called her a country mouse, but she has a sophisticated soul under it all." She turned to Allison. "Anyway, Harold is scraping backers together for his project. I promised I'd be on his staff if he ever gets it off the ground."

"How fascinating," said Allison. "A sophisticated humor magazine, you say?"

"Exactly,' said Ross, warming to his subject. "I used to edit Judge magazine and it was just like all the other humor rags today; just a bunch of corny, slapstick, pie in the face stuff. I want to do something witty and sophisticated."

"What a marvelous idea," said Allison. "And getting Mrs. Parker is a stroke of genius."

"I hate flattery," said Mrs. Parker, "but I love honesty. Isn't she marvelous?"

"So what will you call your magazine?"

"I haven't decided yet," said Ross, "but it will have a name that conveys its sophistication, like New York Wit, the Knickerbocker, or possibly Manhattan Murmurs."

Allison nodded politely. "Well, I suppose that should appeal to the New Yorker."

Ross's face lit up. "The New Yorker. Now that's a better name. Thank you, Allison. I may be contacting you when I get this thing going."

Ross said goodbye to Mrs. Parker and Allison and headed off down the street. Mrs. Parker watched him go, then turned to Allison.

"He sort of resembles a dishonest version of Abraham Lincoln, doesn't he?"

"Well..."

"Never mind. We kid him about his magazine and his lack of a literary background, but he's a talented man. During the war he was editor of Stars and Stripes Magazine and he was still in his twenties. I'm not sure how The New Yorker will work out, but I wouldn't bet against him."

"Mrs. Parker, thank you for describing me as a writer, but I do have one question I have to ask."

"As long as it's not about writing technique, drinking, or sex, go ahead."

"I saw your poems in the Conning Tower the other day, and I was wondering if the country mouse was,... well,... was about me."

Mrs. Parker looked at her in disbelief.

"Oh, God. Is that what you thought? Why, this is marvelous; the first case of posthumous inspiration. I wrote that about a week before you used my name in vain to gain entrance to a speakeasy that would have let you in anyway. You had nothing to do with it. If I had met you first, the poem would have been a lot different. Thank God I didn't."

Allison smiled. "I suppose it was presumptuous of me, but..."

"Presumptuous? Not a bit. It was perfectly logical." Mrs. Parker looked at her watch. "Damn. I have to be going. I promised to meet Mr. Bencheley at three this afternoon. By the way, I see they caught the woman that shot that Connelly fellow. Was that your husband's doing?"

"No. The police found the murder weapon in her apartment."

"In her apartment? Not exactly a master criminal, is she? Well, I must fly. Good bye, Allison. Keep up your writing. I read one of your articles yesterday; the one about bootlegging. Well, see you."

Allison wanted more details about Mrs. Parker's opinion, but was afraid to press the matter.

John Reisinger

Chapter 21
Tom Fulton gets a job

After he got back from the warehouse, Max walked up Broadway to the automat once again and spoke to the manager. With his star waitress in jail, the man was obviously distracted, hard pressed to keep up with the late lunch crowd, but answered Max's questions as best he could.

A few minutes later, Max took the subway back up to West 70th Street to look at the scene of the crime once more and compare it to what he had learned. He didn't think it was fair (or wise) to drop in on Constance Tibbet again, so he observed from the outside. This was an easy task, since the front windows were large and Constance Tibbet liked to keep the curtains open during the day. He looked in and saw the reception room.

He saw the place Connelly had been found slumped in his chair, the hole in wall where the bullet had entered, the table where the letters and envelopes had been found (with one letter missing), and the place on the floor where something had chipped the tiles.

Max walked back and forth viewing the room from several angles, reconstructing the crime in his mind and comparing it with what he had been told by various people.

But still no answers came.

As he turned away from the window, he heard the tooting of a car horn nearby, along with the deep rumble of a powerful automobile engine. A shiny maroon Chrysler had pulled up next to the curb.

"Hey, Mr. Hurlock. Over here," came a voice from an open window of the car. Cautiously, Max walked over, put his foot on the running board and looked inside.

"Tom Fulton? Well, hello again. Say, I thought you came up dry in Connelly's will. Where did you get the new car?"

"Aw, it's not mine. It's Mr. Whitney's car. He lives just up the block. He hired me as his chauffeur just yesterday and I'm bringing the car back from the garage. Ain't she a beauty? It's a Chrysler Imperial E80 touring car, complete with landau roof, white sidewall tires and wire wheels. Yowsah!"

Max smiled. "You seem to be in a better mood than when I last saw you."

"Sure; why not? I liked Mr. Connelly, but he didn't pay so well. Mr. Whitney pays almost twice as much, and there's no driving around late at night chasing women, either. Besides, with Mr. Connelly, I never knew when I'd have to make a getaway from angry husbands and ex-girlfriends. I needed a little less excitement in my life. To hell with Connelly's money. Everything's Jake now."

"Glad to hear it. And you still get to drive by Connelly's house every day."

Fulton looked past Max at the front window of the Connelly house. "The old place still looks the same, even without Mr. Connelly around to run things. I had my differences with Connie Tibbet, but she does know how to keep a house in shape. Well, I'd better get going, Mr. Hurlock."

"Hold on a second," said Max. "One more quick question. What is the name of Mr. Connelly's boat?"

Fulton smiled. "Say, that was a beautiful boat. I was only on it a few times, but I remember all the Mahogany and brass everywhere. It cost a lot of dough, I can tell you that."

"Yes, but what was its name?"

"Name? Oh, well you know how Mr. Connelly was a card expert and all? Well he named it after one of those card terms; you know, like trump card or shuffle. It was sort of a funny name. Now what was it? It sounded like finish or finished, or something like that"

"How about Finesse?"

"That was it! I remember now. Well, I was never much of a card player, myself."

"Never mind," said Max, "you may have helped me get a winning hand. It was good seeing you again, Bill. Best of luck in your new job."

Max stood thinking for a few minutes after Fulton had driven away, then snapped his fingers and walked away. The bootleggers had mentioned a future delivery at Broadway and 49th. Max had to pass by that area on the way back to the hotel, so he decided to look around to see if he could learn anything else.

Broadway and 49th Street was a good hike from the Connelly house, so Max took the subway and was there in less than a half hour. A line of Brownstones with basement entrances looked like possible speakeasies. He quietly passed around to an alley in the back.

The alley was strangely quiet after the noise of the street and was lined with boxes and garbage cans. A thin stream of sluggish liquid marked the center of the paving. Max continued down the alley casually glancing at the trash cans to see if any empty El Castillo rum bottles were showing. They weren't. Then from somewhere inside one of the buildings came the sounds of a band rehearsing, though from the sweet sound of it, rehearsing was the last thing they needed. Though complex, the music was so perfect, Max thought it must be some sort of a recording. Max listened for a moment, decided the building had to be a speakeasy, then went to one of the trash cans and lifted the lid.

"Come on," he muttered to himself, "a speakeasy must have a lot of bottles in the trash. Where are they?"

All he could find were a few empty bottles with the labels carefully removed, and realized the owners were no fools. They were not going to toss illegal liquor bottles where the Prohibition Police could find them.

Max was so intent on his search he didn't notice that the music had stopped, and didn't hear the back door of the speakeasy opening.

"Down on your luck, mister?"

Max spun around and saw several black men emerging from the club and lighting cigarettes. They regarded him curiously.

"I can give you a fin if it'll help," said the tall one, taking a five dollar bill from his pocket.

"Uh, no...thank you anyway. I'm just looking for something."

"In the trash? All you gonna find in there are rats."

"Do you guys work here?"

"Every night," the tall one said. "we're here at the Hollywood Club. We were just rehearsing and thought we'd get us some fresh air."

One of the others chuckled at the fresh air remark.

"We're the Washingtonians. My name's Ellington, but everyone calls me Duke."

"Max Hurlock. I've heard of you. They say your band plays the hottest Jazz around."

"Well, we try. After all; it don't mean a thing if it ain't got that swing. But we don't call it Jazz. To us it's just American music; nothin' like it anywhere else in the world. But you still haven't told us what you were looking for."

"I'll level with you guys. I'm not with the police or with the Prohibition cops, and I'm not out to cause any problems for the club, but I'm trying to find out what brand liquor they use."

Ellington shrugged. "Same as anywhere else, I guess. Lots of stuff from Canada. Anyway, they take the labels off as soon as they get it."

"Any rum?"

"Sure, Bacardi and some El Castillo when they want the harder stuff."

"El Castillo? Any idea where it comes from?"

Ellington gave Max a knowing smile. "That's a question we never ask. It might make people nervous. After all, we're just the entertainment."

The Washingtonians laughed, ground out their cigarettes and filed back inside. The music resumed and Max stood for a while just listening to it in wonder.

When Max left a few minutes later, he had the strange feeling that one day he'd be proudly telling his grandchildren about the time he met Duke Ellington.

Back at the hotel, Allison had returned to the room and started packing for the return to St Michaels when Max opened the door.

"Max! I ran into Dorothy Parker again today. It turns out the country mouse poem wasn't about me after all; and guess what? She's read one of my articles and she referred to me as a writer."

"Well, aren't you?"

"That's not the point."

"Well, what is the point?"

"Max, you're a detective.."

"Investigator."

"All right; investigator. What if you were called an investigator by Sherlock Holmes himself?"

"He's a fictional character."

"All right then, Arthur Conan Doyle."

"He's a writer."

"Then how about..."

Max laughed and hugged her. "Never mind. I know exactly what you mean. That's a great compliment from someone who should know. Congratulations."

"The problem is, she never actually said what she thought of the article. Maybe she hated it Oh well. How did you do today?"

Max looked out the window for a moment, then turned back to Allison.

"I went to that warehouse in Brooklyn today and met some bootlegging gentlemen."

"You what?" Allison's mouth dropped open.

"It was fine. Don't worry. Anyway, the place is definitely being used as a warehouse for illegal liquor. A nearby garage owner verified that the place was a transfer point for booze, and he said something else interesting; he saw Connelly's boat there a few months ago. I'm not sure what it all means; maybe it's just a coincidence, but then I went to the Puncheon Club and found they are using the same brand of rum I saw in the warehouse."

"Are you sure?"

"Of course. I have it from Duke Ellington himself."

"He's that Jazz guy that's tearing it up around here isn't he? It looks like we're both hobnobbing with celebrities."

"Just another strange coincidence," Max shrugged.

"Well, it so happens I found another one of those strange coincidence at the records office," Allison interjected. "I was curious about that warehouse too, so

I looked up the owner in the property records while I was there."

"And?"

"Wait a minute." She fumbled in her purse and produced a slip of paper. "See for yourself."

"Martin Forsythe owns that warehouse? Well he did have some sort of business relationship with Connelly, but I didn't think it was bootlegging."

"So what does it mean?" Allison asked.

"I'm not sure. This is interesting, of course, but it doesn't constitute that connection I've been looking for. All it does is indicate that Connelly and Forsythe were both involved in bootlegging, that is, assuming Forsythe even knew about what was going on in his warehouse. He has a lot of properties and this one might be leased out to someone else who was using it for rumrunning without Forsythe knowing a thing about it for all we know. Besides, what does it have to do with Gwen Perkins?"

"That's the real question. I can't image her dabbling in bootlegging while working at the automat," Allison sighed. "I just don't think she did it."

Max started pacing the room with his hands in his pockets. "I agree. Jazzmen and bootleggers are all very interesting, of course, but it doesn't change the fact that Gwen Perkins has been locked up for killing Connelly. But if Gwen Perkins did it, why keep the murder weapon? Why plant the false teeth in the glass? Why deliver the phony note?"

"It does seem a bit above the odds," said Allison.

"Anyway, I went back to the automat and checked with Gwen's supervisor. He checked the time book. It seems Gwen Perkins was working a double shift when that note was slipped under our door."

"Wowser. Could she have had an accomplice?"

"Not a chance. Gwen is a loner. Besides, who could she use?"

"Maybe another member of the jilted girlfriends club?"

"Well, I suppose it's possible," Max admitted. "But there are more loose ends and strange coincidences in this case. If we could find just one more piece of..."

Max suddenly stopped pacing, frowned, and pulled a piece of paper out of his pocket; the note Detective Darwin had given him authorizing him to enter Gwen Perkins's apartment.

"Allison, I have an idea of the connection I've been missing, but I need a link to tie everything together. How would you like to accompany me to Gwen's place to look for that link? I notice you're wearing that green and black dress you wear when we're flying. Maybe it'll bring us luck."

"Sure thing, but what exactly are we looking for?"

"I don't know yet."

"Then how will we know when we find it?"

"I don't know that either. Let's go."

Allison barely had time to grab her cloche hat and her purse as they went out the door.

"Well, nobody ever said investigation was an exact science."

Chapter 22
Images

"So let's see," said Allison, determined to make sense of everything. "The police have arrested a woman with a strong motive, who had the murder weapon in her apartment, who once physically attacked the victim, and who showed no regret that he was dead. Have I missed anything?"

"No, that pretty much covers it."

"So tell me again how you know Gwen Perkins is innocent?"

"I don't know that Gwen Perkins is innocent, but I think she is. One thing is for sure: there are too many loose ends and too many unanswered questions to send anyone to the electric chair just yet. There's something important that's been missed; something that will tie everything together logically, and we've got to find it."

"And you currently have no idea just what that something might be?"

"I have an idea, but I don't know how to prove it. No."

"And no particular reason to think this something, if it exists at all, should be in Gwen Perkins's apartment?"

"No, but if it isn't there, I don't know where else it could be."

"Well, that certainly clarifies things. I like this plan. I'm glad I asked. We should have these talks more often."

The cop standing outside of Gwen Perkins's place in Soho looked bored. He paced listlessly back and forth occasionally twirling his nightstick, but without any real enthusiasm. He watched several kids up the block playing stickball, then went back to his routine.

"Good afternoon, officer," said Max. Allison said nothing. She just smiled widely.

"Good day to ya," said the cop in a brogue so thick you could have made porridge out of it. "Sure an' it's a foine day."

"Fine indeed," Max agreed. "I have a note here from Detective Darwin downtown. I'm Max Hurlock and he asked me to take a look inside."

"Faith; did 'e now?" said the cop. Frowning at the piece of paper Max showed him. The cop was teetering on the edge, so Max decided to give him a nudge.

"He said the place was being guarded to keep reporters and idlers out. We're not in that category, so he said it would be all right."

The cop rubbed his chin in thought. "Well..."

Max had nudged. Now Allison gave a shove.

"Sure an' it would be a foine thing ya be doing officer. We'll be appreciatin' it, we will."

He looked at her, "Are ye from Ireland, Miss?"

"Me sainted mother was from the auld sod; all the way from County Clare. She was a Murphy."

"Oi'm from County Cork, mesself. Sean O'Grady at your service." The cop was grinning. "Well, I don't see as how a wee look would do no harm. You go on in."

As they mounted the steps, Max whispered to her.

"Where did you pick up that accent?"

"I played a Leprechaun in Goucher's production of Finnegan and the Pot of Gold."

Max shook his head. "You are a woman of many talents."

"Let's just hope finding this elusive link is one of them," she replied.

Gwen Perkins lived in a gloomy one room apartment on the first floor. The door was unlocked so Max and Allison went in. Through the one front window they could see Officer O'Grady on the sidewalk outside, now walking with a spring in his step.

A bed took up a large portion of the floor space. The kitchen was a hot plate on a table next to an ancient ice box. A wardrobe contained Gwen Perkins's clothes and another table held an assortment of books, papers, dishes, and other evidence of life in a crowded place. A dusty chest of drawers in the opposite corner completed the picture

"Well," said Max, "Let's get started. Why don't you look through the clothes and personal things. I'll check the rest."

Allison nodded. "From what I see so far, this shouldn't take long."

While Allison went through the meager collection of clothes, Max looked through the papers on the table. There was the usual assortment of bills, advertisements, and notices, but nothing really unusual. He moved on to the dresser top, where he found a mirror a hairbrush, and some cosmetics. He was particularly interested in a framed photograph on one corner. It showed a young man, presumably Gwen's current boyfriend. The picture was signed 'Robert'. Allison looked over his shoulder.

"Is that one of the suspects?"

"No. Apparently he's just an innocent bystander who is currently seeing our Miss Perkins."

Allison continued to study the portrait. "Of course he would have access to her gun and her earrings. Maybe he heard about Connelly and wanted to knock him off to impress Gwen."

"Maybe," said Max. "Did you find anything else ?"

"I'm not sure. Her clothes, for the most part, are old and well worn, but she has a few newer items from Sachs and Macy's that look to be pretty expensive. Same story with the jewelry; mostly cheap baubles, but a couple of what look like new diamonds in the mix. What do you think it means, Max?"

"It means she's recently come into some source of money she didn't have before."

"Hmmm. Oh, I also saw her earring collection."

"The police already found a match to the one you found that fell off on the stairs."

"I know," she said, "but it didn't fall off."

"What do you mean?"

Allison pushed her hair back and took off an earring. "Let me show you something interesting about earrings that men might not know."

She held the earring up to the light.

"Now, notice that this type of earring has a threaded stem that you turn to allow the earring to clamp onto the ear lobe".

"Sort of like a C clamp," said Max.

"Exactly. As you can see, I unscrewed it enough to allow for easy removal and to make it easy to reattach when I want to. Take a look. There is now a gap of about a quarter-inch under the stem. The earring found on the stairs had a similar gap. But an earring that accidentally falls off a woman's earlobe will have a much smaller gap since it was merely not quite tight enough to hold, not intentionally loosened. The earring on the stairs, however, had a wide gap, so it was obviously taken from Miss Perkins's apartment and dropped to implicate her. It had a wide gap because that's the way the killer found it in her jewelry box since she had loosened it before removing it the same way I just did."

Max whistled. "Then that means the earring you found on the stairs..."

"...was not left by Gwen Perkins," said Allison.

"That's great," said Max, "but it's still not the link we need."

"I'll see what's in the bathroom."

"While you're in there, see if there's anything indicating our Robert was an overnight guest; things like a Gillette, or a shaving brush."

"There weren't any men's clothes in the wardrobe, but I'll check."

Max found a small bed table and idly pulled out the drawer. In the bottom of the drawer a spare clip and dozen loose .45 rounds reflected the meager light.

"I found where she kept the gun. Looks like she was ready for uninvited visitors."

"And I found evidence of some invited ones," came Allison's voice from the bathroom. "So far I have a straight razor, two Gillette safety razors, a cake of shaving soap and two toothbrushes."

Max went to the kitchen area. The icebox was empty and the cupboard contained several cans and a box of spaghetti.

The sink held a dirty glass and a dirty dish.

Allison reappeared, brushing a strand of hair away from her face. "You know, Max, I still don't know what I'm looking for, but I am sure that what I've found so far isn't it."

"I know what you mean. Hey, look at this." He picked up a slightly bent umbrella standing in the corner by the door.

"Do you suppose it's the umbrella she slugged Connelly with?" said Allison, waving it in the air.

"Probably."

"So, is she keeping it as a souvenir?"

"No; more likely she just can't afford a new one. Maybe that's the next thing she's going to buy with her new money."

Max pulled out a drawer of the bureau. Under a piece of cardboard was a bank passbook. Max picked it up and began flipping the pages.

"Ah, here's something that might be enlightening. Let's see. Hmmm. I was right. Miss Perkins has been barely in the black for most of the time, but she's been depositing $100 every week for the last eight months. Everything is starting to fit together. I wonder where that money came from?"

"Maybe she was blackmailing Connelly and he cut her off suddenly?"

"No. I don't think so,"' said Max. "The last deposit was two weeks after he was killed. Besides, what could she have over him? She wasn't blackmailing Connelly, but she was blackmailing someone. I have a pretty good idea of who it was and how it fits in with Connelly's murder, but I need something that ties them together. Otherwise, that person will just deny everything and it will be their word against that of an accused murderer."

"Well, there are no letters or other correspondence here. We've been over every inch of this place and the only really personal thing we've found, other than her unmentionables and the cryptic bankbook, is the picture," said Allison, "and that shows some palooka that probably has nothing to do with anything. Say, where is that picture anyway? I want to look at it again."

"Over on the bureau. I suppose we can look all over again, but as small as this place is it seems.."

"So this is Robert," said Allison, holding the framed photo. : "He certainly looks...say, Max, did you notice how heavy this picture is?"

"Yes. I think it's the frame."

Allison was fiddling with the picture. "No. Here it is. Look. There must be a dozen other pictures here behind the current one."

"Pictures of what?"

"What do you think? More men." Allison was going through a pack of photos like a deck of cards. "Jeepers. Miss Perkins sees more men than an army recruiter." "but so far I haven't found any pictures that are inscribed 'Thanks for killing Ellsworth'."

Max picked up the pictures and started looking through them. "You won't need to. Unless I miss my guess, we'll find what we need right here. Voila!"

"I see what you mean. It's like..Wait a minute."

"You found something?"

Max had stopped shuffling and was staring at a picture. Allison looked.

"There's no inscription."

Max shook his head. "I don't need one. You just found the link we were looking for."

"So what do we do now?"

"We get back to the hotel so I can go through my notes."

"And then?"

"Then we make a couple of calls. If you can say 'thank you' in Gaelic, please give our regards to Officer O'Grady outside."

"What the hell? Max, you can't be serious." Detective Darwin was outraged.

"I'm perfectly serious, Harold." Max's voice was cool and reasonable.

"Damn it, Max. Haven't you been paying attention? We already have the killer. We have motive, means, and opportunity, not to mention the murder weapon, What are you trying to do?"

"Tell you what," said Max. "Get me this information and we'll talk again before I spill everything to the newspapers."

"Before you sp..."

"If you agree, I'll let you take the credit. I get paid either way."

There was a long pause.

"Come on over in an hour and we'll take a look together," said Darwin.

"Thanks, Harold. Oh, by the way; I need to talk to Gwen Perkins one more time, too."

"Sure; why not?" Darwin had shifted into sarcasm mode. "Maybe you'd like me to arrange a little chat with the mayor while you're at it?"

"Harold, if I'm right about this, pretty soon *you'll* be chatting with the mayor."

He hung up the phone.

"Well, did you convince him?" Allison asked.

"Everything's Jake," said Max.

"And you're going to let him take all the credit?"

"Of course. I let Pfeiffer grab the glory in the Taylor-Bradwell case and everyone knew the real story anyway. Word gets around, especially to would be clients. But by doing it this way, I get the eager cooperation of the police. I can't get far without it. I help my reputation and make it easier to do my investigations in the future."

"Max, that's downright Machiavellian."

"Now you watch your language."

"So now what?"

"I meet Darwin at the station in about an hour. If the information he digs up matches with what Gwen Perkins tells me, we put on a little show for certain people."

"Bellisimo!"

Two hours later, Max finished his meeting with Detective Darwin and made his way back to the hotel. The sun was setting, putting the canyons of midtown Manhattan into deep shadows, lightened only by crimson reflections from walls of windows. In the fading light, Allison was waiting at the front door of the hotel. Max thought he had never seen her looking more beautiful.

"How did it go?"

"Darwin and the New York Police department are convinced and have promised their full cooperation."

"My hero! What now?"

"I was thinking of a quick dinner, then we retire to the comfort of our room."

"Now you're cooking with gas."

"Not yet," Max assured her, "but I plan to be very soon."

Later, Max lay next to Allison with his arm around her. The window was open to the night sounds of the city and a barely perceptible breeze. They heard an ambulance siren as it moved up the street, past the hotel, then receded in the distance. On the bureau, the electric fan droned away.

"I hope this works out for you tomorrow, Max. I had some adventures in the literary world and got an article written while we were here, but I'd hate for you to go home empty handed."

"Either way, we get to go home in a day or so. It'll be a nice change of pace, although I'm not sure I'll be able to sleep without the sound of horns and sirens."

"Well, there's always the ducks and bullfrogs. They make a pretty good racket."

"You know, Allison, we make a pretty good team."

"We sure did a few minutes ago."

"I mean about tackling problems together."

"Oh. Well, isn't that what marriage is supposed to be all about?"

"I suppose it is   ."

"Good night, Allison."

"Good night, Max."

Chapter 23
A gathering of interested parties

"Do you think they'll all come?" Max asked.

"They'll be here," Darwin assured him.

"Including the killer?"

"Especially including the killer. I set everything up personally."

Max looked out the window and nodded. He noticed his palms were sweaty.

The group that finally gathered in the reception room of the late Ellsworth Connelly's house on West 70th Street was not a happy one. Only a few were on good terms with each other, so for the most part, everyone sat grimly with arms folded. As each person took one of the chairs set up around the room, he moved it a little farther from the next one. Although it was early evening; the sun was still bright and the room was uncomfortably hot. Soon, handkerchiefs appeared as people mopped their brows impatiently.

As Detective Darwin and Max entered the room, the seated group bombarded them with questions and complaints. Darwin was cool and collected. He just held up his hand.

"Ladies and gentlemen. A little patience, please. All will be made clear in due course. I hope everyone is comfortable."

"We're not," said Helen Arness. "I don't care for either the heat or the company."

"Thank you all for coming. I hope we can clear up this case and be on our way quickly. I know you are all busy people. Now as I--"

Helen Arness interrupted again. "What do you mean 'clear up this case'? You've already made an arrest. What is there to clear up except the date of execution?"

"Well, we usually prefer to have a trial first, Miss Arness, but you are correct that we have made an arrest."

"Then what are we doing here?" Martin Forsythe added his disapproval. "I'm sure that woman you arrested can answer your questions a lot better than we can."

"Let's hear what he has to say," said Von Grunewald. "What's the harm?"

"Yes; let's hear him out," added Mandy Jewell. "I think we owe Ellsworth that much."

"I'm sure you have repaid Ellsworth many times over," Helen Arness remarked.

As the room erupted into arguments, Darwin turned to Max. "With this bunch, I guess we're lucky there was only one murder."

"It's still early," said Max.

"As I said," Darwin continued, raising his voice over the grumbling, "we have a few questions remaining. It's true we've made an arrest and recovered the murder weapon, but this has been a complicated case. We want to be sure we have our ducks in a row before we put anyone on trial. Everyone in this room was closely acquainted with Mr. Connelly and that is why you are here."

Mandy Jewell, clearly in agreement, nodded once. Helen Arness and Martin Forsythe frowned, but were silent. The others sat impassively.

"Now as good as the NYPD is, we can be stretched pretty thin at times, so in a case like this we're happy to accept help. As you all know, Mr. Max Hurlock has been helping us. Mr. Hurlock is a well-respected investigator and he's been cooperating with us since he arrived."

"In the course of that cooperation," Darwin continued, "Mr. Hurlock has turned up some things that have helped our investigation, but have not yet been fully explained. In the interests of clarity I'm going to ask Mr. Hurlock to go through what he's found with you and see if we can clear everything up."

"I still don't see what there is to clear up," Helen Arness muttered.

Max was on his feet now, addressing the people in the room.

"As Detective Darwin said, a suspect has been arrested. The problem is that we have not yet found a set of facts that is fully consistent with Gwen Perkins being the killer."

At that, the room erupted in amazed protests and outrage.

"This is bushwa," said Helen Arness. "She had a motive and the murder weapon. For God's sake, what more do you need?"

"Yes," Martin Forsythe echoed. "The case is clear cut. What more do you need?"

Von Grunewald looked both surprised and uncomfortable. "Max, what are you saying?"

"What more is needed?" said Max. "The answer is simple; consistency. Would a woman who is so impulsive she once attacked him with an umbrella on a public street be able to plan a cold-blooded murder such as this one? And why would she wait so long after her first attempt?"

"Why must it have been planned?" Von Grunewald asked. "Perhaps she became enraged and simply went to his house and killed him?"

"No," said Max. "Whoever killed Connelly planned it carefully and took pains to misdirect the police. Consider the false teeth."

"Did you say false teeth?" Bill Fulton asked.

"Ellsworth Connelly's false teeth were found in a glass of water on his bed table. This would indicate the killer was either someone who came unexpectedly, when Connelly was ready to retire, or someone for whom Connelly did not find it necessary to look his best."

"That would seem to eliminate a woman, wouldn't it?" Bill Fulton ventured.

Max nodded. "Most women, yes. Connelly always wanted to look his best to charm the ladies. But what about a woman he didn't want to charm? What about a woman he wanted to be done with? A woman he wanted to go away and leave him alone? If he wanted to discourage an ex-girlfriend from pestering him, maybe he would leave out his false teeth and present a less appealing picture."

Helen Arness interrupted again. "But wouldn't that support the idea Gwen Perkins is the killer?."

Even Constance Tibbet nodded in agreement. "I've seen Mr. Connelly without his teeth. He is not at his best in such a condition."

Max smiled. "You're all right. Ellsworth Connelly's false teeth in a glass is perfectly consistent with Gwen Perkins being the killer; in fact it implicates her. The only problem is that Connelly didn't put them there."

"What?" said Tom Fulton.

"Someone who didn't know Connelly's daily routine, almost certainly put them there to throw us off and confuse the investigation. There was a wet ring on the wood table top from condensation, but no other water stains. It is obvious the glass was not usually placed there. Miss Tibbet later confirmed that Mr. Connelly actually kept that glass on his marble top dresser."

Constance Tibbet nodded curtly. "Yes. That's where he always put it."

"Oh, for heaven's sakes." Helen Arness was not convinced. "Gwen Perkins put the teeth in the glass on the wrong table. Apparently she wasn't so impulsive after all. What is the problem?"

"The problem," said Max, "is explaining why a killer would arrange a fake clue pointing to herself."

The room was silent.

"Now, we come to another problem; the police found the shell casing at the murder scene. There is no doubt that casing came from the murder weapon. The problem is, what was it doing there?"

Constance Tibbet frowned in confusion. "Where else would it be?"

"If the killer was so cool and calculating he took the trouble to set up the false teeth, why didn't he take the much more obvious and simple precaution of simply picking up the spent casing from the floor and taking it with him?"

"Maybe in the heat of the moment she just forgot," said Martin Forsythe. He turned to Detective Darwin. "Really, Darwin; this is all very interesting, but is it actually leading anywhere? I for one have more important things to do."

Darwin was unfazed. "If the police don't fuss about these things, Mr. Forsythe, you can be sure Gwen Perkins's attorney will, and I know we'd all want to see justice done. Now Max, you were saying?"

Max went on. He was now pacing back and forth in front of the room. The heads followed him, almost like watching an extremely slow tennis match.

From where she was sitting, Allison noticed Von Grunewald mopping the back of his neck with his handkerchief, but whether because of the heat or the revelations she couldn't tell.

"Now we move to a week or so later, when Allison received this note that said the killing was over a horse. A little investigation indicated this was an attempt to send me off in the wrong direction. But the note did indicate the killer was actively following the investigation and trying to misdirect it. This seems out of character for Miss Perkins, who was far too tied down at the automat to have time for such things. In fact, we have determined that Miss Perkins was working at the automat when the note appeared, so obviously someone else sent it. I think when the police compare the typeface to a certain typewriter elsewhere, they will find a match."

"Wait a minute," said Von Grunewald. "Didn't you tell me that whoever left the note lost an earring at the scene?"

"That is true."

"And didn't you say that the police found the matching earring in Miss Perkins's apartment?"

"That's an interesting point," said Max. "Miss Jewell, are you wearing screw-on earrings?"

"Well, yes I am as a matter of fact."

"Would you take one of them off, please?"

She complied and handed the earring to him. He held it up for the others to see, then repeated what Allison had told him about the size of the gap indicating the earring had been planted. He was pleased at the stunned silence that resulted.

Chapter 23
The culprit

Detective Darwin now took up the narrative again.

"We have a careful, calculating killer who is most certainly not Gwen Perkins, but who deliberately leaves clues such as the false teeth, the cartridge casing and the earring that point to her. Now the question becomes more focused. Before it was who had a motive to kill Connelly? The answer is; many people. Now the question becomes who had a motive to kill Connelly and also direct the blame at Gwen Perkins? Go on, Max."

Von Grunewald was increasingly restless. "Aren't you forgetting something, Max? The murder weapon was her gun and it was found in her apartment. What you are saying is theory, but the gun is fact."

"I'm not forgetting the gun at all," Max replied calmly, "but the gun was not the only thing found in her apartment. Although she lives very frugally and has a very small income, Gwen Perkins has several more expensive items in her place, as if she were receiving money from somewhere else. We also found this."

Max produced the bankbook. Mandy Jewell squinted at it as if trying to read it.

"This shows a woman of very limited means- up until several months ago, that is. Then suddenly she started making $100 deposits every month. The most likely explanation is blackmail, but what could Gwen Perkins, a single woman who works in the automat have to blackmail anyone with?"

"Could she have found out some guilty secret from Mr. Connelly?" Bill Fulton suggested.

"I doubt that he ever revealed anything of that nature to his lady friends," Max replied. "Besides, she apparently made two deposits after Connelly was murdered. But you are on the right track. Gwen Perkins was a single woman looking for the right man and never finding him. She met many men, and had been greatly disappointed in love, but Ellsworth Connelly was the worst."

"Finally something I can agree with," said Helen Arness.

Max smiled. "I mean the worst disappointment. She was scorned and hurt, and she reacted. She attacked Connelly with an umbrella, an impulsive but ineffective act totally in keeping with her character. Because of her rejection by Connelly, she vowed she would never let a man mistreat her again. Her exact words were that anyone who jilted her in the future would pay dearly. At the time I didn't realize she meant it literally."

"What are you talking about?" Constance Tibbet asked.

"The fact is that Gwen Perkins was perfectly serious about her vow to make any future cads pay, but she wasn't talking about violence. A few months after her breakup with Connelly, she met another man. Like Connelly, this man seemed too good to be true, and he was. Several months later, when he tried to end their relationship, Gwen threatened to make the affair known to the man's wife and even his business associates. In a way, I suppose you could say the man was the victim of bad timing. If it had met her before her relationship with Connelly, he could have withdrawn gracefully and completely, but now Gwen Perkins was not going to let him off easily. She threatened to ruin him, or at least make his life a lot less pleasant and profitable. He begged her not to, and in the end, offered to 'supplement her income'."

Von Grunewald continued to wipe his neck.

"But this man was a cold and calculating sort. He bought some peace by paying off Gwen, but he knew he was on dangerous ground. She could change her mind at any time and either tell all or insist on more money. He had to put a stop to her, but how? Then he got an idea; a diabolical plan that would take care of two problems at the same time. He would kill Ellsworth Connelly and frame Gwen Perkins for the crime. From his affair with her, he knew about her resentment against Connelly, he knew her work schedule, he knew she kept a gun for protection, and he had a key to her apartment. It was a simple matter to slip in and remove the gun, kill Connelly with it, then replace it and wait for the police to find it. He probably wore light gloves so his fingerprints wouldn't show, but hers would. He may have removed the earring at that time as well. All he had to do was plant a few clues and Gwen Perkins was as good as convicted."

"How did he do it?" said Mandy Jewell.

"He sent Connelly a note, probably offering to reopen a business deal and arranged a nighttime meeting. At the scene the police found six letters Connelly had been reading, but there were seven envelopes. This would indicate that one of the letters had been removed. Since it was Miss Tibbet's day off, she didn't do it, so it was likely the work of the killer. Why? This is speculation, of course, but we believe the letter was sent by the killer to make sure Connelly admitted him. I don't know what was said, maybe 'let's let bygones be bygones', or maybe 'I'm sorry for the way I've acted and I would like to meet you and explain'.

Maybe it was even the offer of a business deal or a new racehorse. Whatever it was, it did the trick. Ellsworth Connelly willingly opened the door to his killer. That missing letter is more evidence of a calculating murderer."

So Connelly let him in and the man pulled a gun. He sat Connelly down on a chair and shot him, taking care to leave the shell casing but remove the letter he had sent. He put the false teeth in a glass by Connelly's bed to make it look like an unexpected and undesirable guest such as Gwen Perkins had suddenly arrived. The next day, he replaced the gun in her apartment while she was at work. That took care of his problem with her and also his problem with Connelly."

"Wait a minute," said Mandy Jewell. "What problem did he have with Connelly?"

"Oh, didn't I tell you? This man had a brief business arrangement with Connelly. He provided a warehouse and a customer when Connelly brought back contraband rum from the Caribbean on his yacht. We have located the warehouse and traced its owner. In addition, we have a witness who will testify that Connelly's yacht unloaded there."

"Not only that," said Darwin, rising from his chair, "but some of my men raided the warehouse last night. We arrested two men who are singing like canaries, and we found contraband liquor by the case along with extensive invoices. We're still putting it all together, but I can tell you that we will be making another arrest very soon."

"Thank you, detective," said Max. "The arrangement with the warehouse ended when Connelly turned his amorous attentions on the man's wife. In a fit of anger, the man terminated the arrangement just as Connelly was coming back with a load of liquor. Connelly was turned away from the warehouse and probably had to dump the contraband. I believe he intended to ask my help in tracing the original customer so he could reopen the trade, but never got beyond sending me a clue in the mail before he was killed. Meanwhile, the husband was still angry about Connelly's attentions to his wife, not enough to do anything drastic, but it ate at him. So later, when he was blackmailed by Gwen Perkins he suddenly saw the chance to get rid of her and the man who had been pursuing his wife in one stroke."

"Wait," Von Grunewald protested. "How do you know all this? Surely you can't rely on the word of an accused murderess."

"In fact, I do rely on her word. She admitted the affair with the man I have in mind, and the fact that she was blackmailing him, but there's much more. This other man is the link that was missing; the factor that made everything else make sense. There were hints; the man had business near the automat; several people suspected he carried on the occasional discrete affair, and his wife suspected he was involved with a waitress. The confirming evidence came when we searched Gwen's apartment. Under a picture of her current boyfriend she kept pictures of her former ones. We went through them and found this."

Max held up the picture from Gwen Perkins's apartment. The effect was electric. Everyone gasped, but no one spoke except for Dianne Forsythe.

"Martin. Is this true?"

Martin Forsythe was on his feet in an instant.

"Damn it, Hurlock. This is outrageous. You're trying to frame me. This is a set up. You planted that picture and that Perkins woman is lying through her teeth to avoid hanging. By God I won't take this lying down. I'll sue. I'll-"

"You'll sit down and shut up," growled Detective Darwin. He called to the back room. "Anderson; you can bring her in now."

Anderson appeared in the rear doorway followed closely by Gwen Perkins.

"Now I'm sure Miss Perkins here can verify everything Mr. Hurlock is saying about the blackmail," said Darwin smoothly, "and about Mr. Forsythe's business with Connelly."

"It's all true," Gwen Perkins said quietly. "Martin was worried about his wife finding out. I didn't even know he had a wife until he dumped me. He was also worried about some of his clients. He handles real estate investments for several big religious groups and any scandal would make them drop him like a hot potato."

"Nonsense," Martin Forsythe protested. "All you have is the word of an accused killer."

"Well, she'll have company in the accused killer department soon," said Max, "but that's not all we have. When I first talked to you, Mr. Forsythe, you mentioned Connelly's false teeth. That was something he never told anyone, so how did you know? My guess is that you found out when you shot him and his teeth fell out. But there's still more. Why don't you tell them what else you found, detective?"

"Gladly," said Darwin, happy to be the center of the show once more. "We've been doing some checking of your clients and found that you do have several large religious organizations on the list, just as Gwen said. We have verified that you own the warehouse we raided. We also have your bank records here. They show a series of $100 withdrawals corresponding exactly to Gwen Perkins's bankbook record of $100 deposits."

Martin Forsythe mumbled something about coincidences, but not convincingly.

"And," Darwin concluded with a flourish, "we have a search warrant for your apartment and your office. I'm sure a comparison of the typing from one of those typewriters and the typing on the note you dropped at the hotel will pretty much seal the case."

Martin Forsythe was considerably less confident now, but still protested feebly.

"I..I was at home the night of the murder. I didn't go out. My wife will tell you. She will vouch for me."

Dianne Forsythe looked at him with fire in her eyes. "I will not! I've been making excuses and explaining away your exploits for years. Well, no more. I will not lie for you.You left at 10 and didn't return until three in the morning. You said you had car trouble."

Now it was Martin Forsythe who was wiping his neck with a handkerchief.

John Reisinger

Chapter 23
Summing up

"*Gott in Himmel*, Max. How do you eat these things? And why is there dirt all over them?" Gunther Von Grunewald was having his first encounter with steamed crabs at Benny's Seafood restaurant in Brooklyn, the only place Max could find that served them near New York.

"That's not dirt, it's bay seasoning. Come on, Gunther; you're a submarine man. You must be familiar with sea creatures."

"But isn't the Blue Crab a scavenger?"

"Not anymore," said Max. "These are dinner."

Von Grunewald picked up a wooden mallet from the table.

"I suppose this is in case any of them aren't dead?"

"No," said Allison, giggling. "You do this."

She brought the mallet down sharply on a claw and was rewarded with a satisfying crack.

"Now look at the nice white meat in there. Have a taste."

Von Grunewald looked dubious, but took a bite.

"Oh my. That is very tasty. Such a sweet delicate flavor."

He picked up his mallet just as Max was breaking off the backfin of his crab.

"Max, I wish to thank you for clearing me of Connelly's murder. I have my life back."

"I just found the truth," said Max, "and you turned out to be on the right side of it. But you made it a lot harder than it had to be. Why didn't you level with me from the beginning? I had to dig up things like your argument with Connelly, things that looked worse for you because you hid them."

Von Grunewald took a sliver of claw meat and ate it gratefully.

"I am sorry for that, but I wasn't hiding, exactly. I just wanted you to concentrate your efforts on the others, not on me."

"What?"

Von Grunewald looked embarrassed and apologetic. "I am sorry. I was afraid that if I told you the full extent of my dealings with Connelly you might think me guilty too. I should have trusted you."

"Yes, you should have. When you hire an expert to do a job, it's not usually a good idea to hamstring him. And you're still doing it. Why don't you ever mention your wife?"

Von Grunewald looked uneasy. "My wife died three years ago."

"But the wedding ring; I saw the sun tan marks," said Max.

"I do wear the ring sometimes in her memory."

Max shook his head. "I guess I can forgive you for not telling me that. I guess you submarine fellows are just used to hiding and keeping your heads down.'

"And you are used to forcing them up again. You were wonderful the way you found out Martin Forsythe was the killer. What will happen to him?"

"I talked to Detective Darwin this morning," said Max. Forsythe has confessed and Gwen Perkins has been released."

Allison cracked open a crab shell. "But wasn't she guilty of blackmail?"

"The DA doesn't see it that way. Since Forsythe offered money first, the blackmail was only implied; almost like entrapment."

"So what about the missing letter to Connelly?" said Von Grunewald.

"It's been destroyed, of course, but Forsythe says it was a promise of a secret business deal. That way, a meeting at one in the morning wouldn't seem so suspicious. When Connelly answered the door, he was facing a .45, and then...."

Max brought his mallet down hard on a crab claw for emphasis.

"And what about the tiger figurine Connelly sent you?" Grunewald asked. "How did that fit in?"

Max smiled. "Oh, yes. The blind tiger statue. At the time, Connelly was only worried about a future market for the rum he was bringing back from the Caribbean, since Forsythe had cut him out. I believe he wanted me to do some investigation to find out where Forsythe had been selling the product so he could deal with them directly. The blind tiger represented speakeasies and the tag represented the rum. He wanted to see if I could make the connection and infer that his problem involved speakeasies and rum. It was part test and part game."

"But why would he hire an out-of-towner like you when there are so many detectives right here in New York?" Grunewald asked.

"That's no mystery: Connelly was a socially prominent man. A local detective would be more likely to talk to some local acquaintance or relative and let it slip that the respectable Mr. Connelly was a rumrunner. Aside from the danger of prosecution, it would ruin his reputation and drive away his upper crust clientele."

"Sort of ironic, I suppose," said Allison thoughtfully, "A blind tiger from a man who was blind to the danger he was in."

After their dinner with the grateful Von Grunewald, Max and Allison strolled back to their hotel down Sixth Avenue by way of Times Square. The lights were just coming on, splashes of flashing color competing for attention. Allison squeezed Max's arm.

"It really is a magical place, isn't it?" she said, looking around her.

Max smiled. "I suppose it is, even with all its dirt, noise, crime and corruption. There's so much life and activity, even the bootleggers can't keep the place down completely."

"Max, I don't know if I'll ever be a great writer, or even a well-known one, but meeting Dorothy Parker and the rest, I'm inspired. Oh, I don't want to be like them, sparring over lunch and throwing barbs at people, but I do hope to write almost as well someday. I'm not going to give up."

Max stopped and pulled her close. They stood like an island in a stream as pedestrians flowed around them.

"I never thought you'd give up, and I wouldn't want you to. You have a gift and gifts shouldn't be squandered."

She kissed him.

"You have a way with words yourself. Somehow, you always seem to find the right ones for the occasion."

A few days later, Max and Allison were back in St Michaels and flying Gypsy high over the Chesapeake once again.

"She's running great," Max shouted into the speaking tube. "Maybe Gypsy just needed a few days' rest."

"I know how she feels," Allison agreed. "Still, it's good to get above the world again."

Soaring low over green fields, they finally returned and Max brought Gypsy in for a somewhat bumpy landing. A few minutes later they were back at the house relaxing in wicker chairs on the front porch.

"Well, Max, my article on speakeasies is finished."

"That's great. Any ideas for the next one?"

"Right now I'm taking a cue from Gypsy and resting between flights."

"Me too, but ever since the Connelly case, I've been getting offers every few days."

"I know. Anything interesting?"

"Nothing I'd be willing to dive into right now; just a few missing person cases. That's like finding a lost cat. Let the gumshoes do it. By the way, are you ready to take a trip into town to get the mail?"

"Oh, I forgot to tell you. We don't have to today. Isis is going in and she said she'd get it."

"Isis?"

"You know; Isis Dalrymple. She runs the library in town."

"Oh. Right. Isis. That woman who is an authority on everything. If you ask her the time she'll give you a lecture on the watchmaking industry. Where did she get a name like Isis, anyway?"

"Oh, her father was an Egyptian archaeology bug. He used to read all about the Pharaohs, and the mummies and the like. So when he had a daughter, he named her after the Egyptian goddess Isis."

"He named her Isis? Was he Osirius?"

"Max, that is the worst pun in the entire history of western civilization."

"Well, I guess the literary stuff rubbed off on you in New York, but not me."

"Obviously."

"Max, I had a grand time in New York, and Today's World is picking up my Blind Tiger article."

"That's great. Your literary light shines brighter than ever."

"And you managed to shine solving the case without making an enemy of the NYPD."

"You just have to let them get a little of the credit and resist the impulse to make them look bad. But you did pretty well for yourself. After all, how many people from St Michaels have ever eaten at the Algonquin round table?"

She smiled at the memory. "That was wonderful. Still..."

"Still what?"

"I wonder what Dorothy Parker really thought of my article? She never said."

"I thought you didn't want to be like those writer people."

"I don't want to act the way they do, but I have to respect their abilities. In that sense, their approval is important. What if she really hated my article? What if she thought it was poorly written? And I'm still not sure that country mouse poem wasn't about me."

"Who cares? Why would you want to write like Dorothy Parker when you can write like Allison Hurlock?"

"Thanks, Max. You always make me feel better.'

"That's my job, lady."

The crunching of tires announced a visitor.

"Hey, It's Isis. Over here!"

The Model T slid to a stop and a slight woman with short hair and glasses emerged.

"Hey, Allison. Hey Max. I got the mail."

"Thanks, Isis."

"So another crime solving caper, eh? We have a bunch of detective books at the library. Most of the stories are pretty unlikely, though."

"If you think they're unlikely, you should try real life," said Max.

Allison, meanwhile, was going through the mail.

"Hey, Max. Here's one from Dorothy Parker."

Isis Dalrymple's eyes widened to an extent Max wouldn't have though possible in a human.

"Dorothy Parker? Of Vanity Fair? You know Dorothy Parker?"

Allison acted casual. "Well, why not? After all, we're both writers."

"But Dorothy..."

Allison opened the envelope. Out came a single sheet of paper.

"It's a note," said Allison.

Isis Dalrymple looked to be bordering on apoplexy.

"Dorothy... Parker... wrote... you... a... note?"

Allison began to read.

I forgot to tell you. Your article was damned good. No wonder you didn't want my advice. You don't need it.

Dorothy Parker
P.S. Regards to Max.

"Well, that should frost the cake for you, eh Allison?" said Max. But Isis Dalrymple was still astonished. Without a word, she drove off in a cloud of dust.

"That's the first time I've seen her at a loss for words. Everyone in St Michaels and Easton will know about it by tomorrow."

"Oh, great. Now I'll be the envy of all the other country mice."

"Well," said Max, "the literary ones at least."

He thumbed through the rest of the mail.

"Here's an official letter from the New York City Police Department. Let's see. They're thanking me for my help."

"Yes," said Allison, "I suppose solving the case for them was a big help."

Max shrugged, "Darwin thanked me profusely before we left. This is the official version. It's more than I expected to get from them."

He shuffled some more letters.

"Here's one from Von Grunewald. I hope he's not in any more trouble."

"Maybe it's another check."

"I'm afraid not. Von Grunewald has already paid up and he's been very generous. Just think, a client that's both grateful and wealthy."

"It sure beats angry and broke," Allison agreed.

Max read silently for a while, then laughed. "Well, it seems Dianne Forsythe has filed for a divorce, Bill Fulton the chauffeur is seeing Gwen Perkins, Constance Tibbet has bought a house with her sister, Mandy Jewell has left for Albany to take a job as a school principal, and Helen Arness......"

"You're not about to say that Helen Arness is marrying Von Grunewald?"

Max looked up. "Von Grunewald likes to live dangerously, but he isn't suicidal. No, I was about to say that Helen Arness hasn't been heard from. As for Von Grunewald, he's enjoying his new found status as a man who is not under suspicion of murder."

The sun was dropping over the marshes, streaking the sky with yellow and pink as Max and Allison walked back to the house. A few ducks floated placidly in a small cove, silhouettes in the fading light. Max reached for her hand, then they turned and kissed.

"So," said Allison. "What do you want for dinner?"

"Uh...How about pastrami on rye? I got to like it in New York."

"I don't know where we'd get Pastrami around here, and the Merkle brothers are the only ones making rye. Well, at least they were."

"Oh..right....Well, then how about your world renowned southern fried chicken?"

"Coming right up. Von Grunewald isn't the only one who can live dangerously."

As they went in the house, Max stole a look at the ceramic tiger on the hall table and was astonished to see that Allison had painted eyes on it.

"What's the idea?" he said, gesturing towards it.

"I felt sorry for him. You brought light to the Blind Tiger case, so I thought I'd bring some light to the blind tiger that started it all."

Max looked back at the tiger once more, and in a trick of the late afternoon light, could have sworn it winked.

The End

Notes

The Elwell Murder case
The Blind Tiger Murder is based on a real life case, the death of Joseph Bowne Elwell in 1920. Elwell was an authority on Whist and Bridge, and made a good living teaching and playing with the wealthy, including the Vanderbilts. His wife both pushed and supported him in these efforts, but Elwell's popularity and eye for the ladies eventually caused them to divorce. This left Elwell free to live a riotous bachelor life much as described in the story. In addition to his house on 70th Street in Manhattan, Elwell owned a yacht in Florida and several race horses. Like Ellsworth Connelly, Elwell's many romantic liaisons included a number of married women. Some have even speculated that Elwell served as one of the models for Jay Gatsby in F.Scott Fitzgerald's novel The Great Gatsby.

On the morning of June 10, 1920, however, Elwell's good life came to an abrupt end when he was discovered sitting in a chair in his reception room dead of a gunshot wound to the head. The case was a sensation in New York and police had no shortage of suspects among the jilted lovers, jealous husbands, and losers at cards that Elwell left in his wake. Although the papers were full of titillating details and breathless revelations about Elwell's scandalous life, no one was ever brought to trial and the case remains officially unsolved.

The crime was the basis for The Benson Murder Case by S. S. Van Dyne.

Chapter 7-
Dorothy Parker and the Algonquin Round table

As drama critic for Vanity Fair Magazine, and later writer for the New Yorker, Dorothy Parker was renowned for her sharp wit and sharper tongue. Along with her confidant Robert Benchley, she spent many nights at local speakeasies, notably the Puncheon Club. Parker and Benchley met with other New York literary people at the Algonquin Hotel most days for a raucous, quip-filled lunch at a large round table the management reserved for their use.

Parker survived three marriages, alcohol dependency, and several suicide attempts before dying in 1967 while writing screenplays in Hollywood. She willed her estate to Martin Luther King, who had no idea who she was. Since she had expressed no preferences for her burial, her ashes remained in a container in her attorney's filing cabinet for almost 15 years. Finally, the NAACP, which inherited Parker's estate when Martin Luther King was assassinated, placed them in a memorial garden at their Baltimore headquarters in 1988. The inscription mentions that Parker's original preference for her epitaph was "Pardon my dust."

The roundtable is still a tourist attraction at the Algonquin Hotel in New York.

Chapter 8-
Edna Ferber and Show Boat

Writer Edna Ferber, a member of the Algonquin Round Table finished her best known novel, So Big, about the time of the Blind Tiger Murder. She later wrote Show Boat, the basis for the long running musical of the same name. She researched Show Boat on the

Adams Floating Theater as it traveled between the towns on Maryland's Eastern Shore. Along with Showboat, several of her works have been made into movies; Giant, Saratoga Trunk, and Cimarron. So Big won the Pulitzer Prize in 1925.

She collaborated with fellow round table member George S. Kaufman on several plays, but feuded with Alexander Wollcott, whom she once described as "a New Jersey Nero who has mistaken his pinafore for a toga."

Chapter 10-
Texas Guinan
"Hello suckers!" was Mary Louise Cecillia "Texas" Guinan's famous catch phrase as she greeted her customers at her club. A silent film actress, Guinan was known as America's first cowgirl movie star before becoming New York's most celebrated nightclub hostess in the 1920s. She reportedly made $700,000 in a single year, but lost much of her fortune in the Depression. She returned to the movies in 1929 in Queen of the Nightclubs, and later New York Through a Keyhole, movies based on her nightclub hostess days. Whoopi Goldberg's character, Guinan, on Star Trek, The Next Generation, is named for Texas Guinan.

Chapter 11-
The Spanish Flu
In the years 1918 and 1919, a worldwide influenza pandemic broke out that was more deadly than the recent world war, or of any disease in recorded history. The Spanish Flu, which probably originated in China, killed between 20 and 40 million people. More people died of the Spanish Flu in a single year than died of the Black Death in four years. So great was the lethality of the disease that the average life expectancy in The

United States dropped by 10 years. Previous flues had a mortality rate of about 0.1 %. The mortality rate of the Spanish Flu was 2.5%, a whopping 25 times higher. At one point, over a quarter of all Americans were infected.

Chapter 17-
Izzie and Moe
Many Prohibition agents were corrupt, incompetent, or both. Two remarkable exceptions were Isidore Einstein and Moe Smith, popularly known simply as Izzy and Moe. These otherwise unremarkable men created the perfect storm of enforcement, using subterfuges, deception and disguises to gain entrance to speakeasies and get served illegal liquor so they could make an arrest. During their careers they disguised themselves as lumberjacks, football players, sanitation workers a society man (and his wife!) and even delegates to the Democratic National Convention. Their announcement: "There's sad news here- you're pinched!" became a New York catchphrase as newspapers covered their exploits.

During their five year career, they made almost 5,000 arrests and destroyed over 5,000,000 bottles of illegal booze. But their high profile ways did not sit well with new Manhattan Prohibition Director Lincoln Andrews who laid them off as part of a reorganization in 1925, keeping men who were far less effective.

Chapter 20-
Harold Ross and the New Yorker
Born in Colorado and a high school dropout, Harold Ross was an unlikely literary person, but during the First World War, he talked himself into the editorship of

Stars and Stripes Magazine. He started up The New Yorker in 1925, with capital supplied by Fleishmann's yeast heir Raoul Fleishmann, but it did not become a success until years later. Much of the Algonquin Round Table contributed to the magazine, including Dorothy Parker. Ross was a demanding editor, insisting on detailed descriptions of people because he believed the only two people everyone was familiar with were Harry Houdini and Sherlock Holmes.

Chapter 21-
Duke Ellington
When God was handing out talent, Edward Kennedy "Duke" Ellington must have gotten in line twice. Though he started out as a free-lance sign painter, he was a superb musician who raised Jazz to an art form. He seldom called his music Jazz, but simply American Music. In addition, he was a prolific composer whose works such as Mood Indigo, Take the A Train, and It Don't Mean a Thing if it Ain't got that Swing have become classics. At the time of the story, Ellington and his band, The Washingtonians, were playing a four year engagement at the Hollywood Club after being recruited from the prestigious Exclusive Club in Harlem. (Ellington had left a successful career in Washington to be part of the Harlem Renaissance.) The Hollywood Club would soon be renamed the Kentucky Club.

Ellington signed several record contracts and wrote pieces for several black-themed Broadway shows. He toured in the US and in Europe, and became a figure of the big band era. He wrote and performed the music for movies such as Anatomy of a Murder. Duke Ellington won the Presidential Medal of Freedom and has a star on Hollywood's Walk of Fame.

Other adventures of Max and Allison Hurlock

Death of a Flapper
How did the most popular girl in town and her ex-fiancée end up dead and half-dressed in her locked bedroom? A distraught parent begs Max Hurlock to find the truth, but another murder occurs and the suspicious local police arrest Max for the crime!

"...fun and interesting, crammed with tidbits of historical information that gives it flavor and captures 1922 and early years of the Roaring 20s with real gusto." Amazon Review

Death on a Golden Isle
Death crashes the party at an exclusive island club for millionaires when a member is poisoned at the club dance. All eyes turn to his new wife and she turns to Max Hurlock to crack the case. But how do you pry secrets out of the most powerful men in America?

"...a delightful visit to an era, long past, with suspicions, secrets and clues woven through summer mansions, the exclusive club, and into shadowy hunting grounds." Amazon Review

Death at the Lighthouse
It's lights out on the Chesapeake Bay when a lighthouse keeper is murdered. Was it local rumrunners, a jealous husband, or something even more sinister? Max and Allison Hurlock must get to the bottom of a case involving rumrunners, jealous husbands, watermen, spiritualists, a corrupt federal agent, and a certain well-known magician.

"Mark me down as a super-fan of John Reisinger. I predict that every lover of an exciting tale told well will agree." Anne Stinson, Tidewater Times Book Review

Death in Unlikely Places

The Florida real estate boom is falling apart and someone is killing the biggest real estate developers in spectacular and impossible ways. One is stabbed in his locked office, apparently while shooting at the killer; one is killed while in a boat on a lake in view of a marina; one is killed in an elevator between floors; one is found draped over a tree branch 15 feet in the air; and one is shot while alone in a private gallery whose only door is in constant view of dozens of witnesses. The killer is so elusive, he is being called The Invisible Man, and a famous aviation pioneer calls on Max Hurlock to get to the bottom of it. Can Max Hurlock make sense of these mysterious events? More to the point, can he stop them? In this fifth Max Hurlock mystery, enter the world of Florida in the Roaring 20s and meet real estate barons, tin can tourists, crackers, bootleggers, and even a Voodoo priestess. As Allison would say "St Michaels was never like this."

"I would definitely recommend this book to anyone who enjoys mystery and desires to brush up on history at the same time." Amazon Review

Death across the Chesapeake

In 1926, the Hurlocks are back on Maryland's sleepy Eastern Shore to settle down to a quiet life after years of solving murders. But when a local stockbroker is killed in his locked office in a building owned by the wealthy and eccentric Stilwells, the Easton police know they have a delicate situation on their hands, and turn to Max and Allison for help. Several unhappy investors, a soon-to-be ex-wife, and a disappointed lady friend of the victim all have motives, and there seems to be some connection to the Stilwells themselves and their mysterious and well-guarded waterfront estate, Casa Leone. Max tries to put the pieces together, while Allison helps the mayor fend off the sensation-seeking press. The pressure mounts, but no one can say who killed the stockbroker, or even how he did it.

Add to the mix a man from Allison's past, an unlikely New York art dealer with a passion for mysteries, some ravenous reporters, a safe that seems to hold nothing of value, a book found at the crime scene that shouldn't be there, and a small, unexplained pile of plaster dust, and it soon becomes clear that Max's retirement from detective work was premature.

Books by John Reisinger

The Max Hurlock Roaring 20s Mysteries
Death of a Flapper
Death on a Golden Isle
Death at the Lighthouse
Death and the Blind Tiger
Death in Unlikely Places
Death across the Chesapeake

Historical novels
Flanagan and the Crown of Mexico
Nassau
Evasive Action
The Confessions of Gonzalo Guererro

Biography
Master Detective: The Life and Crimes of Ellis Parker, America's Real-life Sherlock Holmes

Children's
The Duckworth Chronicles
The Duckworth Papers
The Duckworth Dossier
Duckworth Redux

www.johnreisinger.com

About the author

John Reisinger lives on Maryland's Eastern Shore, and is the author of Master Detective, the true story of detective Ellis Parker and his controversial involvement in the Lindbergh kidnapping investigation.

He also writes the Max Hurlock Roaring 20s Mysteries, based on real crimes of that era, as well as of several historical novels, including Nassau, Evasive Action, Flanagan and the Crown of Mexico, and The Confessions of Gonzalo Guererro.

John has appeared as a panelist or solo presenter at Deadly Ink, Malice Domestic, New England Crime Bake and Bouchercon conferences. Several of his presentations have been broadcast on local television and radio. John has also appeared on the TV series Mysteries at the Museum in a segment based on Master Detective.

Website- johnreisinger.com
Blog- johnreisinger.wordpress.com

Death and the Blind Tiger
Book group suggested discussion questions

1.-How did the more basic communications technology of the 1920s (No TV, no cell phone, no Internet, etc.) affect the pace of life and the investigation of crime or events?

2.-How much of the police suspicion of Von Grunewald was due to his actions and how much was due to his history as a German U-boat commander?

3.-How are Max and Allison's different personalities reflected in their reactions to New York City?

4.-In what ways does Allison help Max in the investigation and Max help Allison with her literary aspirations?

5.-How would you expect the average police department to react to the participation of an amateur detective, and how does Max overcome Darwin's reluctance?

6.-How did Helen Arness help shape Ellsworth Connelly's character and lifestyle?

7.-Why would Mandy Jewell downplay her education and intelligence?

8.-Why did Gwen Perkins (The Automat Queen) so bitterly resent how Connolly treated her?

9.-Was the housekeeper's interest in Connelly professional, paternalistic, or romantic?

10.-How did speakeasies differ from bars, and what was their longer term social effect?

11.-Who did you think was going to turn out to be the killer and why?

12.-How did the Prohibition law lead to so much law-breaking and corruption?

13.-Considering the chauffeur's view of Connelly, do you agree with the expression "No man is a hero to his valet."?

14.-Who was the character you liked the best? The least?